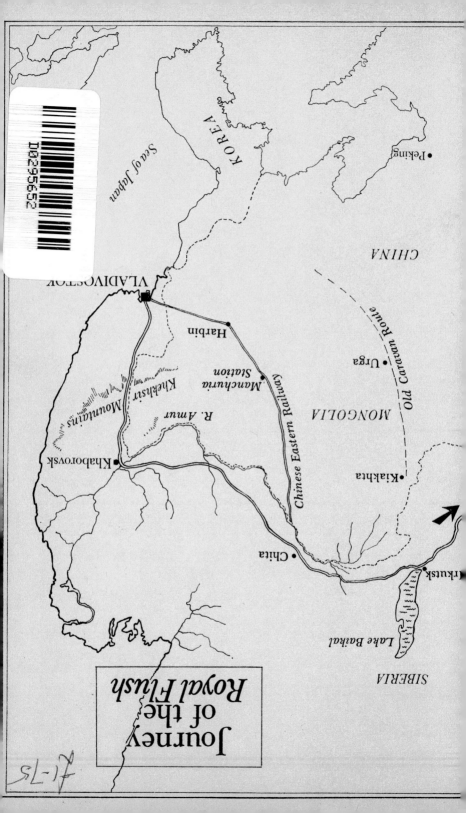

Journey
of the
Royal Flush

The Buckingham Palace Connection

It began in the House of Lords on a hot summer afternoon in 1976.

The Baroness Ward of North Tyneside had asked Her Majesty's Government whether there were any unpublished documents in the archives which related to the murder of the Tsar by the Bolsheviks in 1918, and if any members of the Russian Imperial Family had survived.

The minister replied that there were no such documents, but he added, significantly, *that no one could be sure about the fate of the Tsar's family.* Among the peers who sat listening to this exchange were two men: Viscount Tremayne of Trevellick, and Ted Willis, the author.

Later, they met and talked. And from that meeting there unfolded, bit by bit, the extraordinary story of what really happened in the war-ravaged Russia of 1918. As a young man Tremayne had been summoned to Buckingham Palace and given a special commission from King George V and Lloyd George. He was to mount an expedition to rescue the Imperial Family of Russia from the execution which threatened them.

Here, in graphic detail, is the story of that great adventure. Eastern Siberia was in the toils of civil war and revolution, the countryside a battlefield between 'Red' and 'White' armies and bandits. Tremayne and his companions make their way by armoured train from Vladivostock to Ekaterinburg in a hazardous race against time.

Will he reach the 'House of Special Purpose' in Ekaterinburg where the Tsar is imprisoned in time? Can he succeed in pulling off the rescue of the century?

This thrilling story is, at the same time, utterly credible. History is never disregarded or flouted. Perhaps Tremayne really *did* know what happened at Ekaterinburg. From the first page to the tension-packed climax the pace never slackens.

Ted Willis has been called 'the master story-teller of television': in this book, he establishes himself as a master of the adventure thriller.

THE
BUCKINGHAM PALACE
CONNECTION

Ted Willis

ISBN: 0 333 24177 0

First published 1978 by
MACMILLAN LONDON LIMITED
London and Basingstoke
Associated companies in Delhi Dublin Hong Kong
Johannesburg Lagos Melbourne New York Singapore
and Tokyo

Printed in Great Britain by
THE ANCHOR PRESS LTD
Tiptree, Essex

Bound in Great Britain by
WM BRENDON & SON LTD
Tiptree, Essex

Although this is a work of fiction, many of the events
are a matter of recorded history and actually took place.
In some instances, I have used the names of the people involved,
and these will be easily identifiable. For the rest, the
characters and their actions are imaginary. Their names and
experiences have no relation to those of actual people,
living or dead, except by coincidence.

Ted Willis

A Personal Statement from the Author

*Unlike writers in a number of countries, British writers are not paid for
the borrowing of their books from public libraries, even though the
British public library system is the largest in the western world.
Whether you are yourself a borrower or a buyer of books, please tell your
MP and your local authority that you support Public Lending Right,
under which writers will be paid, from central government funds, a small
fee for each borrowing of their work.*

Ted Willis

For Margaret and George Hardinge,
who have a special interest

Chapter One

The day began badly for me.

I'd been up half the night putting the final touches to a format for a new TV series, and followed this by a heavy morning trudging from one dull appointment to another. By midday I was hot, tired and irritable. Battalions of tourists, slow-footed as followers at a funeral, had taken possession of the pavements, the buses and the taxis, and by the time I arrived at the restaurant for lunch I felt as though I'd been pushed and shoved halfway round London.

The lunch did little to improve my mood. The ice-machine had broken down and I had to put up with a tepid whisky-water, while the food which followed was only marginally this side of indifferent. And to compound the dreariness of the morning, the television executive with whom I was lunching told me that production of the projected TV series, about which he had raved three months before, would have to be postponed for at least a year.

I did not so much receive this information as gather it. The executive had developed to a high art the practice of making the non-definite statement. He blew his light-weight thoughts into the air, like bubbles, committing himself neither the one way nor the other, covering all the options. He put me in mind of a cushion which adjusts itself to each new backside that sits upon it. I had the feeling that he would go far.

In television, postponement is another word for death. Subjects have a way of going cold and once that happens revival requires a miracle. I'd already put three months' hard work into preparing the series, and I'd cleared the decks for the next nine months to write the scripts. So I was looking at a gap in my working life as wide as a five-acre field, a gap which would have to be filled somehow.

My Cockney mother had a mind, stuffed like a ragbag, with tags for all occasions. One of her regular bits of homespun philosophy was to face a disappointment with the phrase: 'Oh, never mind. When one door closes another always opens.' As I left the restaurant, I thought wryly of her words.

I would have been surprised if someone had told me then that the other door was to open almost immediately, and downright incredulous if they'd said that it would be the heavy, embossed, oaken door which leads to the chamber of the House of Lords, the Upper House of Her Majesty's Parliament at Westminster.

2

It was the afternoon of July 21, 1976, and we were at the height of that long, hot summer when Britain sweated and sweltered in its fiercest heatwave for 200 years. The newspapers had relegated the nation's economic troubles to second place; the front pages all carried stories of the drought, with pictures of cracked and empty water reservoirs and of the crops wilting in the fields.

Around Parliament Square the sightseers drooped as

they dragged weary feet over burning flagstones, so exhausted that many of them seemed to lack even the energy to raise and click their cameras at the statue of Winston Churchill, or at the patient policemen who guard the gates of Parliament. The heat and humidity had breached the stolid walls of Whitehall and senior civil servants, slightly shamefaced, walked the corridors of power jacketless and with their shirt-sleeves rolled up. It was rumoured that one official on the Middle East desk at the Foreign Office had presented himself for work dressed like Lawrence of Arabia, in a *galabieh*, the loose white costume of the Arabs. In the City, many of the young men defied the convention of generations and the astonished looks of their elders by discarding their ties.

In suburban houses, old men hunted through battered trunks and came up with baggy, knee-length, khaki shorts, relics of their colonial days. At first, they wore them only around the house, but as one hot day followed another they grew bolder, and their mottled legs were actually to be seen in full public view in the streets. Many pubs ran out of beer, and men, maddened by thirst, drove miles to find and fight over the dwindling supplies.

From every pulpit there were prayers for rain. Self-professed witches held mysterious midnight ceremonies in fields and forests, invoking the mercy of the ancient Pagan Gods. One newspaper suggested that the Government should invite a famous Australian Aborigine water-finder to tour the country with his *yamagulli* – a set of bones which, in his hands, were supposed to be able to locate water in the most inhospitable deserts.

The sun, it seemed, was steadily drying England's green and pleasant land to a dark sepia, and just as steadily driving its people mad.

On this day, against this background, the House of Lords seemed like an oasis. The entrance-hall was shadowed and cool, and in the bar the ice-machine was actually working. I took a long, slow, cold drink, went into the Chamber, and took my place on the back-benches.

Prayers had been said, and the business of the afternoon began, as usual, with a series of four Unstarred Questions. My mind was on other things and I took little notice of the gentle cut and thrust in which the Government and Opposition benches indulged. This is all part of the parliamentary game and the fact that the Upper House plays it in a more genteel fashion does not make it any the less futile.

It was the fourth and final Question which brought my wandering thoughts back to the business of the day. A back-bench peeress, a lady with a long and distinguished career in politics, had risen to her feet from her seat on the Opposition benches, and was going through the prescribed ritual.

'My Lords, I beg leave to ask the question standing in my name on the Order Paper.'

I glanced at the printed question. It read: 'The Baroness Ward of North Tyneside: To ask Her Majesty's Government whether there are any hitherto unpublished documents in the archives of the Foreign Office which relate to the murder of the Tsar and the Russian Imperial family by the Bolsheviks in 1917, and if so, whether they will make an up-to-date statement on this matter, so that the full facts may be known.'

Lord Goronwy-Roberts, the Minister of State for the Foreign and Commonwealth Office, a relaxed, bright-eyed Welshman, rose in front of the Despatch Box. He opened the official red binder and read out a prepared reply.

'My Lords, all the available documents in the possession of Her Majesty's Government relating to the assassination of Tsar Nicholas II and his family are open to the public at the Public Records Office. It is for historians to assess this and other evidence. It is not a matter on which the Government have pronounced or could pronounce.'

He smiled courteously in the direction of the questioner, and sat down. He knew, as did we all, that this was just the opening exchange and waited expectantly for the noble Baroness to fire the next shot. She was one of the few women in the House who still wore a hat and she made a slight adjustment to it as she rose again.

'My Lords, is the noble Lord aware that that is a rather unsatisfactory Answer—'

Several Lords rebuked her with cries of 'No!' Voices are seldom raised in the House of Lords and the interruption amounted to no more than a murmur, but she waited for silence before continuing.

'Is the Minister aware that a new book* has recently been published which challenges the official account of this tragic event and puts forward some interesting new facts? Would it not be possible for the Government to make just a general statement as to these new facts?'

'As I have said,' replied the Minister, 'this is not a matter on which the Government could pronounce. I have no doubt that the book to which she refers is a substantial production, but it is for historians not governments to assess its value.'

Three or four other peers rose and expressed opinions in the form of questions, to each of which Lord Goronwy-Roberts responded with unwavering politeness. However, the formidable Baroness Ward of North Tyneside was not finished yet. She waited her moment and then slipped in a last question.

'May I ask the Minister,' she said, 'whether he is

* *The File on the Tsar* by Anthony Summers and Tom Mangold

absolutely satisfied that all the family were murdered at Ekaterinburg? I am not referring to the well-known case of the Grand Duchess Anastasia, who, as so many people believe, escaped to the West, but to the other three daughters. Is the Minister positive that these are not alive?'

'No, my Lords,' replied the Minister. 'Nor do I think anybody can be absolutely satisfied on that point.'

And that, for the moment, seemed to be that.

3

The House went on to discuss the Aircraft and Ship-building Industries Bill, and after an hour or so I made my way to the Bishop's Bar (so-called because it was formerly the room in which the Bishops changed into or out of their robes) in search of more refreshment. Four or five peers were sitting at the table nearest the door talking, inevitably, about the drought, and apart from these and an elderly peer in a corner at the other end of the room, the place was empty.

I took my drink and an evening paper and sat down in the coolness and comfort of an armchair to relax. I'd scarcely read the headlines when I heard a voice.

'Are you the writer chap?'

Looking up, I saw the peer in the opposite corner glaring at me from under spiky, grey eyebrows. I smiled politely at him over the newspaper.

'You do a bit of writing, don't you?' he asked. His voice was sharp and rasping, and the belligerent tone suggested that professional writing was some form of sin. Which, of course, may well be true.

'A bit,' I confessed humbly.

'I read one of your books,' he said. 'The one about the tigers.'* Again, he managed to suggest by his tone that he had not enjoyed the experience.

'Ah,' I said, in a careful, defensive voice.

'Good yarn that,' he said, to my surprise. 'Rattling good read.'

'Thank you,' I said, aware that my smile was now less neutral. After my experiences of the morning, I was in the mood to welcome a little bit of morale-building.

'Bring your drink over here,' he said. 'Can't talk across the damned room.'

It was a command, not a request, and I obeyed. As I sat down there was a longish pause during which he glared at me again, in that fierce uncompromising manner which is common to the very old and the very young. I guessed then that he was about 70 and discovered subsequently that he was 86, though his bright blue eyes and healthy walnut-brown skin would have done credit to a younger man. I could not recall seeing him before and had no idea of his name, but since only peers may use the Bishop's Bar, I knew that he must be a member of the House.

'You don't look like a writer,' he said. There was no answer to that, so I made none, and he continued: 'Hard work, is it?'

'Not easy,' I said diffidently.

'No.' He nodded thoughtfully. 'How do you get all the background stuff?'

'Research,' I said, 'I go out and dig for it.' Writers are used to this sort of question but I had the feeling that he wasn't asking out of idle curiosity; the fierce old eyes seemed once more to be assessing me. After a moment or two of this, the eyes softened and he relaxed. He sipped his drink and for a good twenty seconds stared down at

* Man-Eater

his copy of the Order Paper, which was open on the table. I saw that the question about the Tsar and the Russian Imperial Family had been ringed round in red ink and in the margin beside it there were a couple of bold exclamation marks.

'They don't know the half of it,' he said, as if speaking to himself.

'The Tsar?' I asked. 'About the Tsar?'

'Don't know the half of it,' he repeated.

I don't know why, but I became conscious of that slight tightening of the spine which always comes when I feel that I am on the threshold of a story. It was as though some sixth sense had switched itself on inside my head, and I was eager to know more.

He seemed about to speak again, and then checked himself, perhaps because the bar was beginning to fill up. He rose abruptly. 'Have to be going. Train to catch. Nice talking to you. Always wanted to have a go at writing myself, but no good. Haven't the gift for it.' He glanced down at the Order Paper and shook his head; then, with an abrupt nod, he moved out, his back upright but walking with the careful steps of an old man.

The Bishop's Bar is run by a capable and smiling woman called Anne, and since she is a mine of information about the House, I asked her the name of the peer I'd been speaking with. She supplied it immediately.

'Oh, that's Viscount Tremayne of Trevellick, my Lord.' She seemed surprised that I did not know him.

'I haven't seen him here before.'

'He hardly ever comes in, my Lord. This is the first time I've seen him in ages.'

I went to the library and looked up Tremayne in the latest issue of Dod's, a sort of Who's Who of members of both Houses of Parliament. It read as follows:

TREMAYNE of Trevellick (6th Viscount of U.K.), James Spring Richard; cr. 1762. C.B., 1926. Born Jan. 13, 1890. Son of General, 5th Viscount, K.G., G.C.B., D.S.O. Succeeded his father 1932. Educated Winchester, Trinity College, Cambridge. Entered Diplomatic Service, 1913. Served in Petrograd (now Leningrad), Vladivostock, Berlin and Foreign Office. Resigned 1927. Heir none. Address: *The Viscount Tremayne of Trevellick, The House of Lords, S.W.1.*

It was a strange little summary. I recalled from my reading of the history of the First World War that his father, General Tremayne, was one of the few military commanders to come out of that particular piece of madness with an enhanced reputation. Yet the son's career, after a promising beginning, seemed to have come to an abrupt halt. He'd been made a Commander of the Bath, a high honour for one so young, in 1926 but in the following year he'd resigned from the Diplomatic Service. It seemed odd. And then again, people in his position, with his background, usually went on to become directors of banks or great merchant companies, and to hold various honorary positions on Trusts, international organisations and similar bodies.

Yet Tremayne appeared to have stopped, reached a dead end, in 1927. In that year he would have been only 36; at the age, one would have thought, when his career was about to take off. And why the silence since that date? I could not believe that this bright-eyed man, so full of life and personality even at 86, had simply idled the intervening years away.

It was not until the outbreak of the Great War in 1914 that the Russian government changed St. Petersburg to Petrograd, and some time after that before it was changed yet again to its present name, Leningrad. So clearly

Tremayne must have served in Russia during the war and this probably explained his interest in the fate of the Tsar and his family.

But did he have a special interest? Had he been personally involved with them? Why had he come to the House on this particular day, after so long an absence? Was it because he'd seen the reference to the Tsar on the Order Paper?

I left the library, my mind full of such unanswered questions, and as I passed through the Princes Chamber, one of the Doorkeepers handed me a note. It was short and to the point, but the few words it contained were written in a fine, flowing hand.

> *Come down and see me if you've a mind to do so –*
>   *TREMAYNE OF TREVELLICK.*

I showed the note to the Doorkeeper. 'He didn't leave an address,' I said, 'and there's nothing in Dod's. When you forward his mail, where do you send it?'

'Cornwall, I think, my Lord,' he said, 'somewhere in Cornwall – I'll look it up for you.'

He consulted a notebook. 'That's right, my Lord. Viscount Tremayne of Trevellick, near Zennor, Cornwall.'

4

I spent most of that evening and the following day reading up, from what books I could lay my hands on, all that I could about the Russian Revolution of 1917 and Tsar Nicholas II. At 6 a.m. the next morning I left for Cornwall, choosing such an early hour so that I could negotiate London before the traffic started to peak.

I love Cornwall and the West Country, and I took with me a bag packed with sufficient clothes and other necessities to last me for a week at least. If my meeting with Viscount Tremayne proved to be a waste of time, I intended to stay on for a while, relax for a few days. I was half-hoping that this was how it would turn out. I hadn't taken a holiday in years and the idea of some time to myself was an appealing one.

I stopped at a motel near Basingstoke for what turned out to be a very good breakfast, and afterwards made good time to Exeter. From then on I got caught up in the swarming holiday traffic which crowds the narrow roads of the West in summer and began to regret the impulse which had prompted me to make the journey. But all the grittiness and irritation dissolved when I reached the coast road which would lead me to Zennor and then on, if I wished, to Land's End. Here was nature at its most formidable and dramatic. The great, bristling cliffs seemed to be like fortresses, surrounded by hostile forces: on the one side they faced the thunderous attack of the Atlantic rollers, while at their backs the moor, its brown and purple crags standing out like watch-towers, surged against them like some more tranquil sea.

Zennor itself turned out to be a sturdy, grey-stone village; most of the houses were clustered around a little square, and there was a beautiful little church just beyond. The building that caught my eye, however, was the local inn, The Tinner's Arms. It took me about two minutes to park the Rover and head for the coolness of the public bar. The service was friendly but not servile; there was ice for my Scotch, and the roast-beef sandwiches were freshly-made and delicious.

The bar was pretty crowded and I made my way over

to a table in the corner where there was a single vacant seat. I looked with an enquiring smile at a man sitting there, and he indicated with a nod that I might join him. He was a big sturdy fellow with black luminous eyes above a prominent nose, and the sort of slight darkness of skin which sets the true Cornishman apart from his English neighbours. It was easy to imagine the strains of race which had made him – Celt with a touch of the Phoenician. He wore a small gold ring in one ear; put a cutlass at his belt, I thought, and he could have passed for a pirate.

He was friendly enough, though conversation proved to be difficult at first, for he responded to my questions with nods or monosyllabic answers. He accepted my offer of a drink with some reluctance, but after that he seemed to relax a little more and I discovered that he was a local man and a fisherman. We spoke about the dwindling fish stocks and about the old, abandoned tin mines which are a feature of the area. It was a pleasure to relax after my long hot drive and to listen to his soft, singing Cornish accent.

The time passed so quickly that I was surprised to hear the landlord call 'Last Orders'. I drained my glass and rose to go.

'I'm looking for a place called Trevellick,' I said. 'Can you tell me which road to take?'

He looked up at me and I was suddenly aware of a hostility in his eyes, as though I'd unwittingly trodden on some forbidden ground. There was a pause of no more than a moment, but it seemed longer.

'I wouldn't know it,' he said.

'Viscount Tremayne lives there,' I said, puzzled both by his answer and its tone. 'Tremayne of Trevellick. I'm a writer and—' I was about to add that Tremayne had invited me to call on him but he interrupted.

'I can't help you, sir,' he said firmly. It was the first time he'd called me 'sir', and he made it sound as though there was a wall between us.

I thanked him rather bleakly and crossed to the bar. The landlord was busy at the till, and as I waited, I could feel that the other man was watching me. When the landlord turned to me with an enquiring smile, I repeated my question. Again, I was aware of a sudden underlying tension; the smile remained, but it had become fixed, professional.

'I reckon you must have it wrong, sir,' he said. 'I don't know of any place called by that name – not round here.' And before I could say anything further he turned away and called: 'Time, ladies and gentlemen! Drink up, please. Time! Time, please, ladies and gentlemen.'

By this time I had begun to think that I probably had made a mistake, and I went out to the car to check my notes; but there was the address as I'd copied it down from the Doorkeeper at the House of Lords: *The Viscount Tremayne of Trevellick, near Zennor, Cornwall.* I was in the right county and the right village. Unless the Doorkeeper had got it wrong – and that was hard to believe – Tremayne must be living somewhere near. Trevellick was not marked on the map, but that did not surprise me. I assumed that it was the name of a house or an estate. What did surprise and puzzle me was that, of all people, the landlord of the local inn should not have heard of it, or of Tremayne.

I put the note in my pocket, locked the car, and strolled over to the church. The door was open and I went inside. Two American tourists were looking at a carving on the end of one of the benches, and a kindly, grey-haired old man with stooped shoulders was explaining its origin. He welcomed me with an easy smile.

'Good afternoon. I was just explaining our local legend

to Mr. and Mrs. Purcell. They're from America. There is a story that, years ago, one of the local fishermen fell in love with a mermaid. This is a carving of the lady. He swam out to sea with her and was never seen again. They say that on mid-summer day each year they come back to Zennor and can be seen swimming off-shore.'

'Have you ever seen them, sir?' asked the American.

'No, I haven't, I'm afraid,' said the old man gravely. 'But then, I can't say I've gone out of my way to look.'

'It's a very nice story,' said the American lady. 'I like it.'

'This land is full of legends and mysteries,' said the old man.

As the Americans moved on, I drew him aside. 'I wonder if you can help me?' I asked. 'I'm looking for a place called Trevellick, where Viscount Tremayne lives.' And as the gentle old eyes clouded over, I added hastily: 'He has asked me to visit him.'

I showed him the note Tremayne had left for me. He gave me a curious look, then took out a pair of wire-framed spectacles and studied the note. He took his time, seemingly going over the words again and again, then he folded the scrap of paper carefully, smoothed it with brown, wrinkled fingers, and handed it back.

'I didn't catch your name,' he said.

'Willis. Ted Willis,' I answered. 'I met Viscount Tremayne in the House of Lords earlier this week. That's when he left me this note.' I turned it over, so that he could see my name.

'Ah. *Lord* Willis.' He emphasised the title. Then he put his head to one side in the manner of a bird, and scratched his ear, clearly considering the situation.

'He does live near here?' I asked, trying to keep the irritation out of my voice.

'I thought I recognised the name. You wrote that

television programme, *Dixon of Dock Green*,* didn't you?'
he said, as though he hadn't heard my question.

'That's right,' I said impatiently. I get a little tired of
being remembered only for that particular series. It
wasn't a bad programme of its kind and for its time but
I have written other things, after all. Still, in this instance
it stood me in good stead, for I could see that he'd
already decided that a man who'd created such a gentle,
homespun character as Police Sergeant George Dixon
was a man who could be trusted.

'I'm sorry it's finished,' he said. 'Always used to enjoy
it. Every Saturday night. Never missed it.'

'Thank you,' I said politely, and waited. Once again,
he went through the motion of scratching his ear.

'Take the coast road towards Morvah and St. Just,' he
said at last. 'Just before you reach Morvah turn inland
on the road to Madron. About two miles on, you'll find
a track on your right. That will take you to Trevellick.
The track isn't marked, but I don't think you'll miss it.'

I almost exploded with relief. Thanking him, I put a
pound in the offertory box by the door, and went out
into the sunlight. When I reached the Rover, I noticed
that the landlord and the man with the gold ear-ring
were standing together at the entrance to the Tinner's
Arms, watching me.

Why had they been so secretive and defensive? As I
drove past, I lifted my hand in what I hoped was a
satirical gesture of farewell.

They did not respond.

*A BBC police-drama series, popular in Britain 1955–76

5

I found the track which the old man had described without too much difficulty, but as the car bumped along it, I began to wonder whether I'd been deliberately misled. The track dipped, rose and curved over a desolate moor in which great outcrops of granite stood out like grey islands. There was no sign of human habitation apart from the roofless ruins of an old cottage. The moor had a certain savage beauty, but why anyone should choose to live there was beyond my understanding.

The track began to climb upwards towards the edge of a high ridge. I changed down to a lower gear and made up my mind that if there were no sign of Trevellick when I reached the top, I would turn back. The Rover was sturdy and reliable but it had had a rough passage and the last thing I wanted was to break down in the middle of this desolation.

It had been a journey full of surprises, yet there was another just ahead of me. Not the greatest surprise of this incredible day, as I was to learn: that was yet to come. But this one was enough to be going on with!

As the car struggled to the top of the ridge, I found myself looking down on an extraordinary valley. It was as though I'd arrived in a different country, as though nature had relented and touched part of the moor with her finger, making it green and gentle. Lush rolling pasture lined the natural hollow, and nestling against the furthest slope, facing south, there was a house. It was partly hidden by a screen of American Lodgepole pine, and its grey stone was so clothed with ivy that the building itself seemed to have put down roots and sprung naturally from the earth. It took me a moment or two to pick it out behind this natural camouflage, but eventually I could see that it looked like a large farmhouse, low, long and graceful, and through the trees I caught the flash of colour from flowers and shrubs.

It had to be Trevellick.

I shut off the engine and got out of the car. At this point, at the top of the ridge, the track was hedged with stern outcrops of rock, and the way forward was barred by a gate on which someone had nailed a large notice: PRIVATE PROPERTY – STRICTLY NO ENTRY.

I opened the gate and turned back to the Rover. The afternoon sun threw my shadow before me and I had only moved a couple of paces when I stopped abruptly, my heart pounding. Another longer and broader shadow had linked with mine and was moving with it: the silhouette of a head and part of a body showed clearly on the track.

In the same moment I heard the lightest of footfalls behind me. I half-turned, had time to catch a glimpse of a burly, bearded man, and then, like a bolt from the blue, I felt a crushing blow to the back and side of my head.

I heard myself scream out in pain, the ground below me seemed to spin madly, like a merry-go-round out of control, and I went down to meet it.

6

When I opened my eyes I had to close them again quickly for the light was too sharp and blinding to bear. My head felt heavy and leaden, and in some way separated from the rest of my body; at the back of my skull I could feel a regular, almost rhythmical throbbing pain, as though a little man had somehow got inside and was striking at a nerve with a tiny hammer.

I was aware of voices speaking in low tones, I heard what I took to be the rustle of curtains. Something cool and sweet-smelling was smoothed across my forehead, and I drifted off into sleep once more.

When I woke again, the room was quietly shadowed and the little man in the back of my head seemed to be resting from his labours. I lay staring at the white ceiling, gradually putting myself and my thoughts together.

I heard a door open softly and looked towards the sound. The movement jarred my head, and my eyes misted over with pain, but when the blur of vision cleared I saw Tremayne moving towards me.

'How are you feeling, old chap?'

I heard a voice answer, 'I'm not sure,' and a moment later realised that it was mine.

He sat down on a chair beside the bed. 'You'll be all right. No serious injury. You'll live,' he said gruffly.

'A man hit me. From behind,' I said.

'I know. It was a mistake.'

'That's comforting.'

'We are jealous of our privacy here. We go to great lengths to protect it. Unfortunately Michael received a message from some friends in Zennor—'

'Michael?' I asked.

'Works for me. As I say we have good friends in the district—'

'Like the landlord of the Tinner's Arms?'

'He's one. A fine man. He knows that we don't welcome strangers here – especially the press. And apparently you told someone else at the pub that you were a writer. They jumped to the conclusion that you were from a newspaper and warned Michael to be on the look-out.'

'And he jumped me,' I said ruefully.

'He's a reliable fellow, but not bright. Getting on a bit now. Tends to act first and think afterwards. You should have warned me you were coming.'

Somehow the situation seemed to have reversed itself so that I was now being blamed for the attack on myself. I could understand the man's desire for privacy but to knock people over the head in its defence seemed to be going a bit far: but I was too weak and weary to argue and I let it pass.

I was aware of a movement behind Tremayne and an old lady came and stood beside him. The face beneath the grey hair was smooth and delicate, the brown eyes gentle and concerned. Even in my battered state, or perhaps because of it, I felt myself respond to the tranquillity, the feeling of peace and stillness that seemed to flow from her. She rested a hand on Tremayne's shoulder and looked down at me, smiling. She did not speak but the smile was beautiful.

'This is my wife,' Tremayne said gruffly.

A thought drifted into my mind. There had been no reference to a wife in the brief biography I'd read in Dod's. I let that pass also.

'We've brought in your car,' said Tremayne, 'and your things are here. You will stay with us for a few days.'

I managed a painful nod. I was in no mood to move or be moved.

'Good,' he said. 'Tomorrow or the day after we will talk. I am sorry for what happened, but I think we shall be able to make it up to you. You meant what you said in the House of Lords, I trust?'

'What did I say?'

'About research. For a story. You said you go out and dig for all the background stuff.'

'That's right,' I said wearily.

'Good,' he said again. 'We can tell you a lot – but

you'll have to do some digging on your own account.'

I nodded once more, not really taking in what he was saying. The little man had started swinging his hammer inside my head again, and I wanted to escape into sleep.

'It has to be told,' he said. 'Before it is too late.' He touched his wife's hand. 'We've waited a long time – perhaps too long.' They moved to the door and he turned and added: 'I don't think you'll be sorry you came.'

I didn't agree with him at the time, but he was right.

It is not really possible to say with any certainty where a story begins. Certainly, the roots of this one spread back into the centuries and across vast continents, and it was to take me many months and many more journeys to unravel even some of the threads.

But I have chosen to start in the two strangely contrasting places where it began for James Tremayne. In the study, at Buckingham Palace, of His Majesty, George V, King, by the Grace of God, of the United Kingdom of Great Britain and Ireland and of his other realms and territories beyond the seas, Emperor of India, Defender of the Faith; and in the bar of a London public house.

The pub came first. And what happened there was crucial to all that followed.

Chapter Two

The young man in the new and elegant civilian suit looked strangely out of place in the crowded bar of the Wellington Arms. Almost all the men around him were in uniform, many of them wearing the wound stripes and medal ribbons which marked their service in one or more of the great battles on the Western Front. From time to time, some of the women with the soldiers cast hostile looks in his direction, but he seemed unaware of this; he sat at the end of the curved mahogany bar, sipping a glass of warm, weak beer, glancing at a pocket-watch from time to time and apparently content with his own company.

A few Australians in their distinctive slouch hats were gathered around a battered old upright piano at which one of their mates was hammering out the tune of *Waltzing Matilda*. Around the walls, on the bare wooden benches, the old people sat and watched, smiling with sad eyes at the antics of the soldiers, thinking wistfully of the sons and the grandsons they had lost. The wiser among them could sense that the high spirits were only skin-deep, that there was a cold edge of desperation, even of despair, beneath the gaiety and the laughter.

For this was April, 1918. Only a few weeks before the papers and the politicians had been saying that Germany's reserves were exhausted, that she was on the verge of collapse.

Yet now news of a new and powerful enemy offensive was beginning to filter through. True, the newspapers tried to play it down, but after almost four years of war, people had learned to understand the language of the official communiqués, to read something of the truth between the lines. They knew that 'strategic withdrawal' or 'shortening the line' meant retreat. They had learned to read maps, the names of almost every town, village and hill in Flanders were as familiar to them as the names of the streets in which they lived. If they read one day of fighting around Armentières and a few days later of a battle at Merville, they knew that this could only mean one thing – the enemy had advanced and the Allies were in retreat.

There were persistent stories, carried for the most part by wounded soldiers returning home from the battle-fronts, of a German artillery bombardment more fearful and terrible than anything ever known, of an attack which had forced General Gough's Fifth Army to retreat to the Somme and beyond. The Somme, of all places, where every inch of ground had been bought at such cost!

All the hope which had come with the new year seemed to have melted along with the winter snow, and in the bar of the Wellington Arms that night it was reflected in the small, serious pockets of conversation which went on under the thumping of the piano and the singing.

War-weariness and disillusion made each man seek his own scapegoat. Some blamed the Americans for not doing enough; some blamed the French for the same reason; some blamed the new Bolshevik government in Russia for concluding a separate peace with the Kaiser, thus releasing hundreds of thousands of German troops for the offensive in the West.

And, not without reason, most people blamed the politicians or the Generals or both.

'Still, and all, I reckon Big Willie will do it for us,' said a corporal in the Royal Artillery reassuringly.

'Big Willie?' giggled a girl at his side. Her thick, red hair was escaping in untidy strands from under a blue felt hat and she swung uneasily on the corporal's arm.

'Tanks, lovey, tanks,' said the corporal.

'Oh,' she said, and giggled again. 'I thought you meant something else.'

'They say old Haig has got thousands of them,' said a private of the Royal Fusiliers in a drunken whisper that could be heard across the room. 'Thousands. Bloke in my mob reckons he saw—'

'That's enough of that!' said the corporal sharply, and nodded towards a wall on which there was a display of posters. One of them was a blunt warning against careless talk, under the heading: THE ENEMY IS LISTENING! It was illustrated by a lurid drawing of a shifty-looking man in a raincoat standing in a public-house on the fringe of a group of soldiers.

'And what about that one?' said the girl. She pointed an unsteady finger at a second poster, which was begining to peel away from the wall. TO THE YOUNG WOMEN OF LONDON! screamed the headline and under it in bold type were three questions:

IS YOUR 'BEST BOY' WEARING KHAKI?
IF NOT, DON'T YOU THINK HE SHOULD BE?
IF YOUR YOUNG MAN DOESN'T THINK THAT YOU
AND YOUR COUNTRY ARE WORTH FIGHTING FOR —
DO YOU THINK HE IS WORTHY OF YOU?

29

'That's out of date,' said the corporal. 'There's conscription now, girl.'

'Not for some,' she said pointedly. 'Some seem to be able to wriggle out of it.' She swayed a little as she turned her eyes on the young man in the corner. Tremayne turned his head at this moment and gave her a polite smile.

'Don't you smile at me!' she said scathingly.

'Give over, Mavis,' said the corporal.

'Didn't you see him? Bold as bleeding brass – grinning at me!'

'Give over, I said.'

The corporal tried to draw her aside, but she pulled away from him, and yelled: 'There's people fighting and dying over there and he sits here like a toff, swilling beer and grinning at the girls! Well, he ain't going to grin at me! If you won't turf him out of this place, I'll find someone who bloody well will!'

A silence fell on the bar, as she stalked up to Tremayne, and glared down at him, hands on hips.

'Well?' she demanded.

'I beg your pardon?' He stood up and compounded his offence by smiling again.

'I warned you not to grin at me, mister!' she shouted.

'I'm awfully sorry,' he said, and sounded as if he meant it.

'I'm awfully sorry,' she repeated, mocking his accent. 'Why ain't you in uniform, eh? Eh?'

'You've taken a drop too much, darling,' said Tremayne. He picked up a soft trilby hat which was lying beside his glass on the bar, prinked the crown with his fingers and gave the girl a little nod. 'Have my seat. I have to go now anyway.'

'You telling me I'm drunk!' She was beside herself with anger now and turned for support to the group of soldiers who had crowded in behind her. 'Did you hear that! Did you hear what he said!' Stuttering with rage, she turned back, seized a half-full glass of beer from a surprised Australian, and threw it at Tremayne, soaking his coat, shirt and tie. He looked down at the spreading stain for a moment, shaking his head, then sank back on to his stool.

The fusilier lurched past the girl and grabbed Tremayne by the lapels of his jacket. 'No, you don't,' he said. 'You can shift. Shift your arse, mate. Pronto.'

'That's right. You tell him!' said the girl called Mavis.

Tremayne looked down at the hands that were holding him. 'Don't do that, please,' he said in a pained voice.

'Don't do what?'

'That,' said Tremayne, and at the same time he took hold of the fusilier's wrists. It looked to be a simple, straightforward hold, but the soldier gave a sudden sharp shout of pain and stepped back, looking down at his hands in astonishment.

'No trouble, gents,' shouted the landlord, 'don't let's have any trouble!'

'Let him go,' said the corporal.

'Never mind him!' said the Australian soldier, 'what about my bloody beer!'

'You keep your nose out of this!' shouted the fusilier.

'What did you say?' said the Australian, in a tone of ominous quietness. 'What was that?'

The fusilier swung a punch in the general direction of the Australian but it was his unlucky night. The other man ducked away, and returned the compliment with a blow to the fusilier's stomach which brought the breath whistling from his body and doubled him up in retching agony. Within seconds the fighting spread; Diggers and Tommies enthusiastically working out old antagonisms with kicks, fists and bottles.

The landlord watched in dismay for a moment, then ran to the door and blew several blasts on a police whistle. Behind him there was a pandemonium of screaming women and grunting men, of breaking woodwork and crashing glass.

Two ordinary policemen and two military policemen appeared out of the night and, drawing truncheons, they waded into the mêlée. It took them about three minutes to restore some sort of order.

'Right,' said the senior of the two ordinary policemen. 'What happened?'

'He started it!' shouted the girl with the untidy red hair, pointing at Tremayne.

The policeman walked over to him and sniffed. 'Hmph! Smells like a blinking brewery.' He turned to the M.P.s and indicated three soldiers who were lying unconscious on the sawdust-strewn floor. 'Right. I'll be generous. We'll take this one and you can have them three.'

He took Tremayne by the arm. 'Come on,' he said. 'Don't make any more trouble for yourself.'

'I'm afraid I can't do that, constable,' said Tremayne politely. 'I've an appointment in half an hour. Rather important. Must keep it.'

The constable tightened his grip on the other man's arm. 'She'll have to wait, then, won't she?' he said heavily.

'I do assure you—'

'Now, come on, come on!' said the constable sternly.

Tremayne sighed, drew a letter from an inside pocket and handed it to the policeman, who sniffed and held the sheet of paper out almost at arm's length, screwing up his eyes. They opened in astonishment at the sight of the distinctive crest at the top, and he glanced at Tremayne and back to the letter as though unable to connect the two. He read the brief note slowly, his lips silently trembling over the words. His face reddened, a fringe of sweat formed on his forehead, and then, as if someone had pulled an inner wire, he jerked to respectful attention and raised a hand to his helmet in an uncertain salute.

'Sir! Sorry, sir. I didn't mean to—'

'That's all right, constable. Forget it.'

'Yes, sir. Thank you, sir.'

Tremayne took the letter from the policeman's shaking hand and put it in his pocket. He stepped carefully over the unconscious body of the unlucky fusilier and raised his hat to the wide-eyed Mavis.

'Thank you for the drink,' he said.

They watched him go in silence. When he reached the street he paused to examine himself in a shop window. The damage to his clothes was worse than he'd thought and even in the fresher evening air he could smell the strong, sour odour of the beer.

He could not possibly present himself for his next appointment in that condition. The only thing to do, he decided, was to go back to the club and change. It would make him late by a half-hour or more but there was really no alternative.

2

Lord Stamfordham, the King's private secretary, was appalled. Young Tremayne had not only appeared late for his appointment, but his clothes were more suitable for a day at the Henley Regatta than for a meeting with the King. He smoothed back his silver hair and composed his face into a look of stern disapproval. It was difficult because he was, by nature, a kindly and tolerant man.

'You are late,' he said. He took out his gold hunter watch – a present from His Majesty – and made a deliberate calculation. 'To be precise, you are exactly 43 and one-half minutes late!'

'Sorry about that, sir,' said Tremayne. His cheerful grin did nothing to ease the other man's irritation. 'Had a bit of an accident on my way here.'

'An accident? And how was that, may I ask?'

'Well, I was in this pub, don't you see. That's why I'm wearing this clobber.' He ran a hand over the blazer. 'Only have the one suit. Sold the rest in Moscow. Great demand for English togs out there—'

Lord Stamfordham raised a weary hand. He wanted to hear no more.

'Never mind. I doubt whether His Majesty will be able to see you now. Which is probably a good thing for all concerned. He is with the Prime Minister, and after that he has to go on to a dinner at the French Embassy.'

'Oh, I see. Well, I really am very sorry, sir. If you would convey my apologies—' Tremayne moved as if to leave, but Stamfordham checked him quickly.

'I did not say you were to go!' Really, he thought, these young men have no idea, no idea of protocol or correct behaviour. 'You will wait here until I have spoken with His Majesty.'

'Jolly good, sir,' said Tremayne.

Stamfordham winced, and with a little shake of his head went through to the King's study.

3

He found the Prime Minister and King George as he had
left them – locked in a discussion which, at times, had
the heat and force of argument. The King was visibly
agitated as he paced up and down, treading a line on the
pattern of the carpet. Lloyd George, standing with his
back to the fireplace, seemed calm and controlled by
comparison; but he was speaking as Stamfordham came
in, and for all his respectful manner, there was no dis-
guising the cutting edge in the singing Welsh voice.

'And I may further remind you, sir, that when
Kerensky asked us last year to give asylum to the Tsar
and his family, it was your Majesty who expressed the
view that it would be inexpedient to do so. I have your
letters of April 6, 1917 with me should you wish to re-
fresh your memory.'

'That was a year ago, Prime Minister! The situation
has rather changed since then!'

'It has changed for the worse, sir. You wrote in your
letters about the mood in the country – and you were
right so to do. That mood has developed. With respect,
there are many who regard the ex-Tsar as an autocratic
tyrant.'

'That is monstrous!' interrupted the King sharply.
'He was weak perhaps – putting up with that rascal
Rasputin, for instance – but he had a genuine concern
for his people.'

'Perhaps – but the feeling is there nevertheless. And it
is growing. And, as you are aware, we have our own
difficulties in France at the moment. If the public were
to learn that we were spending time and effort on an
attempt to get the Tsar and his family out of Russia
while our armies are fighting to survive there would be

an outcry. And if we were to bring the Tsar here, there would be riots in the streets!' Lloyd George straightened his spotted bow-tie in a manner which suggested that, so far as he was concerned, that clinched the argument.

The King had stopped his uneasy pacing and was now looking out of the window at the darkening gardens. When he turned back to face the Prime Minister, his shoulders sagged a little, and his voice was subdued, almost humble.

'This business – Nicky – the Tsar, the girls, has been much on my mind. Perhaps on my conscience also. I was wrong not to help when the opportunity arose last year. But – well – I felt that Kerensky and the Provisional Government were moderate and reasonable, that the Imperial family were in no immediate danger. It is different now. The Bolsheviks are consolidating their power. They will not leave the Tsar unharmed for long. We must do something, Prime Minister. I do not say bring them here, I accept that such a move might not be popular or possible. But we cannot leave them to rot, or to be murdered.'

The King plucked at his beard with nervous fingers, his sad, mild eyes fixed on the Prime Minister. At that moment he looked almost the double of the man he had been pleading for – his cousin, the Tsar. Lloyd George was not a man to be easily disconcerted but he shifted uneasily.

'The situation in Russia is so confused, sir,' he muttered. 'It changes from day to day.'

'There is a young man just back from Moscow,' said the King. 'General Tremayne's son. He was on the ambassador's staff. I was hoping that he might bring some word—'

'He is here, sir,' said Lord Stamfordham.

Lloyd George grasped at the diversion. 'Let's have

him in then!' he said, and added with a little more deference, 'If his Majesty agrees?'

The King nodded and a moment or so later Stamford-ham reappeared with Tremayne. Faced with both the King and the Prime Minister, the two most illustrious men in Britain, some of the young man's cheery brash-ness evaporated and he waited nervously during the formal introductions. With immaculate politeness, both men ignored the striped blazer.

'He has his father's looks, don't you agree, sir?' asked Lloyd George. He studied Tremayne, his head tilted to one side in a characteristic gesture.

'He is much like him,' said the King.

'What brings you back?' asked Lloyd George.

'I've been given a temporary release by the Foreign Office, sir,' said Tremayne. 'For the duration, actually.'

'What on earth for?'

'I'm anxious to get into things, sir. I'm taking up a commission in the Coldstreams,' said Tremayne un-certainly, not liking the glint in the Prime Minister's eye.

'Hmph!' grunted Lloyd George. 'You know Russia, speak the language, do you?'

'It's hard to know Russia, sir. But the language, yes, I suppose I do speak it reasonably well.'

Lloyd George grunted again, backed off slightly, and began to fiddle with his bow-tie. His face was thoughtful, his eyes did not leave Tremayne. He had, to an extra-ordinary degree, the talent of instant recall, and he was remembering what he had heard and read about this young man and his exploits in Russia. Among other things, he had organised a 'Pimpernel' operation follow-ing Lenin's takeover of power, smuggling members of the old Provisional Government to the safety of the South. It was said that he had played a leading part in helping Kerensky escape to the West.

'What is your view of the Bolsheviks, Mr. Tremayne?' asked the King.

'I share Mr. Bruce Lockhart's opinion, your Majesty. He believes that it would be fatal to underestimate them.'

'Do you think that they will be able to retain power?'

'Well, sir, I don't know: I am not an expert in political matters. The Bolsheviks have a great hold on the masses, they are brilliant at organisation and propaganda, and they are dedicated, determined and ruthless. I would say that it will take a great deal, a very great deal, to shake them loose.'

'But they are a small minority, surely? What of those who oppose them?'

'If I may speak frankly, your Majesty—? '

'That is why you are here, Mr. Tremayne.'

'The opposition, the so-called White opposition, is ineffective for several reasons. First, it is largely led by former Tsarist generals and officials who wish simply to return to the sort of régime Russia had in the past. They do not really understand what has happened in their country, and they will get nowhere until they do. Second, they seem unable to agree among themselves. One general wants this, another that, and each wants to control his own private army. They are autocratic by nature and upbringing. Third, they have no adequate supplies of arms or equipment.'

'Not bad for someone who isn't an expert,' said Lloyd George. 'Is that all?'

'One further thing, sir,' said Tremayne. 'Quite simply, they have no leader who can measure up to either Lenin or Trotsky.'

'Those monsters!' said the King. He paused, and then added tentatively, 'What do you hear about the Tsar and his family?'

Tremayne looked surprised. 'All I know is what is in the reports I brought over from the Ambassador.'

'They are still held at Tobolsk?'

'Yes, sir, they are. Or rather, they were at Tobolsk when I left Moscow.'

'Do you believe there is any possibility that the Bolsheviks will let them leave Russia?'

'No, sir. I do not.'

'What do you think will happen?'

Tremayne hesitated a moment and then said: 'I believe – it is only my opinion – I believe that they may be executed, sir.'

The King stared at him for a long moment, then turned away. The Prime Minister cast a glance of sympathy in his direction, and moved closer to Tremayne. He smoothed back the great mane of white hair, then said softly: 'Answer me one question. Why have the Bolsheviks not executed them before? Why have they been kept alive so long?'

'Because they were useful.'

'In what way?'

Tremayne frowned. He found it hard to believe that the Prime Minister was not informed on these matters. Was he being submitted to some sort of test? And if so, why? For what purpose?

'I believe you know the answer to that, sir,' he said defensively.

'Tell me, boy, tell me!'

'The Russian Imperial Family have been useful, so far, as bargaining counters. With the Germans, for instance.' Tremayne lowered his voice. 'The Tsarina is related both to the Kaiser and to the British Royal family. The Tsar is the King's cousin. And Lenin is a practical politician. He has just signed a separate peace with Germany – and I would be willing to wager that

39

part of the agreement was that the Tsarina would not be harmed. In similar circumstances, Lenin might be willing to sign an accord with the British, with the life of the Tsar as part of the deal.'

Lloyd George nodded in approval. 'Good,' he said, 'very perceptive. You have your father's brain as well as his looks. Now a final question. Let's agree that the Tsar is being kept alive simply because he might be useful to Lenin at some future date. How much longer can that continue? When will Lenin decide that he no longer needs the Tsar and his family?'

The King turned to listen for the answer. Tremayne looked from one man to the other before replying. 'Not long, sir. Soon, I should say.'

'How soon is soon?'

'A few months. Once Germany is defeated. A few months perhaps.'

Lloyd George smiled.

'The war will be over by Christmas. Now, where have I heard that before?'

'The situation is different now, sir,' said Tremayne. 'The way I see it is this. Since the Americans came in the Allies have gained an immense superiority in manpower and materials. The Germans have almost exhausted theirs – the Ludendorff offensive is the last fling. Sooner or later they must crack.'

'I wish you could get up in Parliament and say that! So – you want to get in before it's too late, eh?'

'That was rather the idea – yes, sir.'

'Well, you won't!' said Lloyd George briskly. 'You will have other fish to fry.'

'Sir?'

'We can get plenty of officers. What we can't get is young men like yourself who have experience of Russia

40

and can speak the language. You are going back there, Mr. Tremayne!'

'I don't think I can do that, sir,' said Tremayne.

'You can and you will. You can take your commission in the Guards if you wish, in which case we shall simply order you to Russia. Or you can go back of your own volition. Take your choice.'

'With respect, that is hardly a choice, sir.'

'Exactly so. Now—' Lloyd George turned to the King. 'With your permission, sir. If Lord Stamfordham could have Mr. Tremayne shown out of the Palace—'

The King gave the private secretary a puzzled nod, and he stepped forward.

Tremayne tried once more, and this time he addressed the King directly. 'Sir, if I might—'

But that was as far as he got, for Lloyd George intervened quickly.

'There can be no discussion, Mr. Tremayne! The decision has been made. If it is any consolation, you will not be going back to Moscow. The exact nature of your assignment will be made known to you tomorrow.' He softened his tone. 'Don't look so down in the mouth, boy. What I have in mind for you will be a damned sight more interesting than Flanders, and every bit as dangerous.'

And as Tremayne went out with Stamfordham, Lloyd George added, with a smile: 'What you could do in the morning is go out and get yourself another coat. That one won't do at all, you know, not at all.'

4

In the annexe to the King's study, Tremayne made a last appeal to Stamfordham. 'Sir, it isn't fair. I was given a promise. If you would speak to His Majesty on my behalf—'

'There is nothing I can do,' said Stamfordham. He had overcome his initial irritation, and was beginning to like this sturdy, forthright young man.

'I've served three years in Russia, sir. I was promised time and time again that when I'd completed my tour of duty I could go into the Army. Do you think it right that they should go back on their word?'

'It isn't them,' said Stamfordham. 'It is the Prime Minister, and he is a law unto himself. And, if you won't mind my saying so, you did rather bring it on yourself, you know.'

'Sir?' asked Tremayne.

'Had you been on time for your appointment with His Majesty, you would have been gone before Mr. Lloyd George arrived. He wouldn't have seen or known about you.' Stamfordham paused, his eyes twinkling. 'Perhaps there is a moral there. Become a teetotaller – or at least, keep out of public houses.'

Whether it was meant or not, Tremayne did not accept the advice. As soon as he got back to his club, he went straight to the bar and began drinking. It didn't make him forget the interview but it did make him feel a little better.

He was not to leave Britain until almost a month later and there were moments when he began to doubt if he would ever leave at all. While he waited and prepared, it was clear that a violent argument was going on at some high level. But at last the clearance came. Before going he had one more brief interview with the King. He was surprised to find that His Majesty asked no questions about his mission, and simply wished him Godspeed. But as they moved to the door the King paused, produced a ring and handed it to Tremayne.

It was a heavy gold ring, with a beautifully-wrought signet of the Russian Imperial falcon – the emblem which was embroidered on the sleeve of all the former Tsar's official robes.

'Take this with you,' said the King. 'If – if by any chance you should be able to see the Tsar and show it to him, he will know you as a friend. He gave it to me in 1912, two years before the war. It belonged to his father.'

With that, he turned away abruptly and the audience was at an end.

Chapter Three

She had been christened Margaret, but among her friends back in England she was called Meg, an abbreviation which her father, the Rev. Henry Wellmeadow disapproved of intensely. In the Rostilov household and among their friends in Petrograd, she was known as Miss Meg, a title which she accepted as a happy compromise between respect and affection.

Miron Rostilov and his wife Aksinia never ceased to congratulate themselves on having acquired Miss Meg. That she was clever, resourceful and brave did not surprise them. After all, as Miron often remarked to his wife, she was British and those qualities came naturally to such a people. Mr. Rostilov prided himself on being a Liberal, a progressive thinker, and he had a great admiration for the British way of life. He had been a regular subscriber to *Punch* and the *Illustrated London News* for many years.

It was this admiration that had decided him to seek out a suitable English governess for his children, Natasha and Mischa. He had a flourishing business in the fur trade which took him abroad at frequent intervals, and in 1913, on one of his visits to London, he consulted an agency which specialised in such matters.

It was arranged that he should interview two possible candidates. He was strongly attracted by the first applicant, a plump, pretty girl with a smooth, creamy skin, impudent blue eyes, and a lively personality. Miss Wellmeadow, on the other hand, if not exactly plain, could hardly be described as pretty. She was thin – at least by Russian standards – and she was reserved to the point of shyness. Still, he liked her expressive, grey eyes, her honesty, and though she spoke no Russian, her other qualifications and her background were excellent.

But did she have the necessary strength to cope, not only with the rigours of the Russian climate, but with those two young terrors, Natasha and Mischa?

It was an important decision and he worried over it for most of the following night. In the morning, he woke with a clearer mind, ashamed of his earlier procrastination. In general, though not always, he was a loyal husband who tried hard to keep to the vows he had made to Aksinia. He saw now that he had allowed the first girl's considerable physical attractions to sway his judgment; to have her living in the house would be disturbing to say the least, and perhaps, knowing his own weakness, a positive danger.

On this high moral tone, he hurried round to the agency and made arrangements for Miss Wellmeadow to come out to Petrograd as soon as possible.

He laughed now when he remembered those early doubts. The young Englishwoman, who had never before been further than Bournemouth or London, settled down to her new life in this strange country with remarkable ease. She attacked the language with a determination which astonished the easy-going Rostilovs; in six months she had more or less mastered it, and by the end of the first year she could read, write and speak Russian fluently.

She won over Natasha and Mischa within a few days, and from then on, they were devoted to her. Firm but kind, she made the Rostilovs realise how spoiled the children had become before her arrival on the scene. She did not destroy their high spirits – in fact, she appeared to encourage them in their pranks – but their manners and their consideration for others improved beyond recognition, and they seemed positively to enjoy their lessons. The Rostilovs often wondered how the family had managed without her.

To their delight, she showed an enormous, almost insatiable curiosity for all things Russian. For the winter she had acquired (at second-hand and at a sensible price) one of those warm, heavy coats that the Russians call a *shooba*, some long woollen trousers, and knee-length boots. In this outfit she felt proof against the worst the Russian winter could send against her. In her free time, she would wander off to all parts of the city, even to the working-class areas, and return, her face glowing, to bombard them with questions. When they remonstrated with her about the dangers she smiled and showed them the little Union Jack she had sewn just inside the *shooba*.

'I am a British citizen!' she said scornfully. 'If I have any trouble, I shall simply show the flag. No one would dare to insult me while I wear this.'

Mr. Rostilov had his doubts about the ability of the British flag to protect Miss Meg against a peasant with a skinful of vodka, but he kept them to himself, not wishing to hurt her feelings.

On one occasion she came home to the big house near the Imperial Park, her eyes blazing with indignation. While out walking, she had seen a crowd of workers gathered in a small square behind the Finland Station. They were railwaymen who had met to protest at their working conditions and the rising cost of food.

'They were quite well-behaved,' she said, 'listening quietly to the man who was speaking, causing no trouble.

Then, suddenly, I heard the sound of horses. The crowd heard it too, and they fell silent, even the speaker. Then someone shouted "Cossacks! Cossacks!" and everyone began to run in panic. A troop of Cossacks came round the corner and without hesitation, without warning, they charged the crowd, hitting out at them with their long whips.'

'The Cossacks are brutes, barbarians!' said Mr. Rostilov. 'Those whips have metal tips – they can cut through to the bone.'

'It was frightful,' said Miss Meg, 'simply frightful! People were shouting and screaming, running in all directions. And some of the Cossacks were laughing, actually laughing, as though it were a game!'

'We warned you, we begged you not to go out alone!' said Aksinia.

'Oh, I was all right!' said Miss Meg angrily. 'I managed to get into a doorway. Then, when the Cossacks had gone past, I saw this officer sitting on his white horse at the entrance to the square. So I went up, showed him my Union Jack, and told him what I thought of him and his men!'

'You did what!' gasped Aksinia.

'I am an Englishwoman,' said Miss Meg sternly. 'I do not approve of wanton brutality, and I told him so. Why, there were people lying in the snow with blood pouring from the wounds made by those terrible whips. I saw the Cossacks knock down one poor old man and trample on him, deliberately trample on him! Did you expect me to stand by and say nothing?'

'It's a wonder you're here to tell the tale!' said Aksinia, shuddering.

'I should have liked to see that Cossack officer lay as much as a finger on me!' said Miss Meg. 'The British Ambassador would have heard about him!'

'What did he say?' asked Mr. Rostilov.

'Do you know – he actually smiled and saluted me! He asked if I knew Sandhurst and said he'd stayed at the Military College there last year!' Her voice quivered with renewed indignation. 'Well, I was flabbergasted. Those people lying in the snow, those whips – and him sitting up there on his white horse, talking about Sandhurst! I just looked at him with contempt, turned on my heel, and walked away. He called after me, but I pretended not to hear. He said that I should keep away from the Dark People in future. Now, what did he mean by that, may I ask?'

'Working men,' said Mr. Rostilov. 'That's what the workmen are called. Not by me, naturally,' he added hastily.

'I should hope not!' said Miss Meg. 'We are all equal in the sight of God. I shall never forget what I saw today, never. I didn't believe such things could happen!'

'That is Russia, I'm afraid,' sighed Mr. Rostilov.

'It couldn't happen in England!' said Miss Meg proudly. And as she moved to the door she added: 'Do you suppose the Tsar knows that this sort of thing goes on?'

Mr. Rostilov spread his hands and shrugged.

'I shall compose a letter of protest and send it to His Imperial Majesty!' she said firmly.

Months passed and no reply came from the Tsar. Miss Meg realised that he was a busy person but she was surprised by this failure to respond. She made no public comment, but privately she felt that such conduct was odd, even discourteous.

She had never actually written to the King in England (there had been no cause to do so) but she was certain that if she had, some sort of reply would have been forthcoming, if only an acknowledgment from one of his secretaries.

War came, and with it a letter from Miss Meg's father commanding her to come home. He had never liked the idea of her going to Russia and now, more than ever, he felt that she would be safer under his paternal wing.

She replied politely that she had decided to stay on. There was never any doubt about her decision. It had taken every last ounce of her courage and will-power to escape in the first place and she had no intention of going back. It was strange, but she had never felt so free and happy as she did in autocratic Russia: by contrast, the vicarage in democratic England, which had been her home, seemed like a prison, with her father as the jailer.

She was happy with the Rostilovs and proud that Britain and Russia were allies in the fight against those dreadful Germans. She threw herself into war work, organising first-aid classes, the collection of comforts for the troops, and a dozen other things.

As the war developed and the Russian armies were rolled back in defeat after defeat, she became horrified at the complacency and corruption in the capital. The poor stood in long, patient queues for their share of the fast-dwindling food supplies, while the rich, with a few honourable exceptions, lived almost as well as they had before. She admired Mr. Rostilov more than ever. He turned his Petrograd factory to the task of making winter clothing for the troops and would have no part in the profiteering which went on all around him.

So the outbreak of the February Revolution of 1917 did not really surprise her; she only wondered why the people had waited so long to protest. She felt a twinge of pity for the fallen Tsar, who looked so much like her own

King, but on the whole, she thought he had brought the trouble down on to his own head.

Mr. Rostilov was delighted with this new development. He came home in high exultation one afternoon after attending a session of the new parliament, the Duma. 'At last,' he told Miss Meg, 'at last Russia has a real parliament and a democratic system. Just like you have in Britain.'

He was so excited that he forgot himself and taking her in his arms, he danced round the room. Despite the occasion, she was concerned at this show of familiarity, especially since Aksinia had taken the children out for the afternoon. Mr. Rostilov had been drinking, she could smell the alcohol on his breath, and he was holding her far too close. She released herself as soon as it was polite to do so, and went to her room.

She pulled off her house-dress and was just about to change into her warm, outdoor clothes when, to her astonishment, the door opened and Mr. Rostilov came lurching towards her. His face was pink, the bald spot on the top of his head was shining, and his mouth seemed fixed in an inane grin.

'A kiss,' he said. 'I feel so happy. A kiss. Just one kiss, eh? A kiss for Miron.' His eyes dropped to her white drawers and he sniggered.

'You will leave this room at once!' she said sternly.

'Not till you give me one little kiss. My dove, my little white English dove. You've filled out, my dear, do you know that? A real woman, that's what you are.'

'You are being ridiculous! Please, leave this room!' And as he moved yet another step towards her, she added firmly: 'If you are not out of my room in ten seconds I shall tell Madame Rostilov.'

He stopped, swayed a little, and squinted at her, as if he were finding it difficult to focus.

'What?'

'If you don't leave at once, I shall tell your wife! And I shall go back to England immediately.'

He stared at her in silence for a moment, frowning. At last, her words seemed to register, for he lifted a hand and waved it feebly in front of his face.

'Sorry,' he said.

'And so you should be! Now, please leave!'

'Very sorry.' He shook his head as though to clear his thoughts and moved to the door. As he turned back she saw that his eyes were moist.

'Sorry,' he said again. 'Don't know what—' He looked pathetic now, and she felt almost sorry for him. 'You – you mustn't leave us, my dear. You must never leave us,' he continued.

'I don't think you have left me any alternative, Mr. Rostilov,' she said, not unkindly.

When he had gone she locked the door, then went to her bureau to find and check her passport. She would go to the British consul that afternoon and arrange for a passage home. She would not stay in that man's house, under his roof, a moment longer than necessary. If she did so, it would be tantamount to condoning his conduct, he might even see it as an encouragement.

With this resolve, she set about dressing. As she did so, she caught a glimpse of her almost naked body in the long mirror, and paused. Yes, perhaps it was true. She had filled out a little. She pivoted from side to side, hands on hips, for a moment, smiling at her reflection.

It was something she had rarely done before. She had been brought up to believe that vanity was a deadly sin, that one's body was the repository of wicked urges which should be suppressed. Flesh was something to be covered as much and as often as possible.

She felt one of those strange urges now, a kind of

trembling of the blood which was oddly exciting. Yes, she had filled out, there was no doubt about that, and no wonder with all that Russian food! A real woman – that's what he had called her. Well, yes, perhaps. After all, she would be 24 in a few weeks – if she wasn't a real woman now, she never would be! And the years seemed to be leaping by – she was getting old. It was a chilling thought.

Suddenly, as though the old disciplines had reasserted themselves, she drew back, her face flushed. 'Meg Wellmeadow!' she told herself sternly. 'Meg Wellmeadow. You should be ashamed!'

She dressed hastily, hiding from the light that weak and sinful flesh.

3

That afternoon it seemed as if the whole population of Petrograd had taken to the streets. There was a tiny touch of spring in the air, the first hint of the warmth to come. And over all, there sounded the steady hum of human voices locked in argument, discussion, debate. For the first time in their lives people felt free to speak their thoughts and the words came gushing out, flooding the city. The Revolution was already in its third month, yet still the talking went on, as if everyone was anxious to make up for the years of silence.

As always, Miss Meg found herself caught up in the exhilaration of it all. She had the feeling that she was living through a great turning-point in history and she was determined not to miss a moment of it.

On almost every street corner groups of men and

women were arguing fiercely, passionately. On one, she saw a haughty, bearded man in a fur-coat haranguing a group of workmen who wore the band of the Red Guards on their arms. They answered him respectfully at first, calling him 'sir', but as he grew more angry so did they, until his wife dragged him away. One of the workmen grinned at one of his comrades and shrugged wearily.

'They'll never learn,' he said. 'They won't even try to understand.'

At the Mikhailovsky she saw a group of ordinary soldiers, their faces pinched and white, jostling a young captain of artillery, tearing the epaulettes from his shoulders.

'You don't want those!' they shouted. 'We're all equal now, all citizen-soldiers!' They threw the epaulettes down, and pushed him away with good-natured grins. 'Run along, sonny – and remember, rank has been abolished!'

Miss Meg noticed as she continued that many of the officers she passed had already taken the precaution of removing or hiding their epaulettes, which in the eyes of the soldiers in the ranks were a symbol of the former tyranny. Few of the officers wore the swords they had always carried before the Revolution.

Along the Nevsky Prospect, people with arms linked were stretched across the width of the road, a vast cheerful throng in which, here and there, trams and an occasional automobile were stranded like beached whales. An armoured car came into view, its siren wailing, and the word went round that it was carrying Kerensky, the popular Minister of Justice. Like the miracle of the Red Sea, the crowd parted and cheered the car on its way.

Miss Meg cheered with the rest. She admired Kerensky for the way he had stood up to the extremists when they called for the execution of the Tsar and his family.

'The Russian Revolution does not take vengeance,' he had said proudly. She was sure that Russia would be safe while it had men of such spirit at the helm.

She felt herself being borne along by the general mood of exultation. She saw now the source of Mr. Rostilov's enthusiasm and scolded herself for her intolerance and lack of understanding. What he had done was wicked, of course, but it was the only time he had erred in four years and she should be more forgiving. So she abandoned the idea of leaving – it would be unthinkable to go from all this excitement back to the crushing dullness of home!

Outside the palace of the famous ballerina, Kschessinska, she saw another crowd, listening in tense silence to a small thick-set man in a workman's cap, who was addressing them from the balcony of the palace. He began to attack the Provisional Government and Kerensky, accusing them of betraying the Revolution. He demanded that the war with Germany should be ended, that the soldiers be brought back from the trenches.

He was not an orator in the conventional sense, but he spoke clearly and simply, building his argument brick on brick, like a wall, and he was obviously carrying the audience with him. He finished with the cry: PEACE! BREAD! THE LAND! and the great crowd took up his words, shouting them in unison as with a single, mighty voice.

Another man standing beside the speaker, a man with a goatee beard whose glasses glinted in the pale sunshine, stepped forward and shouted: ALL POWER TO THE SOVIETS! This cry too was echoed by the crowd and as if at a signal, hundreds of fluttering banners were lifted into the air. They were all blood-red and many of them bore the slogans shouted by the speakers.

Miss Meg didn't like the look or the sound of this at all. It seemed to her that some people were never satisfied.

They had only just got their new Parliament and democratic government, now they wished to overthrow it! And the idea of Russia making a separate peace with Germany shocked her patriotic soul: it sounded like treachery.

She spoke to a woman on the edge of the crowd. 'Who is that man – the speaker?'

The woman looked at her in surprise. 'You don't know, comrade?'

'No. Should I?'

'That is our Vladimir Ilyich,' said the woman proudly. 'That is Lenin.'

'And the other man?'

'Trotsky.'

'What are they doing in Kschessinska's house?'

'It is no longer Kschessinska's house, comrade!' The woman laughed. 'It has been taken over by the people. It is now the headquarters of the Bolsheviki.'

Miss Meg's attention was momentarily diverted by an old bearded man who looked like a peasant. He was waving a fist at two fair-haired soldiers who were holding aloft a banner on which was inscribed the words: THE SOLDIERS OF THE SECOND LETTISH RIFLES DEMAND PEACE!

'Traitors!' shouted the old man. 'You should be at the front with your brothers, fighting the Germans!'

And quite right too, thought Miss Meg.

'We have just come from the front, grandad,' answered one of the soldiers mildly.

'Then go back!'

'We have come as delegates to the Soviet. We were elected by our comrades.'

'Soldiers have no right to meddle in politics!'

'You don't understand, grandad—'

'I understand only too well. You are cowards!'

55

'Listen, old man,' said the other soldier sternly, 'we lost three-quarters of our men in the last month. Do you know why? Because we had no ammunition, no supplies. Nobody in authority cares about the ordinary soldier, we are just cannon-fodder! Enough is enough!'

'Why are you complaining, grandad?' asked someone else. 'Are you rich?'

'I am a peasant!' said the old man.

'Well, we want to give the land to the peasants. All the land. Don't you support that?'

'Of course I do! But first we must fight the Germans!'

'What for?' asked the first soldier. 'The German soldiers are our brothers. They suffer and die as we do in this stupid war.'

'Let the Germans take care of themselves,' said another soldier. 'They are already forming their own Soviets, soon they will make a revolution also!'

The old man, still protesting, was pushed aside and the crowd began to march off in a long, untidy, noisy column. Miss Meg turned towards home, her mind a battlefield of conflicting thoughts.

4

What was this? The road to the Rostilov house was blocked by a crowd of angry people, many of whom she recognised as neighbours. Some of the women were weeping. They were being held back by a line of armed sailors from the Kronstadt fleet.

Pushing forward, Miss Meg saw that two trucks were parked in the street. The trucks were already half-loaded with ragged, drunken men and women; soldiers with fixed bayonets were propelling others forward, pulling them from the houses, hitting them with the butts of their rifles when they resisted. A litter of broken bottles and china lay in the roadway, a large grandfather clock stood drunkenly against some railings.

'What has happened?' asked Miss Meg.

'The swine, the swine!' muttered a tall bearded man in the uniform of a civil servant, tears glittering in his eyes.

'It is the Bolsheviki!' said a young woman. 'They have been looting the houses!'

'That is a lie, comrade!' snapped one of the sailors, swinging round. 'The Bolsheviks are not criminals.'

'You are scum!' shouted the tall man. 'Scum! Thieves and murderers!'

Angrily, the sailor raised his rifle and pointed it at the man. The people around him stepped back, but the civil servant shouted: 'Shoot! Shoot! I am unarmed, shoot me!'

Miss Meg stepped between them quickly and to the sailor's astonishment, she put her hand on his rifle and pushed it away.

'Stop it!' she said sharply, in her best governess voice. 'Can't you see the man is upset?' The sailor looked at her with puzzled, sheepish eyes, and after a moment he lowered the rifle.

'All right. But we are not thieves!' he muttered.

It was on the tip of Miss Meg's tongue to ask him why, then, they had taken Kschessinska's house, but she checked herself. Instead, she asked: 'What has happened here?'

'It is the Kharash gang. They pose as revolutionaries, but they are criminals, louts. They have been looting the houses. Don't worry, we know how to deal with their kind!'

57

Beyond the sailor she saw some drunken men being herded out of the Rostilov house. One of them started running down the street; a soldier dropped to his knees and fired after him. The fugitive stopped, swung round and crashed to the ground.

'That is how we deal with them!' said the sailor.

Miss Meg closed her eyes momentarily, trying to fight down the rising feeling of fear and panic. Oh, God, please, she prayed, let the Rostilovs be safe, let the family be safe! She opened her eyes and searched the crowd, but could see no sign of them.

'I live there, in that house!' she told the sailor. 'Let me through!'

'All in good time, miss,' he replied.

'I must go now!' She showed him the Union Jack. 'See. I am English. Let me pass!'

Others began to press forward behind her and one of the sailors shouted: 'All clear now! Let them go, let them go!'

The crowd broke, and scattered towards the houses.

5

The door to the house was open and the large entrance hall was littered with bottles of Mr. Rostilov's precious wine, clocks, ornaments and jewellery. At the bottom of the wide stairs, Miss Meg saw Aksinia's ornate jewel-box and a trail of pillage led upwards.

Every room downstairs had been vandalised, the destruction so wanton that Miss Meg felt sickened. No one answered her frantic calls. She went down the back stairs to the kitchens, but they were deserted; all the servants seemed to have fled.

Upstairs, then, picking her way through the scattered loot, to the main drawing-room and the bedrooms, calling all the time. On the landing she saw Kolya, the coachman, a huge Ukrainian, built like a mountain; he was lying across the stairs, and the blood was bubbling out from a wound in his skull, dyeing the light blue carpet to a dark purple. To her relief, he was still breathing, but all her efforts failed to rouse him. She pulled off one of her skirt-petticoats, placed it as a pad under his head beneath the wound, and hurried in search of the others.

She found Mr. and Mrs. Rostilov in the master bedroom. Standing in the doorway, looking into that familiar, peaceful room where she had often helped Aksinia to dress for some special occasion, Miss Meg felt her heart turn to ice and she began to shiver uncontrollably. She knew without moving forward that they were both dead.

Mr. Rostilov was roped to the rail at the end of the big bed. His head hung downwards, and only the ropes prevented him from falling forwards; his shirt was slashed in a dozen places, and it was as red as the banners Miss Meg had seen earlier. He was facing towards the bed, and his blood still dripped on to the white, lace-edged, counterpane.

Aksinia lay across the bed. Her clothes seemed to have been stripped away from the waist downwards so that the lower half of her body was naked, her plump legs spreadeagled. She, too, was stained with blood, and her broad face dark with bruises.

A distant cry brought Miss Meg back to herself. She went back on to the landing and called: 'Natasha! Mischa!'

With a feeling of unforgettable relief she heard an answer come from the upper floor, from Natasha.

'Miss Meg! Miss Meg!'

Moments later, half-laughing, half-weeping, the children came to the top of the stairs with Maria, their old nurse.

'Wait, wait!' called Miss Meg.

Quietly she closed the door on the scene in the bedroom. Then stepping over the still unconscious Kolya, she flew up the stairs and falling to her knees, took the children in her arms.

6

Gradually, over the next few days, the story came out. It seemed that Kolya, big, simple-hearted Kolya, had been the hero. It was he who had hurried the children upstairs with the nurse, and instructed her to barricade themselves in the nursery. Then, it was clear, he had gone back downstairs to challenge the intruders, fighting them off until he was overwhelmed and struck down. What had happened to the Rostilovs needed no elaboration. Maria had heard Mr. Rostilov shouting that he was a Liberal, on the side of the revolution, but it had clearly made no difference.

Many other people in the street were dead or injured and there was little help for Miss Meg. She managed to get Kolya into the English Hospital, and a nurse there offered to look after the children for a few days. With difficulty, for these were busy days for the undertakers, she arranged for the bodies to be removed and all the details of the funeral. Then she set about the task of bringing some order to the chaos in the house. None of the servants had returned and she had to work almost single-handed, for Maria was too old and feeble to give much help.

Miss Meg sent telegrams to various relatives of the Rostilovs, informing them of the tragedy, but no replies came. The lines were overworked, and even inoperative in many places, and it was probable that the messages were never delivered. However it was, she felt more and more alone.

How was she to tell the children, Natasha now 10 years old and Mischa 8? And what of their future? Who would take care of them? The one thing certain was that they could not be allowed to come back to the house; and as for Miss Meg herself, she now loathed this city which she had once adored, and wanted only to shake herself free of it. Even that stern parsonage in Wiltshire would be better than Petrograd. But she could not desert the children, and could do nothing in her own case until they were safely settled.

On the morning of the funeral she told Natasha and Mischa that their parents were dead, giving them none of the grisly details, softening the terrible blow as much as possible. They wept and clung to her, but it was clear that they did not really understand the significance of this momentous change in their lives.

The graveside service at the Cemetery of St. John the Divine was a shortened version of the full ceremony, for the priests were also under pressure and there were many families waiting to bury their dead. A few friends of the Rostilovs turned up to pay their last respects, and to her surprise, Miss Meg saw Kolya there, his head heavily bandaged. And after, as they were about to leave, Kolya came up to the carriage and spoke to the coachman Miss Meg had hired for the day.

'Move over, brother!' he said gruffly. 'I am the coachman to this family.'

He then took the reins and drove them back to the apartment Miss Meg had rented as temporary accommodation until she could take the children away. Kolya moved in with them as though by right and that evening she told him of her plan.

'Mr. Rostilov has a brother in Ekaterinburg,' she said. 'I intend to take Natasha and Mischa to him.'

'I don't know it, miss,' he said, wrinkling his great brow.

'It is a long way, Kolya. Hundreds of *versts*, thousands. In the Urals.'

'The further the better,' he said gravely, and added, 'I shall come also.'

'No, Kolya, that isn't necessary,' she said.

'Begging your pardon, miss, but that is wrong. A lady cannot travel alone in these terrible days. I shall come with you.'

She nodded, finding words hard to come by. The big man's simple, straightforward loyalty touched her, and she felt her eyes fill with tears.

'Thank you, Kolya,' she said at last.

'God help us all, miss,' he answered and bowing in the Russian manner, he went out.

7

It took many weeks before Miss Meg could complete the arrangements for their departure. The house had to be closed up, jewellery sold to raise money, and there was a long waiting list for the restricted train service. Above all, she had to cut and bribe her way through the bureaucracy which still seemed to keep its stranglehold on Russia.

While she was wrestling with these problems, Kerensky, who was now Prime Minister, paid one of his regular visits to the Tsar, who was under house arrest in his palace at Tsarskoe Selo, a few miles south of Petrograd.

He informed the Tsar that the Provisional Government was coming under increasing pressure from extremists, who wished to have the Imperial family put on public trial as 'enemies of the people'. While they remained so near to St. Petersburg, they were in constant danger.

He was, therefore, making the necessary arrangements for them to be taken away into the interior.

'Are we permitted to know where?' asked the Tsar courteously.

'The actual location has not been decided yet,' said Kerensky. 'It will almost certainly be Siberia, somewhere in the Urals.'

Chapter Four

The man from the Foreign Office, sitting back in his chair with his hands behind his head, said three things to James Tremayne by way of farewell.

The first was to remind him yet again that his mission was entirely unofficial and that His Majesty's Government neither could nor would accept any responsibility or offer any help if things went wrong. He gave Tremayne the impression that he fully expected this to happen. Next, he stressed the extreme urgency of the matter.

'Speed,' he said, 'speed is of the essence. We have received information that the Tsar and his family have been taken from Tobolsk to Ekaterinburg, and placed under a stricter regime. The Soviet at Ekaterinburg is extreme and militant and we know that its members have been putting pressure on Moscow, demanding that the Tsar should be executed.'

Speed, thought Tremayne with some bitterness. It's already the middle of May; I've got to get half-way round the world and back again even to reach the Tsar, and you talk about speed! After all the initial bustle and excitement, he had been held up in London for almost three weeks while the interminable discussions and briefings went on. It had soon become clear that there was, at worst, strong opposition to his mission and, at best, tepid enthusiasm.

Finally, the official put out a languid hand and wished Tremayne good luck. He said it as he had said the other things in a mournful, clerical voice as though he personally despaired of the entire enterprise.

Tremayne left the meeting in a mood which was a mixture of anger and pessimism. Some joker in Intelligence, with a passion for butterflies and moths, had given the mission the code name THE SILVER Y. 'Rather neat, don't you think?' he'd said. 'It migrates, don't you see. Flies from one country to another.' Tortoise, Tremayne thought savagely, would have been a much more suitable choice.

He finally got away on May 13, only to find, after an uneventful but boring trip to Bombay on board a troopship, that some genius had fouled up the arrangements and he was forced to spend six blistering days waiting to move on to Vladivostock. In the end, he managed to bribe and cajole himself a passage on an old Swedish tramp steamer which seemed to be tied together with wire and string and whose ancient engines groaned and protested at every sea mile.

His temper was not improved when, at Singapore, an American came aboard and Tremayne discovered, to his horror, that he was to share his tiny cabin. He protested vigorously, which did nothing to help him or his relationship with the new passenger. There was an acute shortage of ships and passenger accommodation, and the American duly moved in, taking the upper berth. Tremayne noticed with distress that the man smoked cheap cheroots almost incessantly, and wondered what they would do to the atmosphere of the cabin.

However, on the first evening out of Singapore, he decided that he would have to make the best of a bad job and he approached the American on deck after dinner.

'Look, old chap,' he said, 'I'm awfully sorry about making all that fuss. Fact is, my people assured me that they'd booked me a cabin to myself right through to Vladivostock. Still, needs must, eh? Since we're travelling together and all that.' He held out his hand. 'Tremayne. Jimmy Tremayne.'

The American, a big rugged, slow-moving man, looked first at Tremayne, then at the outstretched hand. Tremayne thought he saw a hint of mockery in the very clear, light-blue eyes.

'Sure,' said the American, 'O.K. Why not?' He took Tremayne's hand in a crunching grip. His voice was deep and he spoke with a tantalising, deliberate slowness, as if testing each word before using it. 'Tom Story.'

'Glad to meet you.'

'Likewise.'

And that, to Tremayne's surprise, was that. The big man nodded and turned away in what seemed to be a clear gesture of dismissal. Tremayne stared at the broad shoulders in anger for a moment, bereft of words.

At last, he said coldly: 'I'd be grateful if you would not smoke in the cabin. It really is too small for that, you know.' It was weak and it sounded pompous; as he walked away he had the feeling that the American had won that round.

He made two or three other efforts to draw Story out during the voyage but without much success. The American was taciturn to the point of rudeness, answering mainly in laconic monosyllables. And there was always that slightly mocking look in his eyes, as though he were secretly laughing at the elegant Englishman. Still, thought Tremayne, at least he has given up smoking those cheroots in the cabin, and that represented a victory of sorts.

And, fortunately, there were other consolations. A

small group of nurses from the Swiss Red Cross had joined the ship at Singapore, and Tremayne fixed his sights on one of them, a tall handsome blonde named Babette. He had been without female company for a long time and she posed a challenge which helped to relieve the tedium of the long days at sea. She resisted all his more intimate advances at first, but their relationship ripened to a stage where Tremayne felt that success, so to speak, was within his grasp. And not a moment too soon, he told himself, for on the following day they were due to berth, at last, in Vladivostock.

She did not come down to dinner on that last evening. He was surprised, but not unduly so, for the food was abominable. Tremayne hurried through the meal, leaving most of it, and went to look for her. She was not in her quarters, and none of her friends knew where she could be found. After a fruitless search of the ship he went down to his cabin, mentally cursing all women.

The door was bolted from the inside. Tremayne knocked angrily, and after a moment or so, he heard a movement, and the bolt was drawn back. The door opened a couple of inches and Tom Story's face appeared. Tremayne could see enough to note that he was wearing only a pair of pants.

'Hi!' said the American, his face widening into that slow infuriating grin.

'If it's not too much trouble, I should like to use the cabin,' Tremayne said, with as much sarcasm as he could muster.

'Sure. Why not?' Story made no attempt to let the other man pass. 'Give me an hour, huh? Then it's all yours.'

As he closed the door, he gave Tremayne a small wink. Behind him, someone moved and a girl giggled.

Tremayne paced the deck, working off his indignation.

Some time later, he saw Story at the rail with Babette clinging to his arm, laughing up into his face. Tremayne ignored them with studied deliberation and went below.

A faint drift of perfume hung in the air of the cabin, mocking him. He began to pack, furiously stuffing clothes into his two bags. When Story came down, Tremayne was lying on his bunk reading.

The American glanced at him, smiled, and said: 'Thanks.'

Tremayne turned a page deliberately, and made no reply.

2

Vladivostock greeted the ship with a steady, drizzling rain and a chill wind from the Arctic. The date was June 24. It had taken Tremayne seven weeks to make the journey. Even so, he felt the adrenalin begin to pump again, a sense of renewed enthusiasm. At least now the days of idleness were over. And, from his point of view, the news was good. The Imperial Family was still being held at Ekaterinburg, there had been no change. So there was still time.

The dock was crowded with people of a dozen nationalities, most of them sheltering under umbrellas. Japanese guards were posted at various points, standing like small wet statues in the downpour. At an adjoining dock there was a scurry of activity aboard a Japanese cruiser, and out in the harbour the reassuring presence of HMS *Suffolk*, and the American cruiser USS *Brooklyn*.

Babette, a scarf around her head, came up to wish him

goodbye. 'I hope I shall see you again, Jimmy,' she said, and made it sound almost like an apology.

'I doubt it,' he said coolly. And then, because that sounded priggish and stupid, he smiled and added: 'I shan't be staying here long, I'm afraid.'

'Mr. Tremayne?'

A woman, her face half-hidden under a big black umbrella, had come up to them.

'Yes?' he said.

She lifted the umbrella and he saw that she was young, with brown hair coiled up over an oval face; there was a suggestion of the Asiatic in her high cheek-bones, and dark almond-shaped eyes.

'I am from the British High Commission. My name is Maria Astakhov. May I, perhaps, welcome you to Siberia, Mr. Tremayne?' She spoke in a flat, formal tone, as if she had learned the speech by heart, and she had a marked accent. If her words had any humour in them she was clearly not aware of it.

'Thank you,' he said gravely.

Her eyes flickered for a moment from Tremayne to Babette and back again. 'Sergei will take care of your luggage,' she said, and motioned to a small man in a loose-fitting blouse and baggy trousers who stood behind her. 'This way, if it please you.'

'Cheerio, then,' said Tremayne, raising his dripping hat to Babette. Out of the corner of his eye he saw Tom Story coming towards them, and it gave him a certain pleasure to know that the American was watching as he walked away with the delectable Miss Astakhov.

3

They drove to the High Commission in a gleaming Rolls-Royce, a Union Jack pennant fluttering at the front. The rain had driven most of the civilians inside but there were soldiers everywhere. A troop of Cossacks clattered past, harness jingling, faces impassive; a company of the Czech Legion marched proudly behind the flag which was to be the emblem of their new republic; Japanese and Russian soldiers directed the traffic, a sprawling, untidy mixture of trucks, automobiles, horse-drawn carriages and bicycles.

Miss Astakhov sat demurely beside Tremayne in the back of the big car, her hands in her lap, saying nothing. Making conversation with her, he discovered, was almost as difficult as it had been with the American though for a different reason. She was not at home with English, and she had to strain to understand him. At one point he almost slipped into Russian to make it easier for her, but he checked the impulse. At this stage, the fewer people who knew that he spoke the language the better.

'How long have you been with the High Commission?' he asked.

'Beg you?' Her big eyes searched his face. He repeated the question more slowly. 'Perhaps six months,' she replied.

'This is your home? Were you born here?'

'It is now my home, yes, of course. But I was not born here.'

'Where, then?'

'Beg you?'

'Where were you born?'

'Does it matter?' She shrugged away the question. Tremayne noticed for the first time that she was wearing a wedding-ring. He was about to ask about her husband, but immediately thought better of it. In such times, and in such a place, you did not ask these things. He changed the subject.

'What is the situation in the town?'

'In Vladivostock?'

'Yes.'

'Confusion – yes – that is the word, I think.'

'It certainly looks confused. Who is in control?'

She smiled sadly. 'Everybody and nobody. Each looks after his own.'

'And the Bolsheviks?'

'They tried to take the town. Then the Japanese came with troops and the British, so they stopped.' She paused. 'You will please excuse my bad English.'

'It is very good,' he said gallantly.

'Many troops here,' she continued. 'More coming every day. But no places for them.'

'Which troops? From where?'

'I think mostly the Czechoslovaks.' She pronounced the name with great care. 'The Czechoslovak Legion. All the time they are coming on the railway.'

'In that case, they must have control of it?'

'Beg you?'

Tremayne found her continued use of this phrase amusing and he smiled. 'The Czech Legion controls the railway, does it?'

She wrinkled her brow. 'It is possible. I think so.'

That's something, he thought. If he were to get to Ekaterinburg or anywhere near it, the railway was vital.

His thoughts were interrupted by a burst of firing from a narrow side-street. Four Mongolian-looking horsemen, mounted on shaggy ponies, spurred into a gallop and rode past the car in the direction of the firing.

'Semyonov's men,' said Maria with distaste.

'Semyonov?'

'Ataman Semyonov. He is – how you say it? – like a war-lord. Yes, like that. He has even named himself the Duke of Mongolia! Really he is a bandit. His men say they hunt the Bolsheviki, but I think this is a lie. Not quite a lie, but almost. They look for Reds, yes, but they also look for plunder and for women.'

As if in confirmation of her words, two women, one young, one middle-aged, came running from the side-street, zigzagging this way and that in panic.

'Stop the car!' said Tremayne.

'Is better not,' said Maria.

'Stop!'

The driver brought the car to an abrupt halt. The middle-aged woman, her long hair falling about her, ran across the road towards them, arms flailing, pursued by one of the horsemen. Tremayne lowered the window and took the Browning from his inside pocket.

'No. Please!' begged Maria, taking his arm.

Tremayne shook her off and fired a careful shot over the head of the horseman. The effect was instantaneous. The Mongolian reined in his horse and stared in astonish-ment at the car; his companion stopped his chase of the younger woman and jerked his pony to a halt also. Then, very slowly, they edged their mounts towards the Rolls. The middle-aged woman, trembling and breathless, pressed herself against the bonnet, too weak to run further, but the Mongolians ignored her.

They stared down at Tremayne for a long time. He raised the Browning again and smiled into their angry faces. In the long silence which followed he could feel Maria pressed against him, hear her breathing.

The two men exchanged a few puzzled words and then, with a shake of the head, they put spurs to their ponies and rode away, back into the side-street. Tremayne got out of the car and went up to the middle-aged woman.

'Are you all right?' he asked in Russian.

She looked up at him, sucking in her breath, fear and wonder at her release etched on her face. She straightened up slowly, took one more long, deep breath, then her eyes swept over the Rolls, the damp flag hanging on the bonnet and back to Tremayne himself. The look of fear had now turned to one of bitter contempt. Without a word she turned and walked away, disappearing into the little crowd that had gathered to watch.

'They don't like the British,' he said as he got back into the car.

'They do not like any foreigners,' said Maria. 'Why should they? The foreigners say they come here to keep the peace. Is not true. They come here for their own purposes, is it not so? The Japanese are taking the land, they want to control whole provinces. And they give money to Ataman Semyonov – to this barbarian – so that he will help them do this thing. The people fear that they will never go away, even when the war is over.'

'We're not the Japanese!' protested Tremayne stoutly.

'No.' She gave him a little apologetic smile. 'But even so – you also have your purposes, no? You do not come because you love Russia.'

'As a matter of fact,' said Tremayne seriously, 'I do.'

'Beg you?'

'I love Russia.' It was the truth and she knew it by his tone. She gave a little nod as of recognition.

'Ah. Then you have been here at other times.'

'On and off. Never to the east before.'

'Why are you not telling me that you speak Russian?'

He spread his hands and the lie came easily. 'I have a few words only, a few phrases.'

'More, I think,' she said, but to his relief she did not pursue the subject. As they slowed down to turn into the drive of the big house which was the home of the British High Commission, the boom of artillery sounded in the distance and the grey sky over a low range of hills on the outskirts of the city flared with intermittent flashes of fire. Maria gave a deep sigh.

'Welcome to Siberia,' she said sadly.

4

Klaus Striebeck met Tom Story at the docks with the Bulldog, the Model AC Mack truck which was his regular means of transportation. Although Klaus was an Austrian and a prisoner-of-war, he had learned, at some cost, the traditional rites which are essential to a Texan greeting and he waited for the American to make the first move.

'Hi,' said Story, 'how goes it?' He slammed a huge hand down on the Austrian's shoulder with a force which would have rocked a lesser man. Klaus merely twisted his thick pug-like face into a grin of delight, adjusted the wire-framed spectacles which were forever sliding down his snub nose, and planted a fist in Story's stomach. It was the American who winced. Klaus, though a good six inches shorter, was built like a bullet.

He had been taken prisoner in the early days of the war and posted to various camps, finally ending up at Khabarovsk. After Trotsky signed the separate peace with the Germans at Brest-Litovsk, he was put on the list for repatriation and sent to Vladivostock: but there were no ships available, and the prisoners were now camped in one of the parks, waiting with a patience born of long experience for a miracle to happen.

They were left very much to their own devices. There was no point in guarding them too strictly, for they had no desire to escape, except to their homeland. Some of them, like Klaus, had found work and girls in town, discarded their P.O.W. garb, and settled down to make the best they could of the situation. Vladivostock was not Vienna or Salzburg but it was a whole lot better than Khabarovsk. They could, at least, see the ocean and dream of what lay beyond.

Story had seen Klaus one day at the railway yard, admiring a *bronevik*, one of the great armoured trains which patrolled the Trans-Siberian railway and other vital rail links. Klaus, it turned out, was a railway engineer from Vienna, a practical man yet a romantic. He understood the mechanics of a locomotive better than anyone Story had ever known, but it went beyond that. Klaus loved the iron monsters with a consuming passion, and they responded to him in a most extraordinary way. Under his hand, the most maverick of engines became disciplined and reliable.

Klaus had patiently explained to Story that the locomotive of this particular *bronevik* was in the wrong position. It should not be at the front of the train but in the centre: that way the engineer and fireman would have better protection, and the engine itself would be in a push-pull position, able to reverse or go forward with greater ease. Impressed, Story had taken him on as a sort of general assistant, and from that time on, Klaus had more than proved the wisdom of this decision.

As Klaus put the Bulldog in gear and drove away from the dock, the rain began to ease and there was even a hint of pallid sunshine beyond the grey mist which hung over the town.

'How long has the weather been like this?' asked Story.

'For weeks. Almost since you left,' said Klaus. It wasn't strictly true but it had seemed like that to him. He worshipped the American and Vladivostock had not seemed the same without him. 'Now it is getting better already,' he added happily. 'You have brought the sun.'

Story was not impressed. 'This is a bastard of a town,' he said.

'A bastard,' agreed Klaus.

Story lit two cheroots and passed one over. Klaus nodded his thanks and put it in the side of his mouth. It had taken him some time to accustom himself to these powerful, foul-smelling things, but he had looked upon it as a challenge, a matter of pride. He had observed Story in the act, and now he smoked as he did, talking through the cheroot and chewing the end to a soggy pulp.

'How's Tama?' asked Story, through the smoke.

'Ah!' said Klaus happily. Tama was the woman he lived with, a plump and sultry 35-year-old Eurasian. Klaus had moved in with her in the apartment behind Svetlandskaya Street, taking the place of her husband, who was a prisoner-of-war in Germany. After almost four years in prison camps, Klaus welcomed the regular routine of domesticity, and knowing his own wife, he liked to think that he was simply squaring the account.

And now that the preliminaries were over, Story came, as Klaus knew he would, to the subject which was closer to them than anything else.

'How's the train coming?'

Klaus grinned. 'Finished. Ready.'

'I don't believe it.'

'You wait. You see,' Klaus said confidently.

As they drove into the railway yards, Story frowned and Klaus frowned with him. A white Mercedes 4/2 limousine had drawn up just inside the entrance. It flew the pennant of Ataman Semyonov and lined up alongside there stood his personal guard, a dozen fierce-looking, swarthy men in black Cossack uniforms, armed with sabres and Mosin-Nagent rifles. An orderly was polishing the already gleaming paintwork of the car by the simple method of spitting on it and then rubbing the spittle away with the sleeve of his blouse.

'What the hell!' said Story.

'They have been here many times in the last weeks,' said Klaus.

They drove over to the siding where the train was standing. Story sat in the Bulldog for a full minute, looking, just looking, and Klaus watched his face expectantly.

'Beautiful,' said Story, 'beautiful.' His voice was little more than a whisper. He got down and paced the length of the train.

The locomotive, a Class F Mallet twelve-wheeler, was almost hidden behind the one-inch steel protective plating, which, like the rest of the train, had been camouflaged with brown and green paint. On each side of the engine, back and front, there was a machine-gun wagon, similarly armoured with firing ports for six guns. Each opening could be closed off by a steel flap.

Then came a flat-bed truck holding two Goda machine-guns, with steel shields, mounted on swivels, and beyond this another flat-bed with a field gun housed in a turret. At each end there were two armoured coaches with rifle ports and gun turrets. Huge steel girders to be used as battering rams had been bolted on at the front and rear of the train, and projected forward in the shape of an inverted V.

'Beautiful,' said Story again, as he came back to Klaus.

'Hell's bloody bells! Semyonov!' murmured Klaus

and made a little gesture with his head. A tall man, with the dark look of a Tatar was moving towards them. A bandolier of ammunition and a row of medals fought for room on his thick chest, and on the immaculate brown uniform he wore the epaulettes and insignia of a full general. He was about the same height and build as Story, but his magnificent white fur hat made him seem taller. A heavy automatic pistol was thrust into his belt on one side and from the other there hung a holstered revolver. The belt and his long tan boots shone like mirrors. Two men in Cossack uniform, armed with rifles and sabres, walked impassively behind him.

Semyonov stopped alongside Story and his eyes looked along the train. He nodded twice in approval, then turned to the American.

'Is magnificent,' he said. His face broke into a careful smile, but the narrow green eyes were cold, watchful.

'Not bad, is she?' said Story.

'She?' Semyonov laughed. 'You speak of this as if it were a woman. No, no. It is masculine, a Samson, a Hercules!'

'Have it your way, General,' said Story easily.

'I do not like the painting – the colour,' said Semyonov. 'Only that – otherwise, magnificent!' He turned to one of his escorts, a young captain. 'What you think, Dukhonin?'

The captain came smartly to attention. 'As your High Excellency has said – magnificent.'

'The colour! The colour!'

'It should be white, all white.' The captain gave Story an arrogant look. 'His High Excellency has a fondness for white.'

'White! All white. Then it would be truly a marvel. They would see us coming then, eh, Dukhonin? They would know who rules here, eh?'

'Exactly so, your High Excellency.'

'Buy it, Dukhonin. Make the arrangements with this man.'

Dukhonin saluted. Semyonov turned as if Story and Klaus did not exist, and began to move away.

'Sorry,' said Story, 'but she's not for sale.'

Semyonov stopped and swung round slowly. He put his head to one side and puckered his face in a little, puzzled frown. He paced slowly back to Story, tapping a shining boot with his riding-crop.

'I wish to buy the train,' he said, as though explaining something to a child.

'I heard you, General,' said Story. 'Maybe you didn't hear me. No deal.'

'If your High Excellency will permit—' began the captain, but Semyonov silenced him with an angry lift of the hand. He looked at Story as though he were seeing him for the first time.

'You are the American?'

'That's right.'

'You are in command here?'

'I guess so.'

'Then you can sell the train.'

'No.'

Semyonov sighed. The captain and the other man, a sergeant, tightened ominously.

'We will pay you well. In Kerensky money – kerenkas, if you wish. Or gold. It is as you say.'

'Sorry. No sale,' said Story.

'That is a pity,' said Semyonov sadly. 'You see, if I wish I could kill you and take the train. I am a man of thrift and the idea appeals to me. On the other hand I am a man of honour also. So I will buy the train, at a fair price. What do you say?'

'If you'll excuse me, General,' said the American,

'I've had a long trip and I've a lot to do.' He turned casually and deliberately, showing his broad back. He had moved two paces only, when the sergeant went after him, swinging his rifle like a club.

Klaus gave a warning shout, but it was not necessary. Story had already swivelled round; he seized the rifle in mid-air and wrenched it almost nonchalantly from the soldier's grasp. In the same movement he smashed the weapon against a nearby wagon, shattering the wooden stock. The sergeant came at him with a bellow of rage, but Story sidestepped with loose-limbed ease and cracked him neatly over the back of the head with the rest of the rifle. The sergeant gave him a look of astonishment and collapsed slowly at his feet.

Story sent the barrel of the rifle wheeling into the air, and it fell with a crash against a pile of sleepers. When he turned and faced Semyonov, he was holding an automatic. He took out a cheroot, thumbed a match, and blew a casual plume of smoke into the air.

'General,' he said, 'maybe you didn't understand me. I'll give it to you once more. The train is not up for sale. And if you have any other ideas, hear this. This particular piece of rolling-stock has been bought and paid for by the U.S. Government. You might say it belongs to President Wilson, and I guess he rates higher than a General or even a Duke.'

'It has been a pleasure to talk with you,' said Semyonov.

'Any time,' said Story.

'I hope we shall meet again.' Semyonov said. He raised a hand to the white hat in a mocking salute and strode away. The captain crossed to the fallen sergeant and kicked him in the ribs angrily. The sergeant groaned, crawled to his feet and staggered away, zigzagging like a drunken man as the captain pushed him from behind.

'Does the train really belong to the United States?' asked Klaus.

'As of now,' said Story. 'American troops will be landing in force soon. They'll need all the transportation they can get.'

'They are coming to fight?'

'Nope. Not unless it's necessary. They're being sent to help keep the railways and communications moving and assist the evacuation of the Czech Legion.'

'And what about us – the prisoners-of-war?'

'I guess you'll have to hang on until the war's over, Klaus. I just enlisted you in the U.S. Army.'

'You are not serious!'

'Yep. Down in Singapore they made me a temporary major with orders to look after all this, and keep the lines open. I guess I can't do that on my own. So you're in.'

'With which rank?'

'Sergeant suit you?'

'Hell's bloody bells!' said Klaus happily.

Story stood contemplating the train, chin in hand. 'You know, we got to think up a name for this thing.'

'It is done,' said Klaus proudly. He walked to the cab and hauled down a long white board, which he held up for Story to inspect. On it was inscribed in large black letters: THE YANKEE.

'Jesus!' murmured Story in disgust.

'You don't like?'

'Where I come from that's a dirty word!'

Klaus grinned and turned the board over to reveal another name: THE ROYAL FLUSH. 'This is better?' he asked impishly.

The American studied the board in silence.

'Royal Flush, like it is in poker,' said Klaus anxiously. Under Story's direction he had become an enthusiastic convert to the game.

'You're a comedian,' said Story. 'You ought to be in vaudeville.'

'I remember you are telling me about the time in New Orleans when you are holding a Royal Flush,' said Klaus.

'Four years ago,' said Story, with a sigh. It had been one of the great moments of his life. 'Everyone had folded except for this one little guy. I knew I had a cinch hand, so I bet the limit. That's one of the golden rules, Klaus. If you're holding a cinch, never check – go the limit. The little guy raised, and we went on for ten minutes before he called me. He was holding a straight. I took 1542 dollars from that pot!'

'I have been making a calculation,' said Klaus seriously. 'The chance of a player being dealt a Royal Flush is almost 650,000 to one.'

'I've only ever drawn it that one time,' said Story.

'Now you have it again,' said Klaus. He crossed to the locomotive and slipped the painted board into two metal slots. Then he stepped back to admire his handiwork.

'The Royal Flush,' he said happily.

'Tonight we'll christen her,' said Story.

5

The British High Commissioner in Siberia was a thin, craggy man, with a mop of untidy grey hair and the look of an academic. He handed Tremayne a Scotch, and went to the huge map which almost covered one wall of the office. He swept along the thick blue line of the Trans-Siberian railway with a long, elegant finger.

'Up as far as Lake Baikal and Irkutsk, there is really no problem,' he said. 'Beyond that, the situation is confused, constantly changing. Most of the line is controlled by the Czech Legion or the Whites, but we cannot be sure. The main towns en route, like Novosibirsk and Omsk are held by the Whites. Between Omsk and Ekaterinburg – a distance of 400 miles – there is fighting between the Bolsheviks and a White army group under General Diterikhs.'

'How is that going, sir?' asked Tremayne.

'The Reds are weak and disorganised. Diterikhs has already made significant advances. He is expected to take Ekaterinburg within a matter of weeks.'

'The Tsar is still there?'

'According to our latest reports.'

'And his family?'

'Also.' The High Commissioner walked back to his desk and with some care selected a pipe from a circular rack which stood there. He tapped it on his palm and taking some tobacco from a silver container he filled the pipe and lit it. Only when the blue smoke was curling around his head did he speak.

'Does London understand what they are asking you to do?'

'I doubt it,' said Tremayne.

'Last year they could have lifted the Tsar from Tsarskoe Selo without any problem. They didn't. Why have they changed their minds now?'

'I think you'd better put that question to Mr. Lloyd George, sir. I'm not a politician.'

The High Commissioner went back to the map, and made a sweeping movement of his hand.

'We are speaking of Siberia, a country so big that it could swallow the United States and Europe as a main course and still have room for dessert. We are speaking of a distance of 4000 miles, more or less, between here and Ekaterinburg, a journey in today's conditions of ten days. At least. If – and I say if – you can find a train, and that train can get through. We are speaking of Ekaterinburg, where the Bolsheviks are strong and have little notion of international politics. Lenin and Trotsky may think it expedient to keep the Imperial Family alive as political bargaining counters with the Allies or with Germany, but the Reds in Ekaterinburg know little of such things. They will not let the Romanovs fall into the hands of the Whites or anyone else, if they can help it. They will move them – or execute them. More likely the latter.'

'So we have to get to them before the White army reach the city,' said Tremayne.

'We?'

'I was told in London that you were in touch with – with certain highly-placed people.'

'I have been approached by many groups, all with plans to rescue the Imperial Family. Their ideas range from the lunatic to the impractical. I have kept London informed.'

'I am interested in a man called Kasakov, sir,' said Tremayne, 'Colonel Zakhar Kasakov.'

'One of the lunatics,' said the High Commissioner.

'London has agreed to his plan.'

'Kasakov!' The High Commissioner took the pipe from his mouth and stared at Tremayne in astonishment. 'Kasakov!' he repeated.

Tremayne turned to the map, and picked up a pointer. 'A gunboat, HMS *Chatham*, will berth here in the Gulf of Obskaja, at Novyi Port. The Imperial Family will be taken southwards towards Omsk, towards the advancing White army. But that will be a feint. At Talica – here – we shall turn northwards and strike across country to the River Ob. A river-boat will be waiting at this village – Krasno – to take us up-river to HMS *Chatham*. *Chatham*

84

will head north into the Kara Sea, through the Ovano-vaja Straits here, to Archangel, where the Romanovs will be taken aboard a British cruiser. After that – it will be up to the British Government.' Tremayne replaced the pointer, and smiled.

'Simple,' said the High Commissioner drily, 'you make it sound so simple.'

'Not simple,' said Tremayne, 'but feasible.'

'Haven't you overlooked a couple of things?'

'Sir?'

'First, you have to get to Ekaterinburg. Second, you have actually to lay your hands on the Romanovs.'

'I appreciate that there may be certain problems, sir,' said Tremayne cheerfully.

'God in heaven!' said the High Commissioner. 'And you are proposing to do all this single-handed, are you?'

'Not quite, sir.'

'You surprise me.'

'I shall want to meet this man – Colonel Kasakov. Is he in Vladivostock?'

'He has a house in Karetnaya Street.'

'Can he be trusted?'

'Zakhar is a madman,' said the High Commissioner, 'but, yes, I think you can trust him.'

'Can you arrange for me to see him – as soon as possible?'

'I can but I won't. My orders are explicit. Officially, we know nothing of your mission.' The High Commissioner smiled. 'However, I think Miss Astakhov may be able to arrange matters for you.'

'That will be my pleasure,' said Tremayne. 'Tell me about her.'

'She works here. A useful young lady. She acts as interpreter, secretary, contact woman, general dogsbody. Most useful.'

85

'You have many Russians working here?'

'Not many. A dozen perhaps. We could not manage without them. My English staff has been cut by half in the past year. I keep protesting but London won't listen. If we do intervene against the Reds, they'll have to do something.'

'The Russian staff – they are safe?'

'Oh, yes.' The High Commissioner smiled. 'What is the new-fangled word Intelligence has thought up?' He wrinkled his nose in disgust.

'Screened?'

'That's it. They have all been screened.' He picked up a note from his desk. 'One other thing. If you want to get to Ekaterinburg, you'll have to ask the Americans.'

'The Americans? I thought the Czech Legion controlled the line?'

'Read that.' The High Commissioner handed him the note.

Tremayne read it through and nodded. 'Good,' he said, 'that will make things easier.'

'In my experience,' said the High Commissioner, 'change never makes anything easier.'

Tremayne glanced at his watch. 'If you will excuse me – I've come straight from the ship. I need a bath, a change of clothes.'

'Of course,' said the High Commissioner. He put his hands on the desk, pushed back the chair and got to his feet. 'Tell me,' he said. 'Unofficially, of course. But when is the Navy supposed to arrive?'

'It will be at the mouth of the Ob at dawn on July 17. Ostensibly, the gunboat will have put in for minor repairs. There is little Bolshevik activity in the area so she should be all right. She will wait two days.'

'July 17. And it is now June 24. You have less than a month!'

'Doesn't sound much, sir, does it?' said Tremayne. 'Not when you put it like that.'

After he'd gone, the High Commissioner broke a self-imposed rule which had remained inviolate for over twenty years. He drank a second large Scotch before dinner, and wondered, not for the first time, about the idiocy of governments and politicians.

He did not expect to see Tremayne again.

Chapter Five

I

Every hotel in Vladivostock was like a Tower of Babel, packed wall to wall with an infusion of refugees, army officers, diplomats, and the wheeler-dealers who invariably turn up in any war and just as invariably profit from it. In the ornate lobbies of the two main hotels it was possible to hear ten or twelve different languages.

By some miracle, Maria Astakhov had managed to get Tremayne a room at the Nevsky Palace, a building so extravagantly lavish, so overflowing with marble, crystal chandeliers, ormolu furniture, and Turkish carpets that it seemed to him as if he were moving on to a stage set for some magnificent but improbable play.

At 6 p.m. she brought Zakhar Kasakov to the room. Tremayne's first impression was of youth. Although Kasakov wore the field uniform of a Colonel in the crack Chevalier Guards, he had the face of a teenager. Tall, slim and handsome, there was a touch of impudence in his lively hazel-coloured eyes as he put out a hand to greet the Englishman. The grip was firm and strong.

'I am pleased to meet you – at last,' he said. He put a mocking emphasis on the last two words.

'It is my pleasure, Colonel,' said Tremayne.

Maria had told him that Kasakov had taken part in the great battles against the Austrians in Poland in the first months of the war and been promoted from Captain to Colonel on the field by the Tsar himself. Captured at Vilna in 1915, he had escaped at the fourth attempt, and found his way through to the Allied lines. Until the Tsar's abdication he had served as a Liaison Officer, first with the British Army, and then with the Japanese. After the Bolshevik revolution, he had returned to Russia, consumed by one over-riding purpose – to rescue his beloved Tsar. Looking at the smooth young face, fresh as a new-laid egg, Tremayne found it hard to believe that Kasakov was a man of such experience.

'I hope you bring good news?' said Kasakov.

'Perhaps we can talk alone?' Tremayne nodded towards two soldiers who had come in with the Russian. They wore black woollen hats, shaped like flowerpots, loose tunics, belted at the waist, and baggy trousers tucked into brown felt boots; both had flaxen hair, blue eyes, and wispy, fair moustaches and the same cast of features.

'You do not like my Circassian twins?' asked Kasakov.

'I would rather we talked alone,' Tremayne answered.

Kasakov nodded to the two men. 'Remain outside.' They looked at him uncertainly for a moment, saluted smartly, and went out.

'I shall leave you also,' said Maria.

'That isn't necessary, my dear,' said Kasakov.

'It will be better, I think.' She turned to Tremayne. 'If there is anything further you want, you know where to find me.'

'Perhaps we could meet later,' he said, a little too eagerly and realising this, he added weakly: 'There may be one or two things arising from my talk with Colonel Kasakov.'

'I will come back then. In one hour, perhaps?' There was no expression on her face; if she had read any meaning into his eagerness she did not show it.

'Better make it two. Thank you.'

When she had gone, Kasakov dropped into an arm-chair, straddled a leg over one of the arms, and unbuttoned the top of his tunic.

'She is a beautiful woman,' he said.

'Very,' said Tremayne carefully.

'And a widow.'

'Really?'

'She lost her husband at Tannenberg. Not the only one. My poor Russia! So many widows.'

'It is the same everywhere,' said Tremayne.

The weather had changed with dramatic suddenness, and a hot white sun was beating through the windows. Tremayne crossed and lowered one of the blinds. It seemed to cool the room immediately, flooding part of it in a gentle, golden glow.

'We received your plan in London,' he said. 'We are prepared to co-operate, under certain conditions.'

'You have taken your time,' said Kasakov. He took a slim, gold case from his pocket, clicked it open, and held it towards Tremayne, who shook his head. Kasakov put a black cigarette into a long black holder and lit up. 'What are the conditions?'

'The British Government is not to be involved officially.'

'And the ship?'

'That has been arranged. As you requested.' Kasakov nodded, and stabbed at a smoke-ring with his cigarette, as if part of his mind was on other things. Tremayne fought down a feeling of irritation. 'But the Tsar and his family will only be taken aboard if they specifically ask for British protection. They will then be in the position of refugees, and my Government can respond to their request on humanitarian grounds.'

'Do you suppose that the world will not know that

the rescue was planned, and that the British were involved from the beginning?'

'If we are successful, that will not matter. It will be a *fait accompli*.'

'And if we fail, you will deny everything.'

'We shall deny everything.'

'A strange people, you British. So straightforward in little things, so devious in big ones. Don't worry – we shall not fail.'

'I wouldn't wager on that,' said Tremayne.

'And the other conditions?'

'The actual rescue must be undertaken by Russians, loyal to the Tsar, as you indicated in your plan.'

'Also no problem. I have a hundred good men who are prepared to give their lives for His Imperial Majesty.' The Russian's tone was calm, matter-of-fact, without any suggestion of theatricality.

'A hundred?'

'Two hundred. Three hundred. Four hundred. Whatever we need.'

'No, Colonel,' said Tremayne. 'I meant, even a hundred may be too many. The more people we use, the greater the danger of discovery, betrayal.'

'My men may be trusted absolutely. They have risked their lives many times already. Some of them have fought their way across thousands of miles to join this enterprise. The majority of them are Georgians from the Circassian Horse Regiments and my own Chevalier Guards.'

'The Circassians,' Tremayne said. 'The Wild Squadrons.'

'Ah, you have heard of them! Good. You will know then that they are the best, most fearless fighters in the world. They are mountain-bred, fierce and disciplined.'

'Is it true that they don't drink?'

'Their religion forbids it. They are Moslems. But even the others have pledged themselves against drink and debauchery until we have completed our task.' He smiled wryly. 'For some, it is a great sacrifice.' He paused and added: 'And what of you, Mr. Tremayne?'

'Yes?'

'I cannot believe that you have come all this way simply as a messenger.'

'No.'

'Well, then?'

'I shall want to be involved in the planning and the operation itself. From start to finish, from top to bottom.'

'Is that also a condition?'

'I am afraid it is, old chap,' said Tremayne.

Kasakov drew on his cigarette reflectively and smiled. 'Mr. Tremayne, we had given up hope of the British. It is months since I proposed our plan to your government. Did you expect us to sit on our backsides and wait for your Mr. Lloyd George to make up his mind? Wait so long that, in the end, we should be too late? No. We have been training, working, planning. We are ready to move. I am sorry, you understand, but we really have no need of you.'

'Nor of our cruiser?'

'It would be useful – but there are other alternatives.'

'And you don't need the Americans either?' Tremayne smiled amiably.

'The Americans?' For the first time, Kasakov looked puzzled, less confident of himself. He straightened up in his chair. 'The Americans? What have they to do with this?'

2

At about this time, Miss Meg, tired but happy, was cycling back into Ekaterinburg. She had spent the entire afternoon riding round to the outlying villages in search of food, bargaining and arguing with the peasants until her voice was husky; but the effort had not been in vain. In the bag dangling from the handlebar of the ancient cycle she had two great cow-cabbages, a loaf of black bread, and a pound of potato flour. And, most precious of all, in the little basket at the front, there were six beautiful brown eggs safely tucked into a nest of hay.

Since the time in Petrograd, her appearance had changed. She had grown thin again – though perhaps not so thin as before she left England – and her skin was sunburned and freckled. In the old days, she had always taken care to carry a parasol to protect herself from the sun and to ward off the freckles, but she had long since given up caring about such things. It was sufficient to survive, simply to survive.

Her clothes and hair marked the alteration. The neatly-tailored skirts which just brushed the ground, the white blouses with their starched cuffs had long since been locked away with the neat button-up boots, the dark hair was no longer plaited into a bun at the top of her head. It was slightly shorter now, as was the skirt, and she wore a peasant blouse and birch-bark sandals.

These changes had been made partly out of necessity, and partly as deliberate policy. It was politic not to look too different, too smart in Ekaterinburg, where the Soviet was strong and militant. Men and women had been arrested simply because of their bourgeois appearance, real or imagined. It was better not to call attention to oneself, and to try to merge into the background as much as possible.

Of course, many people in the town, including some of those in the Soviet, knew that she was an Englishwoman, and, naturally, Miss Meg never denied the fact if challenged. In a way, the people were amused by her presence, even respected her.

On her arrival in Ekaterinburg with the children, she had taken them immediately to the home of Boris, Miron Rostilov's brother. Her intention was to stay a few days, see that her charges were safely settled in, and then, somehow, make her way back to England where she intended to enrol in FANY, the women's First Aid Nursing Yeomanry. But all that had now become a dream which with every passing day seemed to recede further into the distance.

In the first place, Boris, who was a reserve officer in the artillery, had been called up for service some months before, and taken prisoner by the Germans in Galicia. Or at least, that is what his wife, Seraphina, chose to believe. No word of his fate had come either from her husband or the authorities, which was not surprising since over a million Russians had been killed or captured in the fighting in this area alone.

In the second place, although Seraphina welcomed Miss Meg and the children with cries of joy, and wept copious tears at their dreadful experiences, it soon became clear that she was quite unable to cope with the situation. A hypochondriac, neurotic to the extreme, she spent half her time in bed nursing imaginary ailments and the other half rushing around the house in a fever of activity, disorganising everything, accomplishing nothing. Since her husband had left for the army, all the servants except one old man had deserted her one by one, unable to stand her capriciousness. At her best, she was a kindly, generous soul with a genuine love for the children, but as time went on, her better moments became less and less frequent.

Miss Meg realised that she would have to stay on longer than she'd planned, but still nursed the hope that things would settle down and she would be able to leave the children with a clear conscience. But month followed month, autumn turned to winter and winter to spring, the Bolsheviks seized power, civil war broke out, and she was trapped. In April 1918, her hopes were crushed by yet another blow. The local Soviet commandeered the imposing house on Circular Place, for use as an emergency hospital, and gave Seraphina and the others 24 hours to get out. It was Miss Meg who found a small house in a poorer district on the outskirts of Ekaterinburg, and bribed the widow who lived there to let her have it. She raised the money by selling some of the Rostilov jewellery to a merchant who, with an eye on escape, was busily turning all his available cash into such solid valuables.

The widow, richer than she had ever been in her life, went happily off to live with her sister. The old man-servant returned, just as happily, to his native village, glad to get away from the town and the revolution. Kolya, who had stubbornly refused to leave, found a room nearby, and a job as a labourer in a local sawmill. He hired a horse and cart and he and Miss Meg made three trips, ferrying furniture and other essentials from the one place to the other. The Soviet had ordered them to take nothing, to leave everything in the house, but Miss Meg argued with the Chairman, Ivan Kalugin, so vehemently that he had given way. He had heard of the strange Englishwoman who had arrived out of the blue with two orphaned children and had chosen to stay and care for them in what was, for her, a strange, alien land and he admired her spirit.

A miner, who was respected in the town as a decent, kindly, moderate man, he had listened to her with a twinkle in his eyes. 'Take what you need, woman,' he said as she paused for breath, 'only leave me in peace. You're worse than my wife Katyusha, damn you!'

'Thank you,' replied Miss Meg, 'but there is no need to use bad language!'

The children quite enjoyed the new house and the adventure of moving, but Seraphina took to her bed as soon as it had been made up and stayed there for two weeks, certain that this latest misfortune had strained her heart. On that first night, Miss Meg came finally to terms with the fact that she would never be able to leave the children. Slowly, she began to make another plan.

She could not go to the west because it was an uncertain, constantly changing battlefield and she could not go south because the Germans were there; to be beholden to them was unthinkable. Eastward, then, to Vladivostock was the only answer. She had read that some allied troops were already in that city and that made the idea all the more attractive. Once in Vladivostock she would get herself and the children to England somehow; what happened after that didn't matter, it was a bridge she would cross when she came to it.

She had spoken of her plan with the British Vice-Consul in Ekaterinburg, a brave man who had stuck resolutely to his post in spite of all harassment and he had promised to try to get her the necessary travel permit and other essential documents.

'But don't build your hopes too high,' he told her. 'The relationship between the British Government and the Bolsheviks is not good – and it is getting worse. They are convinced that we are supporting the Whites against them.'

'And are we?' she asked.

'That is not for me to say,' he replied carefully.

As she bumped over the dusty road on the ancient bicycle with its solid tyres, Miss Meg decided that she would go and see the Vice-Consul later in the week to see what progress he had made. She also thought happily of the food she had garnered; tonight there would be cabbage soup for supper, and some hot potato cakes. She made up her mind to say nothing to Seraphina about the eggs: the children were more in need of them. They should have one each every other day starting tomorrow, and in that way the eggs would last almost a week.

Two figures appeared, trudging down the road, and as she drew nearer Miss Meg saw that they were novices from the Convent of the Resurrection, Sister Elizabieta and Sister Lyudmilla, whom she knew slightly. The bicycle had no brakes and the only way to stop was to push the pedals of the fixed gear backwards. She did this expertly, dismounted, and greeted the Sisters. Their normally pallid, wax-like faces were flushed, their shoes and the hems of their robes red with dust. They were carrying empty baskets, and seemed glad to see her, to pause in the shade of the fringe of birch trees at the roadside and chat. She leaned the bicycle against a tree and all three sat down on the grass bank.

'It is too hot for walking, Sisters,' she said. 'Have you come far?'

'From the town,' said Sister Elizabieta. 'We are going back to the Convent now.'

'Have you been to see Them?' Though they were alone on the road, surrounded only by woods and fields, Miss Meg lowered her voice as she spoke. 'Them' was the local shorthand for the Tsar and his family. The

whole town knew that they were prisoners in Ekaterin-
burg, locked up in the old Ipatiev House on Voznesensky
Avenue, which the Bolsheviks now called the House of
Special Purpose.

'See Them?' Sister Lyudmilla shook her head sadly.
'No one can see them except the guards. We take them
food each day, and we have to hand it to the Guard
Commander. We have no idea if they get it or not.'

'Do you know the latest thing?' asked Sister Elizabieta.
'It is disgraceful, a scandal! All the windows have been
whitewashed over so that the poor things can not even
look out on the town. They are forbidden to open the
windows either by day or night. One of the older guards—'

'Voikov,' interrupted Sister Lyudmilla. 'A good man,
not one of the worst, certainly. What he is doing in such
company I shall never know!'

'His name is of no consequence!' went on Sister
Elizabieta, giving her colleague a reproving look. 'As I
was about to say, this man told us that one of the Grand
Duchesses opened a window on to the courtyard yester-
day, and one of the other guards actually fired at her!
The bullet only just missed, he said.'

'At any rate, they are all still alive. That is something
to be thankful for,' said Miss Meg.

They fell silent at this. Miss Meg was thinking of that
strange day at the end of April, when she had gone to
Ekaterinburg Station to visit a woman who worked as a
clerk in the ticket office. She had been told that the
woman might help her get the tickets for the proposed
journey to Vladivostock. Suddenly, dozens of Red
Guards had descended on the station, cleared it of all
passengers, and ordered the staff to remain in their
offices. Miss Meg had been locked in with the woman
clerk, but by lifting a corner of the curtain they were
able to satisfy their curiosity about what was going on.

And, to her astonishment, she saw the Tsar himself as he was brought in from the train.

She could hardly believe that this small shrunken man, with the sad eyes, had once been the mighty Emperor of All the Russias, a despot whose every wish and word were to be obeyed without question. He wore a simple soldier's tunic buckled at the waist, a peaked cap, and his long leather boots were worn and shabby. He waited with quiet dignity, while two Red Commanders argued briefly. Outside the station, a crowd was pressing against a double line of soldiers, chanting: 'Show us the butcher! Show us Nicholas!' There was something terrible and menacing in their hate-filled shouting.

Yet, in a way, she understood this hatred. Terrifying things had been done in this man's name; oppression, cruelty, corruption, pomp and unbelievable poverty had been the hall-marks of his regime. It was said of him that he was weak and easily influenced; perhaps, therefore, it was not entirely his fault, just that he had happened to be the wrong man, in the wrong place at the wrong time, a prisoner of the system and the title which he had inherited.

It was also said by some that he was, in essence, a simple man, who disliked the pomp and ceremony with which he had been surrounded, that he was a loving father and a good husband who liked nothing better than to be with his family. He loved manual work, to saw logs or to make up furniture in his carpenter's work-shop. It was not the Emperor, but this other man that Miss Meg saw at the station, and her heart went out to him.

How are the mighty fallen, she thought, and how much better for the poor man if he had been born in humbler circumstances, perhaps in Britain, where he could have lived according to his simple nature! She remembered

Kerensky's words: 'The Revolution does not take vengeance!' How different now! Kerensky had gone, his name now only a footnote in history, and outside the station the crowd was baying for the revenge he had repudiated.

She had seen the Guard Commander step forward, heard him say with heavy sarcasm: 'If your Imperial Majesty would deign to follow me?' The Tsar looked at him without expression, and followed quietly. A strange silence fell on the mob as he appeared and then the roar broke out again, a mingling of booing and curses which was frightening to hear.

On that April day, watching that small bearded figure walk away, Miss Meg had experienced an overwhelming premonition of doom. Some lines from Shakespeare slipped into her mind:

'For God's sake, let us sit upon the ground
And tell sad stories of the death of kings . . .'

How did it go on?

. . . . for within the hollow crown
That rounds the mortal temples of a king
Keeps Death his court. . . .'

Yet it was now nearing the end of June and the Tsar and his family were still in the House of Special Purpose, still guarded and hidden from sight by the tall palisades which had been erected around their prison. Perhaps, she thought, King George V has intervened on their behalf. After all, he and the Tsar were cousins; she could not believe that the King would do nothing to help his relative and loyal ally. Even the Bolsheviks would not dare to incur the displeasure of the King of

England, to challenge the might of the British Empire! Miss Meg had an unquestioning faith in both her King and his Empire; she commended them to God each night in her prayers, and never forgot to thank Him for the privilege of having been born an Englishwoman. The thought sustained her and gave her courage.

She was brought back from her thoughts by the voice of Sister Elizabieta.

'Have you heard about Ivan Kalugin?'

'No.'

'He has been deposed as Chairman of the Soviet. It is rumoured that he is under arrest.'

'They say he has been too easy-going,' said Sister Lyudmilla. 'He will be shot – that's what they always do.' There was a note of satisfaction in her tone.

'Poor man,' said Miss Meg.

'He is a Bolshevik!'

'Does that matter?' She felt truly sorry for Kalugin. There had been enough blood, enough death. She did not want to see one more person die; not the Tsar, nor Kalugin, nor Lenin, nor even the Kaiser, though she blamed him most of all for the violence that had been released to spread like a plague over the whole world.

'And who has replaced Kalugin?' she asked.

'A man called Gromeko, Viktor Gromeko.'

'Is he from Ekaterinburg?'

'No. At least I've never heard of him before. He seems to have popped up from nowhere.'

'They say he is cold, like ice, that he never smiles,' added Sister Elizabieta.

Miss Meg rose and plucked a twig from a rowan tree which seemed to have found a place among the birch trees by accident. The berries were not yet ripe; she stripped them off and let them fall through her fingers. A dragon-fly skimmered by on translucent wings. She felt suddenly sad, homesick for the English countryside. Names, the English names of her childhood, rang in her head like bells: Allington, Great Cheverell, Beechingstoke, Morgan's Hill, the Avon. Oh, the smooth and peaceful Avon! And almost immediately she set the feeling aside. Self-pity is a sin, this is no time for such weakness, she told herself sternly.

'I must get back to the children,' she said aloud.

'Goodbye. God's love go with you!' said the Sisters in unison.

'And with you,' she said, as she cycled away. God's love be with everyone, she thought, as she pressed down on the pedals. But where was God?

Had he turned his back on the whole human race in disgust?

3

Kasakov removed his cigarette from the holder and stubbed it out in a large onyx ashtray. Tremayne smiled inwardly; for the first time he had pierced the Russian's calm, the air of casual indifference which he had found so infuriating. He did not let his satisfaction show.

'The Americans, you say. Do they know of our – our plan?'

'They are our allies. Naturally, they have been informed. Through the usual channels. At the highest level.'

'And?'

'They have approved – unofficially.'

'Like the British.'

'Exactly.'

'Unofficially,' said Kasakov waspishly. 'Always unofficially. What is the phrase? Heads I win, tails you lose. If we succeed you take the credit, if we fail you wash your hands and deny everything!'

'Something like that,' said Tremayne.

'We can do without the Americans also!' said Kasakov.

'Can you?' Tremayne strolled to the window and lowered the blind a little more, creating a deliberate pause before he continued: 'Ekaterinburg is 4000 miles away – how do you propose to get there?'

'The Commandant of the Czech Legion has agreed to make a train available. Of course, he doesn't know our real purpose. He has never forgiven the Bolsheviks for trying to disarm his men. He thinks we wish to go west to join up with Diterikhs and his White army.'

Tremayne hesitated. Then, he thought, what does it matter? Tomorrow it will all be public knowledge. 'As from noon tomorrow, Colonel,' he said slowly, 'all rollingstock between here and Lake Baikal will come under the direct military control of the Americans, acting on behalf of the Joint Allied Commission in Vladivostock. Two hundred US Marines from the *Brooklyn* will take over the trains, the station, the railway yards, the repair shops – everything. No locomotive will move in or out without their say-so.'

'How do you know this?'

'I heard the news only a few hours ago from the British High Commissioner. The Americans are taking over from the Czechs – official.'

Kasakov frowned. 'But I understood that President Wilson was opposed to any American intervention in Russia. Has he changed his mind?'

'No. The Americans have undertaken simply to protect the railway and keep the line open.'

'With two hundred Marines?'

'Within a few days, two Infantry divisions and a regiment of engineers will arrive to reinforce them. They will be stationed at all key points along the route between here and Irkutsk, at least. They may extend the operation as far as Omsk.'

'And this is what they call non-intervention!' said the Russian bitterly.

'Politicians have their own language,' said Tremayne. 'Would you rather have the Japanese in control of the Trans-Siberian?'

'The Japanese! They would use it simply to build their Empire in the East!'

'Then, perhaps that explains why the Americans are moving in,' Tremayne said. 'I believe it is called maintaining the balance of power. Whatever the motive, there is this to be said, Colonel. When peace comes, when the time comes to rebuild Russia, you are going to need the Trans-Siberian.'

Kasakov paced the room in silence for a few moments. He stopped and tapped his fingers on a table, drumming out an intermittent rhythm, his eyes on Tremayne.

'So it comes to this,' he said at last. 'I have to go to the Americans and ask them for a train.'

'No,' said Tremayne, 'I do.'

'And will you get it?'

'I told you – the plan has been approved at the highest level. The American representative in Vladivostock will have been instructed to give me the fullest co-operation. Top priority. A matter of the utmost urgency.'

'So.' The Russian's face opened in a boyish grin. 'It seems that I have to take you along whether I wish to or no!' He held out his hand, still smiling. 'Then let us seal the bargain.'

'As long as we understand what it is.'

'How is that?'

'I am not coming just for the ride, Colonel. I am to be completely involved in the planning of the operation – and in its execution.'

'I thought you said our plan had been approved.'

'In outline. It is the detail that I am concerned with. And the people. Let me put it this way, Colonel. Last year, a group of well-meaning patriots made an attempt to liberate the Imperial Family when they were imprisoned at Tobolsk. The idea was bold and imaginative, the planning and execution diabolical. It was a disaster.'

'So,' said Kasakov, 'it comes to this. We are to imitate the Bolsheviks. I will play the Commander, and you will play the Commissar.'

'If you want to put it like that.'

'The Bolsheviks appoint Commissars because, very often, they don't trust their military commanders. I take it you don't trust me?'

'I don't know you,' said Tremayne evenly.

'Nor I you.'

'Then we start on even terms, Colonel.' This time it was Tremayne who smiled and extended a hand.

4

When Maria Astakhov came back for Tremayne she looked quite different. She had changed into a long white evening dress which enhanced the glowing beauty of her light-brown skin and dark eyes, and let down her hair so that it made a perfect frame for her oval face. He had thought her beautiful when she'd met him at the dock, but now that word seemed inadequate; she seemed somehow to have wrought a subtle change in her personality, to have left the efficient, highly-organised secretary behind at the High Commission and emerged as a total, lovely woman.

She stood in the doorway to his room, smiling at the astonished admiration in his eyes. 'You did ask me to come back,' she said.

'Of course. Thank you,' he said awkwardly. Now there was another problem; he could not leave her standing there, but on the other hand, to invite her into his room would suggest a familiarity, a lack of good manners which she might find offensive. In England, at least in the circle in which he had been brought up, it simply wasn't the done thing to compromise a lady in this fashion – not unless she was of a certain type or one was on terms of some intimacy with her.

She solved the dilemma for him. 'May I come in?'

'Yes – yes, please. I'm sorry.' He stood aside as she entered, bringing with her a delicate hint of perfume which emphasised her femininity. He wondered now about the door. To leave it open would appear too obvious, to shut it could also smack of familiarity and could embarrass her. He left it slightly ajar.

'You said you might need me,' she said.

'Ah, yes. Yes,' he said.

'Your talk with Colonel Kasakov went well?'

'Excellent.'

'There is perhaps something else you wish me to do?'

'I don't think so.' He hesitated. He was not usually shy, or ill-at-ease with women, but he was still slightly stunned by the dramatic transformation in her appearance. 'Unless—' he added.

'Yes?'

'Nothing,' he said, trying to sound as casual as possible. 'Obviously, you've got an engagement for this evening. If you hadn't, I was going to suggest that we might –

well – perhaps we might have dinner together, that's all.'

'No,' she said.

'I quite understand,' he said.

'No,' she repeated, smiling. 'I am not engaged for this evening. It would be a happiness to join you.'

'Marvellous!' he said, with an enthusiasm which brought another smile to her face. 'Do you mind? I'm afraid these are the only togs I have with me.'

'Beg you?'

'I haven't a dress suit – dinner-jacket.'

'You look very pretty.' Seeing his look of amusement, she frowned. 'Pretty? No? Is wrong?'

'Wrong. It doesn't matter. A woman can be pretty, but not a man. I could say you were pretty – but even that wouldn't be quite right.'

'I am not pretty?'

'More, much more. Stunning. Absolutely spiffing!'

'Spiffing!' She put back her head and laughed at the word. 'Spiffing! Is nice. I like.'

Downstairs, the great restaurant was crowded, tables packed into every conceivable square metre of space, between which the white-coated waiters wriggled like eels, carrying trays laden with wine, bortsch, caviar, salmon, roasted meats, cucumbers, herring, fresh rye bread, potato salads, and assortments of steaming vegetables. On a dais in one corner a small gypsy band played Tzigane music, trying desperately to make themselves heard over the babble of noise. There seemed to be no shortage of women; their voices echoed in the general hubbub, shrill as a dawn chorus of birds.

At one long table a group of drunken White officers was indulging in some sort of celebration, bawling out a song in competition with the gypsy band, banging the table with their fists and turning from time to time to throw bread rolls and other missiles at some Japanese nearby. The Japanese accepted these donations with solemn politeness, drawing back their lips in cold, oriental smiles.

A mixed party of Czechs and French seemed to be having an equally merry, though slightly more subdued party at another table. And all around there were smaller groups, couples and foursomes, adding their quota to the clamour. In one corner, as though on an island, an Italian captain sat with a beautiful Eurasian girl, holding her hand across the table and looking deep into her eyes. They seemed to be the only silent people in the room.

Tremayne looked at the scene in dismay. He caught a passing waiter by the sleeve. 'Is there a table?' he asked, but the man merely shrugged him off. Maria gave Tremayne a little smile.

'Wait,' she said.

She moved to the desk near the door and he saw her speak with a head waiter. He nodded, bowed, and came back with her.

'If monsieur would not mind to wait a few minutes,' he said. He disappeared into the throng before Tremayne could answer.

'You seem to be able to fix anything,' Tremayne said.

'They know me,' she answered, with a little shrug of the shoulders.

'Is there nowhere else?'

'They are all the same,' she said, 'Vladivostock has gone mad.'

'No wonder the Bolshies have made such headway,' he said.

'Beg you?'

'All this. I thought there was a food shortage.'

'Only for some.' She gripped his arm suddenly, in excitement. 'Wait. You must hear this.' Her voice dropped to an awed whisper. 'Lydia Elman!'

A handsome middle-aged woman was standing on the dais in front of the little orchestra. She wore a low-cut black dress, with a single red rose, like a splash of blood at her bosom, and she waited majestically, as if by right, for silence, her dark eyes slowly scanning the room. It was theatrical but enormously impressive.

Slowly the roar of conversation and laughter dropped, the cry for quiet moved from table to table, and even the waiters stopped work and lined the sides of the room, waiting.

Silence. A violin started, almost inaudible at first, the sound growing slowly, haunting in its sadness. The other musicians joined in and then the woman. At first her voice seemed hoarse, almost tuneless, but gradually it took on a kind of magic. She sang of youth, of first love, of sorrow and, above all, of Russia; the sadness, the beauty, the despair of Russia. The words were simple but they tore at the nerves like a drill. Tremayne stood taut and spell-bound, unable to take his eyes from this woman, whose voice seemed to be able to capture the very essence of this strange land and the agony through which it was living.

As she finished, they greeted her with a frenzy of cheers, but she would give no more. Inclining her head, she turned away, and disappeared through some curtains behind the dais. When Tremayne turned to Maria, he saw that she was weeping. He put a hand on her arm and she gave him a little apologetic smile.

The head waiter came up. 'Your table, monsieur – this way.'

But to Tremayne's surprise, she held back. 'No,' she said. The uproar had started again, the magic of that voice forgotten. She shook her head. 'No,' she said again.

'We are very busy, as you see,' said the head waiter.

'We've changed our minds – thank you,' said Tremayne. He gave the man a tip, and then drew Maria aside. 'Are you all right?'

'Yes,' she whispered. He could feel her trembling under his hand.

'We could – we could go back to the room. Have something sent up.'

She nodded quickly, and turned towards the stairs. When they reached his room, and the door was closed, she said: 'I am sorry. It was the songs – Lydia – everything. The last time I am hearing her was in Moscow. So much has happened since then—'

'You don't have to explain,' he replied awkwardly. He put out a hand to ring the bell for room-service but she checked him.

'Wait,' she said.

5

He woke in the early hours, aroused by a slight movement. Maria was standing naked by the open wardrobe, and he was about to speak when he realised that she was searching through his clothes. He lay silent, watching her through half-closed eyes, as she checked his keys.

She put his document case on the floor, unlocked it, and rummaged through the contents, glancing every now and then at the bed to satisfy herself that he was asleep. He turned over to one side, simulating a snore, and she paused, waiting for him to settle. She locked and replaced the case, put the keys back in his jacket pocket, gently closed the wardrobe door, and began to dress.

He watched her, thinking how graceful and beautiful

she was, feeling the tension growing in his body. Opening his eyes as though for the first time, he said, 'What are you doing?'

'I must go,' she said calmly.

'No. Not yet.'

'Really,' she said, and came over to him in her chemise.

'Not yet!' he said, and pulled her down to him. It was not as before. This time there was no giving on her part and no tenderness, simply a passive acceptance. He entered her fiercely, quickly, as if to punish her, and it was soon over. Afterwards he felt a sense of disgust and shame. She dressed quickly, and slipped out with just a brief, cold word of farewell, leaving behind only the faint imprint of her head on the pillow beside him and a hint of perfume clinging in the air, as the only reminder that she had been there at all.

He rose and checked his things. He was not concerned about the document case; there was nothing of any importance there, most of the papers were simply a cover for his real mission. The gold ring with the crest of the falcon was still nestling safely in the hollow compartment in the heel of his left shoe, and the ten-rouble gold pieces in the false bottom of his travel-bag had not been touched. Her search had been so perfunctory that he was pretty sure that she had not found these rather obvious and clumsy hiding-places.

She had gone through his wallet, but the money it contained was still there – a fair amount in English notes and Russian roubles. That did not surprise him; whatever else Maria might be, he knew that she was neither a whore nor a thief.

That left only one possible conclusion. And one big, unanswered question.

Who was she working for?

Chapter Six

I

Over a large breakfast, for he was ravenously hungry,
Tremayne pondered the problem of Maria Astakhov.
The more he considered it, the more certain he became
that she was working for Colonel Kasakov. She clearly
knew him well; had she been acting for anyone else, she
would have tried to be present at the first meeting
between the Colonel and Tremayne, but she had herself
volunteered to leave. And last night she had asked him
no questions about their discussion or its purpose, she
had appeared quite uninterested. That also seemed to
fit his theory. Why should she bother to ask questions
when she already knew the answers, or would get them
from Kasakov? So much, he thought grimly, for the
British High Commissioner's so-called screening!

He recalled her emotional reaction to the singer in
the restaurant, the tears glistening in those lovely eyes.
That had been genuine enough, it could not have been
faked. And their first love-making, when she had come
to his room, there had been nothing fake or contrived
about that either; he would not have described himself
as an expert on sex, yet he fancied that he knew enough
of human nature to tell the real thing from the false. She
had loved him expertly, yes, with a gentle skill which
had been as surprising as it was delightful and which
must have been born of experience; but the mixture of

passion and tenderness which she had revealed, her frenzied response to his final advances was certainly not assumed. It was probable, he thought, that she had come to the room with no other motive than to make love, and had simply seized the opportunity afterwards, while he slept, to run a check on him.

He found himself smiling, amused by this trend of thought. It had been a very clumsy manoeuvre out of which Kasakov had gained little or nothing, whereas he had spent some delightful hours in the company of one of the loveliest women he had ever met. Much the better of the exchange, he thought, congratulating himself.

An hour later, when Kasakov came to his room for a further meeting, the Russian's change of attitude towards him seemed to add force to this conclusion. Gone was the diffident, almost off-hand manner; the boyish face was bright with friendship and he shook Tremayne's hand warmly. Maria must have given me a good report, Tremayne told himself wryly.

'You look as if you have had some good news, Colonel,' he said.

'Of course! You are the good news, isn't that so?' He spread his hands deprecatingly. 'And I owe you an apology.'

'Yes?'

'Yesterday I did not know – or rather, I did not realise – exactly who you were. Last night I had dinner with a friend, Count Malkov. He remembers you well from Moscow and Petrograd. He knew you then as James Ivanovich, no? You helped him and many others. I am proud to know that you will be with us, James Ivanovich!'

'I'm glad you're satisfied,' said Tremayne coolly. 'No doubt Miss Astakhov also helped you make up your mind?'

'Maria?' Kasakov looked at him with what seemed to be genuine astonishment.

'Let us not play games, Colonel. There is no time for that.'

'But really – I do not understand.' A note of impatience entered the Russian's voice. 'Come, my friend – tell me what has happened. This could be serious.'

Tremayne studied the other man's face for a few moments, concerned now that his own assumptions might have been wrong. In the end, he decided that there was nothing to lose anyway, and he told the story, omitting only its more intimate details.

Kasakov's face seemed to grow older as he listened. He asked one or two brief questions to which Tremayne made equally brief answers, then he shook his head.

'Now you understand, James Ivanovich, why we have forsworn drink and debauchery until our task has been accomplished!' he said chidingly.

'It was hardly a blasted debauch!' retorted Tremayne.

'She is working for the Bolsheviki. That is obvious.'

'Impossible!'

'Nothing is impossible in Russia. The Reds have their agents everywhere. There is no other explanation. You should have dealt with her!'

'I watched her. She found nothing of any importance. I thought it better not to arouse her suspicions, or put her on her guard. As a matter of fact, I decided that she must be working for you.'

'If I needed to check on you or anyone else, I should use different, more efficient methods!' Kasakov moved to the door and opened it. The Circassian twins were standing in the corridor, and Tremayne caught a glimpse of a small, well-dressed man waiting nearby. Kasakov held a whispered conversation with the twins. When he had finished, they both saluted and hurried away. Kasakov motioned the civilian into the room, and as he turned back to Tremayne he was smiling again.

'Now, James Ivanovich – I have brought someone to see you.'

The small man came forward, moving with little nervous steps. He was bald except for a fringe of greased black hair, he smelled strongly of eau-de-cologne, and not even the well-cut coat could disguise his big, round stomach. He was carrying a Gladstone bag which he placed carefully on the table, then he turned to peer at Tremayne through gold-rimmed pince-nez.

Kasakov closed the door. 'This is the Englishman,' he said. 'You may speak freely.'

The little man extended a hand. 'Ipatiev,' he said, 'Mikhail Ipatiev.'

'Ipatiev?' Tremayne frowned. 'From Ekaterinburg?'

'Exactly so.'

'Then it is in your house that the Tsar is being held prisoner?'

'Exactly so.' Ipatiev removed the pince-nez which were attached to a strip of black ribbon and began furiously to polish them on a silk handkerchief. 'It is a beautiful house. I designed it myself. A house of beauty. Then the Bolsheviks came and stole it from me – told me to get out, like that! They came with bayonets, guns. I was forced to leave everything, we were fortunate to escape with our lives! It is a terrible thing, no? That house of beauty and peace – they have turned it into a prison for our beloved Emperor!' He put the handkerchief to his eyes and shook his head.

'You lost a house,' said Kasakov sternly, 'other people have lost far more. You are neither dead nor starving! And I haven't brought you here to bleat like a sheep over your misfortunes!'

Ipatiev gave him a hurt look, and replaced the pince-

115

nez. He carried the bag to the table, drew a long silver key chain from his pocket, and selecting a key with care, he unlocked the bag. From it, he withdrew some drawings, which he unrolled on the table.

'The plans of my house,' he said with pride. 'Everything is here, the complete layout, even the thickness of the walls and the materials we used. Everything!'

2

At 10 a.m. Moscow time, on that same day, a Mercedes limousine drew up outside the Embassy of the Imperial German government in Denezhny Street in Moscow. It flew no pennant and bore no crest for the Germans were still hated by the Muscovites and it was not wise to flaunt their presence in the city. It was enough that only a few months before the two countries had been at war; now to add to the agony of Russia's huge losses in battle, the Germans had forced down Lenin's reluctant throat the humiliation of the Treaty of Brest-Litovsk, under which he had to cede to them an area of territory almost as large as Europe itself, and enormous natural resources.

The picked Red Guards outside the building did not bother to come to attention as the German ambassador, Count Wilhelm von Mirbach, came out with two armed aides and got into the car, which drove away immediately.

Six minutes later, the Mercedes arrived at the Kremlin, and Count Mirbach was shown into the office of Georgy Chicherin, the Soviet Commissar for Foreign Affairs. The room was a mess; papers and documents littered the desk, and were piled around the walls and on the chairs, the air was heavy with pungent smoke from the

Commissar's pipe, which he smoked ceaselessly. Chicherin, in rolled-up shirt-sleeves, greeted the Ambassador politely, but without warmth. His face was grey with fatigue. He cleared a chair by the simple expedient of tossing the papers on it into a corner and Count Mirbach sat down.

'And what can I do for you this time, Mr. Ambassador?' asked Chicherin, relighting his pipe. There was a faint irony in his tone.

'I have had a communiqué from my Government. They have asked me to seek specific assurances from you concerning the Tsar and the Imperial Family.'

'The ex-Tsar,' said Chicherin gently. 'I believe I know the nature of the assurances you require. Allow me to inform you that I am in touch with Ekaterinburg regularly. The ex-Tsar and his family are alive and well.'

'My government is concerned at certain reports which have come through. We understand that the Chairman of the local Soviet has been replaced by a man called Viktor Gromeko.'

'You are well-informed. And you are correct.'

'We hear that Gromeko is a fanatic.'

'It is a question of definition, Mr. Ambassador. A fanatic to some is a dedicated and single-minded worker to others. In any case, this is a matter of our internal politics. I do not see how it concerns your government.'

'Simply that Gromeko has consistently agitated for the public execution of the Tsar and his family. It is a matter of record.'

'He is not the only one,' said Chicherin mildly. 'The ex-Tsar is not a popular figure.'

'I have been asked to remind you of our agreement—'

'That is not necessary,' interrupted Chicherin. 'It is engraved on my heart. You may inform your government that we shall continue to adhere to it.'

'And this man, Viktor Gromeko?'

'Will be kept under control. No harm will befall the Romanovs.'

'We are informed that they are being submitted to many humiliations and unnecessary restrictions.'

'Mr. Ambassador,' said Chicherin sharply, 'they are prisoners. No doubt they find the present regime irksome after their previous life. But they have a doctor in residence to attend the ex-Tsarevich Alexei, a maid, a cook, and two other servants. Milk, eggs, fresh bread and vegetables are sent in every day from a local convent. They eat better than I did when I was in the Tsar's prisons – better than ninety-nine per cent of the people in Ekaterinburg today, I assure you. And, within certain limits, they are allowed to move freely around the house and the yard. We can do no more.'

He rose, pushing himself up from the desk with the action of a weary man. Count Mirbach stood up also. 'You will understand that His Imperial Majesty, the Kaiser, is personally interested in this matter, Commissar.'

'Of course,' said Chicherin in an off-hand manner. 'He is concerned about his relative, the former Empress. Tell him that we shall continue to protect her. Her death would be of no benefit to us. In any case, we have other problems, other fish to fry.'

Shortly after the Ambassador had gone, Chicherin received two other visitors. This time it was a friend and colleague, Felix Dzerzhinsky, the head of the newly-formed Soviet secret police, the Cheka, and one of his senior deputies. The deputy, a stockily-built man in uniform, stood to one side, taking no part in the conversation. Dzerzhinsky, neat and precise, frowned at the untidiness of the room, and fanned the smoky air with a newspaper, in mock disgust. 'How can you work like this, Georgy? Everything disorganised! And this air – you could cut it with a knife!'

'Because each day is different, Felix! Nothing stands still, everything changes, hour by hour, minute by minute.' He waved a hand at the documents on his desk. 'Yesterday's bag of paper. By tomorrow, it will be out of date – and there will be another bag! That, too, will be out of date within 24 hours.' He sighed. 'Nowadays, one cannot even rely on a map. Now – why have you come – to add to my troubles?'

'I thought you might be interested in a piece of news from Vladivostock.'

'Vladivostock is the least of my worries.'

'The Cheka representative there has friends in the telegraph office – good comrades. We learn a great deal that way. At any rate, he has sent a message through to the effect that the British agent, James Tremayne, has arrived in the city.'

'Tremayne?' Chicherin frowned. 'I must be getting old – I am losing my memory for names.'

'He was in Moscow and Petrograd from 1913 until early this year. Officially he was an attaché at the British Embassy, but we suspect that he helped organise the escape to the West of several highly-placed people – we believe Kerensky himself was one of them.'

'I remember the man now. Or at least, the name.'

'Interesting that he should return now, don't you think?'

'Is it?'

'One of the first things he did on arrival was to make contact with Zakhar Kasakov. Kasakov is a former member of the Corps des Pages and the Chevalier Guards. His family were members of the inner circle of the former Imperial court, very close to Nicholas himself.'

'So.' Chicherin sighed again and dug at his clogged pipe with a penknife. 'Perhaps they plan to rescue the Romanovs. All that is your department – why bother me?'

'Because I want your support for a proposal I wish to put to the Political Bureau at tomorrow's meeting.' Dzerzhinsky moved nearer the desk, his voice crisp and urgent. 'Georgy, I want to propose that we rid ourselves of the problem once and for all. As I see it—'

He broke off suddenly as an inner door opened. A short, stocky man entered, carrying a handful of telegrams. There were tiny traces of grey in his moustache and beard and he, too, looked weary, but the keen, sharp eyes emitted a feeling of enormous power and energy. Chicherin stood up as he entered.

'Vladimir Ilyich,' he said respectfully.

Lenin looked from one to the other, a hint of a smile on his face.

'I see, comrades,' he said. 'You haven't enough to do – you have time to gossip.'

'Felix has a problem,' said Chicherin.

'Only one? He is fortunate!'

'It is more in the nature of a proposal,' said Dzerzhinsky, a little uneasily. 'Listen, Vladimir Ilyich, it concerns Nicholas.'

'You want his head, is that it? Another one.' Lenin smiled openly now.

'There are sound political reasons.' Dzerzhinsky's voice took on a stronger, argumentative note. 'So long as Nicholas lives, he will remain the focus of every White general who wants to restore the old regime, every royalist adventurer, every foreign agent. Alive, he is their flag, their Imperial falcon, their rallying-point. Only this morning I had news that there may be yet another attempt to liberate him. Execute him, and you execute the problem.'

'Do you imagine that the Whites will run away if we kill the Tsar?' asked Lenin.

'Of course not. But it will weaken them politically.'

'Felix, my friend, it is not like you to be so naïve. Kornilov, Wrangel, the other White leaders – they don't want the Tsar back on the throne. They know what a mess he made of it before! And besides, they have their own ambitions in that direction!'

'Possibly. Nevertheless, the point remains – so long as he lives he is a rallying-point for counter-revolution. And there is another consideration. The military situation in the Urals is becoming critical. If Ekaterinburg should fall—'

'I know the military situation.'

'So if the Tsar should land up in the lap of the Czechs or Diterikhs? Or of some foreign agent?'

'We must make certain he does not. Felix, we need Nicholas alive for the time being. It is a practical question, nothing more. We must be objective. Georgy here will tell you – kill him or Alexandra and we shall have the Germans at our throats again. And we can say goodbye to the revolution.'

'The Germans are almost finished,' said Dzerzhinsky.

'Perhaps. I will believe it when it happens – one should never underestimate the Germans. They have a genius for organisation – and survival.' Lenin tossed the telegrams on to Chicherin's desk. 'These are for you, Georgy.' At the door, he turned back to Dzerzhinsky.

'Who is the best man you have in Moscow?'

'They are all fully extended, Vladimir.'

'That is not what I asked.' He turned to Dzerzhinsky's deputy for the first time. 'What do you think, Sergo? I want a good man to handle this Nicholas business.'

The deputy considered for a moment. 'This is certainly not something that can be handled by an amateur. If Comrade Dzerzhinsky approves, I will go myself.'

'Good.' Lenin nodded. 'You will leave for Ekaterinburg immediately.' He waved a hand to the others. 'Give him full authority to take whatever steps may be necessary to ensure the security of the Romanovs. If he thinks it necessary to move them to a safer place, he is to do so. And Sergo – remember this. If anything should go wrong, you will pay for it with your neck!'

Late that night, a train was due to leave Moscow loaded with bolts of cloth, spare parts, vodka, ploughshares, pots and pans, nails, pins and needles – anything that could be scraped together. The commander of the Red Army detachment on board had instructions to go as far to the East as was necessary and possible and to barter his cargo with the peasants in exchange for the wheat and other cereals which the capital badly needed.

At the last moment, on direct orders from the Kremlin, the arrangements were changed. The goods wagons were detached, and armoured trucks put in their place. A passenger coach, formerly the property of one of the Grand Dukes, was put between two of the trucks. Although it was divided into a luxurious sitting-room and bedroom, and had its own small kitchen, bathroom and lavatory, the passenger coach contained only one occupant.

His name was Sergo Mogilov. He was aged about 35, a burly, thick-necked man with a friendly, genial manner, and he wore the uniform of a Political Commissar. He had one curious physical feature. A scar disfigured part of the left cheek, extending to his forehead, so that it cut the bushy eyebrow in two. This tended to give his face an odd, sinister expression, particularly when he smiled.

The train commander's troops were reinforced and he was given new instructions. He was to take Commissar Mogilov to Ekaterinburg with all possible speed.

Vladivostock makes up its own mind about the weather; in that unpredictable city it is possible to experience three or four seasons in a single morning. On this day, after the mixture of chill drizzle and occasional sunshine of yesterday, it had decided to be singleminded. It was hot, very hot, with the sun baking the streets with temperatures which by noon were pushing towards 38° Centigrade.

Maria Astakhov felt the heat as she stepped from the comparative cool of the British High Commission building into the open. It was like walking into an oven. She put up her parasol and began the short journey to her small flat which was in nearby Sumskaya Street. She had a two-hour break from her duties and she looked forward to a relaxing wash and change of clothes. There wouldn't be much time, for a man, a very important man in her life, was coming to see her at 12.30. Among other things, she wanted to ask him for permission to leave Vladivostock. After what had happened last night, she was beginning to doubt her own reliability.

It was Tremayne who had, unconsciously, prompted her to think in this way and it was his face that she kept seeing in her mind as she walked through the sizzling streets. She had not gone to the hotel last night with the intention of seducing him, or of being seduced. It had simply happened and she found it difficult to explain this even to herself. Part of it, she knew, was due to the haunting singing of Lydia Elman. That voice had breached her defences, reminding her of her loneliness, releasing a flood of feeling. And she had admired the cool courage with which the Englishman had stood up to Semyonov's bandits the previous afternoon.

Yet she still could not fully understand. After all, he stood for everything she detested; a privileged aristocrat who also happened to be a dangerous and determined enemy. How was it that she could be attracted to such a person, and that he had been able to stir her emotions as no other man since her husband? The truth was that she was desperate to see him again, and she found such longing shameful. We must be like iron, hard and ruthless, she had been told, we must not allow ourselves to give way to personal feelings. How easy to say! Perhaps it was not in her nature to be so strong and objective. How difficult it is, she thought, to divide human beings into friend and enemy, black and white – or even Red and White!

With these thoughts teasing her mind, Maria took a key from her purse to open the door to her flat, and immediately tightened with shock and fear. The lock had been broken, the door swung gently ajar on twisted hinges. She pushed it open cautiously and peered inside. The small sitting-room was in chaos. The curtains had been ripped away from their moorings, the upholstery slashed open, furniture smashed to fragments as if by a giant fist, slivers of china and glass were scattered everywhere.

As she stood in the open doorway taking in the disaster one of the Circassian twins appeared from the bedroom. He grinned at her, showing white teeth, one of which was capped with gold.

'You Red cow!' he said.

She turned and fled down the corridor screaming, but he came after her with long, nimble strides and caught her at the top of the stairs. She swung round and hit out at him with the parasol, but he seized it one-handed with an ease which made a mockery of her effort, and tossed it over the stair-rail. He struck her with his fist and as she fell he grabbed her arm and slung her across his shoulder like a sack of potatoes.

As he carried her back down the corridor, a neighbour's door opened, and a woman peeped out. She took one look, and shut herself in again, pulling the bolts tight, trembling with fear. In such times, it was wiser not to interfere, to see nothing, hear nothing.

The Circassian carried the moaning girl into the bedroom, and threw her on to the bed. A cloud of feathers rose like snow as she fell on the slashed mattress. The other twin wedged the front door closed with a chair and joined his brother. Maria struggled to get up, but the first man put a hand across her neck and held her down. Her eyes were bright with fear as he smiled and lowered his face towards her.

'Now, you little Red bitch, you will tell us everything!'

She had often imagined what it would be like at this moment, when by some chance she fell into the hands of the enemy. She had told herself that she must be brave, stoical, that she must be prepared to suffer anything for the revolution; but, on the other hand, she knew that she had a low threshold of pain and in her nightmares she had seen and heard herself break with terror, babbling out all her secrets in a string of incoherent sentences.

But now, astonishingly, she found a little strength. As he breathed down on her, she felt the anger rise in her blood, and she spat contemptuously into his face. Oddly enough, he continued to smile. Still holding her with one hand, he ripped at her cotton dress with the other, and used the strip of flimsy cloth to wipe the spittle from his face. He glanced at his brother, and together they tore the clothes from the struggling girl.

Naked, she was turned over and her face pressed into the mattress, feathers cascading round her head, filling her mouth. While one twin held her, the other took off his broad leather belt. He ran an exploratory finger, hard as a stick, over the smooth back and rounded buttocks, then standing back he brought the belt down with his full force on the soft skin. Her body exploded with agony, the shrill scream stifled by the mattress. Again and again, the belt rose and fell.

They turned her over, and she saw their faces as in a misted distorting mirror, blurred but menacing. From a great distance she heard a voice say, 'Now will you speak?' She moaned, the words almost came as they had in her nightmares, but she bit them back. She remembered the man who was to call, and found her mind doing a strange thing. She was praying, not that he would come and save her, but that he would be delayed, that somehow he would not fall into the hands of these animals.

They turned her over again, and she heard them laugh. The down from the mattress was sticking to her bloodied flesh and one of the Circassians said: 'Look, she's like a half-plucked chicken!' She stiffened herself for the pain that was to come, but for a long, agonising moment there was silence.

She felt herself being pulled towards the edge of the bed, so that her feet touched the floor. Then each man raped her in turn, mounting her from behind like dogs on a bitch. She could feel their burning heat inside her body, and the tears came now, tears of outrage and shame. When they had finished, there was another silence, and she lay there inert, wishing only for the benevolence of death.

Suddenly, violently, she was picked up and thrown bodily against the wall, crashing into the dressing-table. Miraculously, she managed to stagger to her feet, swaying like a drunk. Then, as they came at her again, terror lent her a new and momentary strength. With a scream, she ran across the room, dashing herself against the window. Glass and frame shattered under the impact and she went through and down, hurtling towards the street below.

The Circassian twins, occupied with their pleasure, had not heard the slight, scraping noise from the other room and now, looking towards the fallen body, they failed to see the man standing in the doorway of the bedroom. He was of middle height, with silver-grey hair, and the stooped, untidy, but respectable look of a professor.

When the twins turned to escape, it was too late. The man was holding a Mauser pistol and he fired twice, taking deliberate aim at each man's crutch. Then quite calmly he stood over the fallen, writhing bodies and fired into the flaxen heads.

He went back to the disordered sitting-room and crossed to the wall at the right of the fireplace where a framed picture of the Tsar hung crookedly from a thin supporting chain. He slit open the back of the picture and removed a small sheaf of documents which he put carefully in an inside pocket. He replaced the pistol in the shoulder-holster inside his jacket, glanced round the room and shook his head, as though in disbelief.

An International Patrol of Japanese, Czech, Italian and Belgian soldiers approached the building as he reached ground-floor level.

'Quickly,' he said, 'upstairs. Third floor!' He spoke with the clear voice of authority and they dashed past him without hesitation. In the street outside a small crowd had gathered around Maria's body. Again, the man spoke with authority as he pushed his way to the front. 'Make way, please. Make way!'

Maria lay crumpled as she had fallen, the blood still

oozing from the ugly, feathered stripes on her back. He stooped down like a doctor and gently turned her over. There was still a faint pulse beat; her eyes fluttered open and she recognised the man's face, read the question upon it.

She made a faint negative motion of her head and breathed the word, 'No.' She saw him smile just before her eyes closed again and when he tried the pulse again, it had stopped. A woman came through with a blanket; he took it from her and carefully covered the girl's body.

He straightened up and stood for a moment as though in salute, and then, pushing back through the crowd, he walked briskly away.

4

The Japanese commandant of the International Patrol took a perfunctory look round the apartment, and ordered the bodies to be scooped up and taken away. He made a few enquiries of the other tenants but without too much enthusiasm. There were many such killings in Vladivostock, it was a waste of time and effort to investigate in any depth.

He showed more interest in the apartment itself, for accommodation was hard to come by, and the rooms would be ideal for one of his own officers. With this in mind, he instructed that the door be sealed.

When he got back to headquarters he filed a short, official report to which he added the laconic opinion: 'Probably the work of Semyonov's men.'

Nothing of the incident was reported in either of the two newspapers published in the city, and the British

High Commissioner did not hear about it until the following morning when, puzzled by Maria's absence, he caused enquiries to be made. It was late in the afternoon when he received a copy of the Japanese commandant's report.

By that time, Tremayne and Kasakov were on their way to the west.

Chapter Seven

I

At 14.30 hours on June 25, Tom Story, newly-created
Major in the U.S. Army, went aboard the battleship
USS *Brooklyn* and was conducted immediately to the
quarters of Admiral Austin Knight, Commander-in-
Chief of the American Asiatic Fleet. The Admiral was
poring over a map with two staff officers and he continued to do so for two or three minutes, ignoring Story.
Eventually he went behind the desk, sat down and examined the new arrival silently. The two staff officers
ranged themselves on either side of their chief, and they,
in turn, surveyed Story in silence. He hadn't yet
got around to acquiring a uniform; he was wearing a
blue shirt and Levi pants, and from the look on their
faces, he guessed that they disapproved of this unmilitary
gear.

After a moment or two of this, Story felt that someone
should break what appeared to be a deadlock and that
maybe it was up to him. 'Story, Admiral, sir,' he said,
with as much military precision as he could command.
'You wanted to see me?'

'At ease, Major,' said the Admiral, and the flicker of a
smile passed across his face. The smile tightened as Story,
taking the order literally, dropped into a chair facing
the desk and crossed his long legs.

'Thanks, Admiral,' he said. The two staff officers

froze as he brought out a pack of cheroots and offered them round in turn. Knight took one and examined it carefully; the officers shook their heads both in refusal and disapproval.

'Burma cheroots, Admiral, sir,' said Story reassuringly. 'I picked up a supply in Singapore.' He leaned forward and gave the Admiral a light, then lit his own cigar and leaned back. 'Sure is a great ship,' he said.

'Glad you like it,' said Knight drily.

'Hell, Admiral, sir,' Story said. 'Tell the truth, I hate ships. I was born and brought up on the land, know what I mean? But seeing the *Brooklyn* out here in Vlad harbour – gives me a kind of right good feeling.'

'You've been here some time – know the place well?'

'Vlad? I guess I know it as well as anyone can. Been here three years. Sure is a strange town, changeable as a prairie fire. Take yesterday – like Chicago in the fall. And today it's high summer, hot as billy be durned.'

'And how well do you know the Trans-Siberian?' asked Knight.

'Pretty well, I guess. Been over the track, all the way, a half-dozen times, maybe more.'

Knight coughed on the cheroot for a moment and looked at it in suspicion. He laid it in an ashtray and pushed that gently to one side. His voice took on a sterner, more official tone. 'Major. The first thing I have to say is that what passes between us in this cabin is Top Secret. Top Top Secret. Understood?'

'If you say so, Admiral, sir.'

'I do. The second thing is that I have an assignment for you. An assignment of extreme urgency and vital importance.'

'Anything I can do—' said Story.

'Can you have an armoured train ready to leave at 06.00 hours in the morning?'

Story thought about this for a moment. 'How big, how many wagons?'

'Sufficient to take a detachment of 24 US Marines, a Russian officer named Colonel Kasakov and his staff, 50 White Russian cavalrymen and their horses, and a British official.'

'What about the crew – the train crew?'

'You will provide the crew, and take personal command.'

'You want I should go along?'

'That's the idea. Can you arrange it?'

Story chewed on the cheroot thoughtfully. 'A train ready to go in – say – 15 hours? I reckon so. Where will we be heading?'

'For the first stage, you take the Ussuri line to Khabarovsk. Then you turn west, following the Amur. About 100 miles from Khabarovsk, at Yakeshi, you will pick up the cavalrymen and their horses. At that point, the British official will give you further verbal instructions – and you will do everything within your power to carry out such instructions without question or delay.'

'You mean this limey – this English guy – gives the orders?'

'I do.'

Story shook his head reflectively. 'Never been much inclined to the British. Never met one I could rightfully understand.'

'You'd better try to understand this one, Major.'

'If you'd say so, Admiral, sir.'

One of the staff officers cut in. 'You must be clear, Major, quite clear, that the United States has taken up a neutral position in regard to the present conflicts in Russia. You will not involve yourself or your personnel in the fighting on either side.'

'And if some bastard tries to shoot up my train?'

'Naturally, you have a right and a duty to defend yourself and US property.'

'Thanks,' said Story. 'Thanks a lot.'

'Officially, you will be making a reconnaissance of the eastern section of the Trans-Siberian,' said Knight, 'and you will keep a log to that effect. But your main task will be to convey Colonel Kasakov, his cavalrymen and this British official to their destination – or as close to it as you can get.' He handed Story an envelope. 'In there you will find two documents. The first is a copy of the President's Declaration, which states quite clearly that the US is opposed to intervention and to any interference in Russia's internal affairs. I advise you to study it. The other is a letter signed by the Secretary of State requesting all persons to give you free and unhindered passage along the railway.'

'When do I get to meet this Colonel – and the Britisher?' asked Story.

'Now is as good a time as any,' said the Admiral. He nodded to one of the staff officers, who crossed to the inner door and opened it. 'If you will step this way, gentlemen,' he said.

As Tremayne entered with Kasakov, Story swivelled round in his seat. He was not easily surprised, but when he saw the Englishman, the cheroot dipped from his lips and he had to put a hand up to save it from falling. 'Jesus!' he whispered, 'oh, Jesus!'

Tremayne had been forewarned, and enjoying the moment, he stepped forward with a smile. 'Hello, old chap,' he said.

Each morning Miss Meg went to Trunov's shop in the Market at Ekaterinburg to join the queue for anything that was going – bread, meat, sausage, coffee, flour. Very rarely did she come away with anything more than the black bread to which her ration cards entitled her, but occasionally she was lucky. On one occasion she had been able to get hold of a bag of veal bones, from which she made a stew that lasted three days; on another, Trunov, in a benevolent mood, had let her have some real coffee, a pleasant change from the ground roasted barley and chicory which was now the common substitute.

But there was another reason for joining the Market queues. It was there that one could hear the latest news, the sort of thing which was never published in the official Bolshevik news-sheets. Miss Meg always treated what she heard with caution, for she knew that much of it was rumour, inspired very often by self-delusion and wishful thinking; and she was careful not to say too much herself for the place was full of Bolshevik supporters and, much more dangerous, people who were only too anxious to ingratiate themselves with the Soviets by informing against anyone suspected of nursing hostile feelings towards the regime.

On this particular morning, she heard it whispered that the Czech Legion was advancing against the town, and that a White army under General Diterikhs had thrown back the Red Army on another front and was within 40 miles of Ekaterinburg. Someone said that their advance patrols were even nearer than that. It seemed that everywhere the Soviet regime was on the point of collapse. Trains were still coming in from the west, from

Moscow, but nothing was going eastwards except a few troop trains, for the lines were held by the Czechs and the Whites.

Miss Meg listened to all this with mixed feelings. Deep in her heart, she had long realised that her plan to take the children east to Vladivostock was nothing more than a dream, something with which to keep hope alive. In every direction there were battle-lines, armies facing each other, it would be impossible to get out. If and when the Whites or the Czechs arrived, there might be a chance; but before then the town would be turned into a battlefield. She could only hang on, hope to survive. And she prayed that it would be the Czechs who came first, for she knew that the Whites could be as indiscriminate and ruthless as the Bolsheviks, that they would take a terrible and bloody revenge. Not for the first time, she wondered about the strange contradictions in the Russian character. She had seen how genuinely warm-hearted and generous they could be, she had enjoyed their rich sense of humour. But underneath there was this other, darker side which made them capable of terrible, barbaric, inhuman acts of cruelty. It was as if the whole nation had a split personality.

As if to confirm the whispered rumours, a Red Guard patrol entered the Market and came to a halt. Their commander, a tired-looking middle-aged man with a stubble of grey beard, shouted an order and the patrol split up. A young Guard, little more than a boy, pushed his way through the queue in which Miss Meg was standing and nailed a printed leaflet to the door of the shop. Forgetting about their places in the line, the crowd pushed forward. An elderly man read the notice aloud in a slow, faltering voice.

TO THE BARRICADES!

The counter-revolutionists of the so-called Czech Legion and the renegade troops of the murderer, Diterikhs, are threatening our beloved city. The Army and the Red Guard of the Revolution are in need of the immediate support of all citizens.

Accordingly, the Soviet of Soldier and Worker Deputies of Ekaterinburg have issued the following Order of the Day.

ALL ABLE-BODIED MEN, WOMEN AND YOUNG PEOPLE BETWEEN THE AGES OF 12 AND 70 WILL REPORT IMMEDIATELY TO THEIR LOCAL STREET OR FACTORY COMMITTEE, BRINGING WITH THEM TOOLS NECESSARY FOR THE DIGGING OF TRENCHES AND THE ERECTION OF BARRICADES. NO EXCEPTIONS WILL BE ALLOWED.

Workers, Soldiers, Citizens – Defend Your City!
Long Live the Revolution!

There was a murmur of anger from some of the women, and one of them was even bold enough to seize the young Red Guard by the arm.

'What's this! Don't you think we have enough to do! If you want trenches, you dig them!'

'It's an order, mother,' said the boy uneasily, taking off his cap and scratching his shaven head. Without the cap he looked even younger than before.

'Don't call me mother!' shouted the woman, 'I'd be ashamed if you were one of mine!' She turned to the crowd. 'Look! We're being led by children now, the kids have taken over!'

'Do you want the Whites to come?' murmured the boy.

'I want peace!' said the woman. 'You lot promised we should have peace! That's all I want – peace!'

'The revolution has many enemies,' said the boy. He replaced his cap and slipped away. Miss Meg hurried across to the Commander, who was standing in the centre of the square waiting for the patrol to reassemble.

'Excuse me,' she said, 'this new order—'

'Well?' He looked at her with weary, red-rimmed eyes.

'I am English—' she began.

'I know. I know you.'

'Then the order cannot apply to me!'

'No exceptions!' he said curtly.

'But I have just explained. I hold a British passport—'

'You live here!' he interrupted roughly. 'You draw your rations fast enough. So you can work also!' He turned his back, dismissing her, and she could see that it was useless to argue further.

That afternoon a Red Guard patrol came to the street with two trucks and moved from house to house collecting up the people. Many of them went willingly, fervent supporters of the Soviets who stood in the first truck with their spades and mattocks singing a popular revolutionary song:

'Banker and boss hate the Red Soviet star,
Gladly they'd build a new throne for the Tsar.
But from the Steppes to the dark British sea,
Lenin's Red Army brings victory!'

The second truck was loaded with those who were less willing, the so-called bourgeois reactionaries, among them former merchants, members of the old Tsarist country councils (Zematvos), the wealthier peasants (Kulaks), and small shopkeepers. These went because they were afraid to do otherwise; they were treated with open mockery and contempt by the Red Guards and, in contrast to the people in the first truck, they stood in sullen, frightened silence.

Seraphina was in bed, enjoying one of her headaches, and she was shocked when a guard opened the door without ceremony and ordered her to get dressed. She drew her bed-jacket around her shoulders and protested: 'I am a sick woman! I'm not allowed to work, I mustn't leave the house.'

'Get dressed, comrade!' said the guard. 'A bit of fresh air will do you good!'

'Can't you leave her, please?' pleaded Miss Meg. 'I am willing to work – but she isn't strong.'

'No exceptions!' said the guard. 'You keep out of this!' He turned back to Seraphina and said: 'I'll give you three minutes to put your clothes on. If you're not ready by then, we'll take you as you are – in your night-dress!'

He left them to it. Miss Meg helped the wailing Seraphina to dress. For some reason she kept blaming her absent husband Boris for her present troubles. 'It's his fault, it's all the fault of people like him with their stupid, liberal notions. They put ideas into the heads of the workers and peasants, and now there's no controlling them! What a disaster! I shall die, I know I will. It will kill me! And then what will happen to you and the children, eh? Tell me that, give me an answer to that!' Miss Meg swallowed what seemed to be the obvious retort.

She took Natasha and Mischa with her on the truck, for they were frightened and could not be left alone in the house. They had developed an utter dependence upon her and were terrified if she was away for any length of time; she knew that she had become the one fixed and secure point in their strange, ever-changing lives, and this bound her to them more strongly than ever.

The Red Guards, so harsh to some of the adults, were kind and playful with the children and it wasn't long before they began to enjoy this unusual excursion. The trucks were driven about 15 miles beyond the town, to the edge of a wood. Several other gangs of conscripts and volunteers were already there, digging trenches or lopping trees to provide props and camouflage, and Miss Meg and Seraphina were allocated the task of dragging the heavy leafy branches to the trenches.

She made a game out of it in which the children joined quite happily, and she even began to enjoy the unaccustomed exercise. It was broiling hot in the area where the trenches were being dug and it was a relief to be working in the shade of the sweet-scented wood. A young Red Army officer, a former student, directed the operation, helped by a small squad of Red Guards. He was a handsome, spirited young man, who wore his cap at a rakish angle. He moved along the line, exhorting and encouraging the workers, so that even the most reluctant found themselves smiling at his rough jokes. And when the going was hard he led by example, taking off his coat to lend a hand with the heavier tasks.

He saw Miss Meg, Seraphina and the children struggling to drag a sapling towards the trenches and went to help them. When it was in position, he hoisted Mischa on to his shoulders.

'You've worked well,' he told Miss Meg. 'Take a break. Come, I'll get you some tea.'

Galloping like a horse, he ran with the laughing Mischa towards a field kitchen which had been set up in a small clearing. A huge samovar was boiling over a bed of glowing charcoal, and they were issued with mugs of tea and rice-cakes. He sat down on a tree-trunk with

Miss Meg, sipped the tea cautiously and said: 'I am told you are English.'

'Yes,' she answered.

'Why are you here then? Are you a comrade, a Communist?'

'I most certainly am not!' she replied acidly. 'As to being here, it is not through choice, I assure you!'

'I see,' he said. 'Then you don't believe in our revolution?'

'I don't believe in violence,' she replied. 'All this bloodshed. You talk of freedom, liberty, but you conscript people, you hunt down and imprison or kill those who don't agree with you. I most certainly do not believe in that!'

'We have no choice,' he said. 'When you meet a pack of wolves, it is a question of kill or be killed, isn't that so?'

'It seems to me that you are all wolves,' she said.

'You don't understand,' he said sadly, 'but I will tell you this. When we have thrown out the enemies of the revolution, then you will see a Russia that will surprise the world! We have everything here – raw materials, resources and a nation rich in talent. Look at those people – not the bourgeois – but the others. See how they work? And do you ask yourself why? It is because now they know they are working for themselves! Not for a landlord or a merchant or a Tsar but for the people, the whole people!' He stood up, his eyes shining, and raised his hands to the sky. 'Our Russia!' he cried. 'Ours! It is ours, all ours!'

'Not yet, not quite,' said Miss Meg.

He grew angry then. 'You are all the same, all you petit bourgeois! Here, before your eyes, history is happening! A new world is being born, and all you can do is spit upon it!' His eyes were sharp with contempt.

Miss Meg felt a twinge of something like envy for the

young man. How wonderful it must be, she thought, to believe in something so completely, to be so caught up in a cause that everything fell neatly into place and one could divide people, without question, into good and bad, friend and enemy. And yet how terrible! For she could only see people as people, human beings; each man and woman were products of their birth, background, and of the times in which they lived, of circumstances beyond their control. They could only be understood, judged, loved – and pitied – in that context.

'Don't be angry,' she said, 'I am trying to understand.' Suddenly she had a vivid mental picture of the Tsar standing in his shabby leather boots at Ekaterinburg station. 'May I ask you one question?'

'Of course.'

'If the decision were in your hands – if it were up to you – what would you do with the Tsar?'

He laughed. 'The Tsar! Nicholas the Blood Drinker! I would parade him in the Red Square in Moscow, before the whole population, and hang him!'

'Why? What harm can he do now? Why not let him go in peace?'

'Let him go? What are you saying? Don't you think he should pay for his crimes?'

'But it wasn't his fault that he was born a Tsar, was it?'

'Your Protector – Oliver Cromwell – he didn't say that when he had King Charles beheaded!'

'That was a long time ago,' she said primly. 'I should hope we would behave in a more civilised manner now.'

A shout came from the direction of the trees, interrupting them. This was immediately followed by the sound of a single shot and more shouting. A few moments later, two of the Red Guards came into the clearing, dragging between them a red-faced, panting, middle-aged man.

'What the devil goes on?' said the officer.

'We caught this fellow trying to escape, comrade – trying to slip away through the woods.'

'No,' stammered the prisoner, in a cultured voice, 'no. They have it wrong, believe me. I was – I went into the woods simply to obey a call of nature, to relieve myself. That's the truth, I swear, I swear it.'

'He's a liar,' said one of the guards. 'He was sliding from tree to tree like a shadow. Then, when we shouted, he took off like a hare. Only stopped when I fired after him.'

'And look, comrade,' said the other man, 'look what we found on him.' He produced a revolver and handed it to the officer, who weighed it carefully, judiciously, in one hand.

'Do you know that it is a crime for enemies of the regime to carry arms?' he asked.

'It is for protection, nothing more,' said the prisoner. 'I am not an enemy, I assure you.'

'Why were you running away then?'

'I – I was frightened – when I saw the guards, when they shouted at me.'

The officer cocked the revolver and, smiling, held it to the prisoner's cheek, pressing the soft flesh inwards with the cold metal. 'Do you know the penalty for your crime, citizen?' The man closed his eyes in terror, unable to speak.

'No! No! Stop it, stop it at once!' Miss Meg seized the arm holding the gun and pulled it down. The officer continued to smile.

'Ah,' he said, 'a request for clemency from the British.' He put a finger to the tip of his nose, pushing it flat, and looked at Miss Meg mockingly for a very long moment.

'It is obvious that this gentleman—' She checked, regretting her use of such a word. 'I mean, this man, this citizen, had a moment of panic. Nothing more.' She spoke with a calmness she did not feel.

The young officer nodded and turned to the guards. 'Well, what do you think, comrades? Shall we show the Englishwoman that the Soviets know how to temper justice with mercy?' They stared at him blankly, and he accepted this as assent. 'Good. A democratic decision. Take him back to the trenches and see that he does a treble shift.' And as they marched the man away he called after them: 'See that his friends are searched! All the men who came in the second truck, search them for arms!'

He thrust the revolver into his belt and smiled at Miss Meg. 'You see, we are not devils.'

'Thank you,' she said, the words coming out as no more than a croaking whisper. Now that the moment had passed she felt a huge emptiness in her stomach. She trembled violently, uncontrollably, and he looked at her curiously.

'Why are you shaking?' he asked. She shook her head, unable to reply, and as she turned away, he put a hand on her shoulder, in a gesture of sympathy. 'You're very brave, comrade. You have courage.'

'Me?' She smiled wanly.

'I wish you were on our side,' he said.

'I am sick of sides.' The reply came from the depths of her heart. His hand still rested on her shoulder, his brown eyes searched her face.

'What is your name?' he asked.

'Margaret. Margaret Wellmeadow.'

'Margaret.' He savoured the name, repeating it slowly, gently. 'Margaret Wellmeadow.'

'I am usually called Meg.'

'I prefer Margaret. It is more – more poetic.'

'And yours – your name?'

'Dukov. Nikolai Dukov. We shall be friends then, what do you say, Margaret?' The emptiness had gone now and she felt a warmth rising in her body. She was unable to stop the blush which came unbidden to her cheeks.

'Of course,' she said, and immediately rebuked herself for the absurd shyness of her manner. It really was too ridiculous that she should behave like a silly schoolgirl in front of this young man with his impish brown eyes.

Later, as she was working in the wood, she became aware that he was standing to one side, watching her. When she caught his eye, he responded with a broad, boyish grin, and she looked away quickly, angry yet again with herself because of the strange excitement which his presence seemed to generate within her. He came slowly, almost tantalisingly, towards her.

'Margaret.'

'Yes?'

'Here.'

He drew her away from the others, through the high sword fern, towards a clump of alders. When they were screened from view, he stopped, and took a pistol from his pocket, a tiny toylike thing with a gleaming pearl-shell butt.

'For you,' he said shyly.

'I don't want it!' She drew away from him.

'Take it!' he said roughly. 'In these times – it could be useful. One never knows. It's a proper lady's pistol – probably belonged to a Countess or even a Grand Duchess! And see, I have written a permit for you – official!' He showed her a scrap of paper torn from a notebook. In a bold hand he had written: *This is to certify that Margret Willmeado, British citizen, is officially licensed to carry a pistol for the purpose of self-defence. Signed: Dukov, Company Commander, 2nd Regiment, Red Army Engineering*

Corps. Over the signature was the impression of the regimental stamp.

She smiled at his mis-spelling of her name, but did not remark upon it. Instead, she said: 'A pistol. Honestly, I wouldn't know how to use it.'

'It is simple.' He showed her the mechanism, the safety-catch, how to load and fire. She pointed the pistol down the slope, where the ground opened up and a small blue lake shimmered in the distance.

'Don't fire it now!' he said, 'you'll bring them all running. Practise some other time.' He nodded with approval as she applied the safety-catch and put the pistol in the capacious pocket at the side of her skirt, together with the permit.

'You'll need these also,' he said, and gave her a pouch filled with cartridges.

'Where did you get it?'

'From one of those.' He waved a hand towards the trench area. 'We found it when we searched him.'

'Then it is not yours to give away!'

'Do all Englishwomen argue as you do?' he said, and before she could answer, he drew her to him and kissed her. She was so astonished that she did not resist at first, but then she pushed him away, her cheeks glowing.

'Just to seal Anglo-Soviet relations,' he said cheekily, and strode away. As her eyes followed him, she saw Natasha and Mischa standing by a tree, and she suddenly realised that they had been watching the scene. She took out a handkerchief and blew her nose vigorously, trying to collect her thoughts, but they still waited, as though too shy to come forward.

'What are you staring at?' she asked angrily.

The children came slowly to her. 'Why did that man kiss you?' said Natasha.

'It was not a kiss!' She rubbed her lips with the back

145

of a finger and corrected the lie. 'At least, not a proper kiss. He was – he was just saying goodbye.'

'Is he going away then?' said Mischa.

'I hope so,' said Miss Meg briskly, 'I sincerely hope so.'

She saw no more of Dukov that day, but the incident remained in her mind, and whenever she thought of it, she felt the blood tingling in her cheeks. The extraordinary thing was that she had enjoyed – well, almost enjoyed – the moment; she knew that she had been attracted and fascinated by the young man's personality. All this, she told herself firmly, was not only incomprehensible, but downright disgraceful. She knew only too well what could happen to young women who allowed themselves to be drawn into such situations. It was time, high time, for her to pull herself together.

As they climbed on the truck at the end of the afternoon's work, a dull boom, like the echo of a roll of thunder, could be heard in the far distance. It was repeated again and again. When Mischa looked at Miss Meg questioningly, she put her arm around him and said: 'Don't worry, my darling. It's only a storm.'

'Of course it isn't,' said Natasha, the forthright one. 'It's cannon – guns. Everybody knows that! They are coming.'

'Hush,' said Miss Meg, drawing the girl to her, so that she was holding both children in a protective gesture.

3

The *Royal Flush* seemed to be as happy as Klaus Striebeck to be on the move. He sang as he stood at the controls, and the locomotive sang beneath him, swaying

146

as though in a dance. They were hitting a steady 25 miles per hour which considering the sheer weight of steel and men was good going; certainly better than Klaus had expected.

Petka, the big fireman, whose beard and fierce moustaches were continually being scorched by flying sparks, did not understand what Klaus was singing but he understood why. He also felt happy. A member of the Russian Railway Service Corps, he counted himself lucky to be on a train which carried the American colours and was under the command of an American. He felt both relieved and secure; he could so easily have been pressed into service by that bandit, the self-styled Ataman Semyonov, or by one of the many other warlords who seemed to have sprung up like weeds since the Revolution. Most of all, he was travelling west, and every mile in that direction took him nearer to his home at Samara, on the Volga, and to the wife and children he had not seen for almost three years.

Tom Story came out on the observation platform of the first coach, raised a hand to Klaus by way of greeting, and lit up a cheroot. Between them was the huge tender, loaded with coal and built up with protective planks five or six inches thick. Inside the coach, the Englishman and Kasakov were locked in private conversation, poring over maps, calculating times and distances, arguing in low, secretive voices. They appeared not so much to resent his presence as ignore it, as though he were a piece of furniture, and their attitude irritated him. It irked him to think that they knew more of this mysterious mission than he did, that he had to wait in the wings until the Englishman summoned him forth and issued his orders.

The view did something to ease his mood. The line ran through the Khekhsir Mountains, which rose on either side, green and brown and magnificent. Here the sturdy pines of the north grew shoulder to shoulder with big red cedars and trees which were usually only seen in the softer south. In these mountains, among those trees, lived the Udeghe, the Forest People, an ancient independent race which had inhabited the area for centuries and had staunchly refused to forgo their hunting and fishing and accept the seductive embraces of civilisation. My kind of people, thought Story, but then he remembered the Indians of his own country, and wondered how much longer the Udeghe could hold out, survive the pressures.

The train took a sharp bend, slowing slightly, and entered a long straight section where the thickly-wooded ground sloped more gently upwards. As it did so, there was a sudden, urgent clanging of alarm bells in each coach. 'Hell's bloody bells!' shouted Klaus and brought the *Royal Flush* to a screeching, slithering, sudden halt.

The engine hissed gently and then there was a silence. In the surrounding forest only the leaves of the trees seemed to be moving.

Story scrambled across the tender to the cab. Klaus was already speaking on the field telephone which connected him to the steel-clad front coach, where a US Marine Sergeant named Kelly and six Marines were on duty. Since the locomotive was in the centre of the train, Klaus had to drive by sticking his head outside the cab to watch the track ahead, or by the use of a complicated array of mirrors which he had positioned with great care. The system worked well enough, but it was Kelly's job to act as an extra eye, a front observation post.

'The line is blocked!' said Klaus.

Story clambered up a narrow iron ladder to the roof of the cab and peered ahead. Across the track, about a yard from the pointed nose of the train, he could see a barricade of trees, trunk upon trunk. He climbed back down, as Tremayne and Kasakov came out on to the platform of the coach behind the tender.

'What is it? Why have we stopped?' shouted Tremayne.

'We're going to make a cup of tea!' said Story. 'Do you take it with milk or lemon?'

'Look!' called Kasakov.

A horseman was moving on one of the further slopes, appearing and disappearing as he circled through the trees, moving towards the train. Story put his field-glasses on the trotting figure; the fur-hatted rider was in uniform, a rifle slung across his back, a sheathed sabre at the horse's flank, and he was carrying a white flag. Story dropped on to the track.

'What are you doing!' said Klaus.

'I'm going to take a walk. Tell those Marines to keep me covered and watch out for tricks.'

He began to move towards the front of the train, his boots crunching on the loose gravel. The horseman changed course and rode towards him. Story went impassively forward until he reached the barricade: he walked all around it, and then climbed to the top where he perched himself nonchalantly and lit a cheroot.

As the man reined in, Story recognised him as the officer who had been with Semyonov at the railway yard, the captain he had called Dukhonin, but he, in turn, gave no indication that he knew Story. He simply surveyed the American in silence for a moment, his eyes narrow and watchful. Before either could speak a sudden release of steam from the locomotive stirred the horse. He lay back his ears, kicking and prancing wildly. The horseman rode out the moment firmly but easily, and slowly the horse settled down. Story gave a slow nod in appreciation of the man's obvious skill.

'I have a message,' said Dukhonin, 'a message from his High Excellency the Ataman Semyonov.'

'You guys sure move around,' said Story.

'His High Excellency urgently requires your train for certain military operations. He looks upon America as his friend, and it is not his wish to spill American blood.'

'Make that two of us,' Story said.

'If you will evacuate the train with your men, his High Excellency will guarantee to provide you with alternative transport to Khabarovsk. The train will be returned to you in due course, naturally, or adequate recompense paid to the American authorities. His High Excellency is a man of honour.'

'I appreciate that,' said Story, 'I surely do.'

'Then it is agreed?'

'No,' said Story. He spelled out the word. 'N.O. – no.'

'Sir,' said Dukhonin evenly, 'your train is surrounded. I have more than 500 men in those woods. Very hard, very strong fighting men. If you think perhaps you might reverse the train and go back, please understand this.' He pointed down the track. 'Around that bend my men are already blocking off the line. You cannot go forward or back.'

'We'll figure out something,' said Story calmly.

'Be realistic. How many men have you? Can you fight five hundred?'

Story took the cheroot from his mouth, examined the soggy end with deliberate care, and then spat on the track, a few inches from the still restless horse. Dukhonin looked at the ground and then, slowly, back to Story. Suddenly he put spurs to his horse, swung its head round, and went galloping away into the trees: he tossed the white flag into the undergrowth and unsheathed the sabre, which glittered like a mirror in the bright sunlight for a moment, and then was lost in the shade.

Story was running down the track now, towards the

locomotive; a bullet pinged against the plating as he reached it and was hauled aboard by Klaus.

'Back off, back off!' he shouted.

Klaus put the engine into reverse and the train began slowly to move away from the barricade. Bullets were now drumming against the armour along the whole length of the train, and from the flat-bed trucks and gun wagon there came the answering chatter of machine-guns as the Marines raked the woods with fire. From either side, groups of Mongolian horsemen on shaggy ponies burst from the forest, firing and screaming as they closed in.

The rifles and machine-guns took a terrible toll, but reinforcements kept coming and some of the horsemen gained the track and rode alongside it, firing directly into the ports. At least a half-dozen of them leaped on to one of the flat-beds, and became locked in a fierce hand to hand struggle with the two Marines who were manning the Goda machine-gun. Tremayne and Kasakov came through from the enclosed gun-wagon as the last of them was sabred down. As one of the Mongolians tried to swivel the machine-gun round, Tremayne shot him through the head, and Kasakov took care of another. Tremayne leaped on to the truck and turned the gun on another party of boarders. A huge invader, with a thin, greased black moustache framing his chin, was caught midway between horse and train and fell screaming beneath the wheels.

They had almost reversed to the bend now, and in the locomotive, Story yelled: 'Kill it, Klaus, kill it!' The train stopped sharply. Story was already holding the field telephone, and he rapped out an order to the Marine sergeant. 'O.K., Sergeant. Give it all you've got.'

The steel shutter over the gun port in the first car slid open and the three-inch gun edged forward until its barrel extended through the port, pointing towards the barricade like a grey accusing finger. The range was about 300 metres. A dozen horsemen were riding down the track and the first shell ripped through them and whistled over the obstruction ahead. Two of the attackers fell, the others wheeled aside, out of the line of fire. The gun was lowered, and the next shell smashed into the barricade. Splinters and branches flew in all directions and two of the topmost trunks rocked and fell aside, but the rest held firm. Shell followed shell, and the recoil from the gun could be felt along the whole length of the train.

Story shot straight into the face of one Mongolian as he tried to board the locomotive and Klaus brought another down with a crack on the skull from a big engine spanner. They grinned at each other and made an invisible mark in the air. Petka was doing valiant work with a shovel, swinging it round from side to side and yelling like a dervish.

Story climbed the ladder and squinted along the track. The first assault had, for the most part, been driven back, although isolated battles were still going on. The barricade was still in position but it looked smaller now, and as he watched a shell landed plumb on target, cracking the trees like matchsticks. Story grabbed the field-telephone and wound the handle urgently.

'Hold it, Sergeant,' he yelled, 'hold it, or you'll tear up the rails.' He replaced the phone and turned to Klaus. 'Right. Full steam ahead. We'll smash our way through.'

Klaus eased the brakes. The train edged forward then began to gather speed. It hit the remainder of the barricade at no more than fifteen miles an hour. There was a shudder, as the steel nose bit into the logs, a crash, and then they were through, swaying and swerving as Klaus opened the throttle.

Semyonov's men came on again, screaming their frustration, but the *Royal Flush*, trailing black smoke as though in triumph, hurtled on its way and they fell back. Klaus pulled the whistle cord in mocking farewell, then he reached into a tin locker-box, brought out a pack of cheroots, and held it out to Story.

'Have one of mine,' he said, smiling.

Chapter Eight

Story was in grim mood by the time the *Royal Flush* reached Khabarovsk. He had toured the train and counted the cost of the encounter with Semyonov; six good men dead, four US Marines and two Russians, plus seven wounded, one of them so seriously that it was doubtful if he would survive. He became grimmer still when the local Station Controller, a nervous, excitable little man, told him that the two hospitals in the town were already overflowing and urged him to take the wounded men on to Chita. A doctor would be brought to the train, but that was really the limit of what he could do. He did not say so, but it became obvious that the sooner Story moved on and out, the happier the local citizens would be.

In the end, it was Tremayne who solved the problem. He came into the office at the station just as Story was about to break loose and announced that he had commandeered a truck in the street outside and that it was waiting to convey the wounded to a hospital attached to the Convent of the Resurrection. He was reliably informed, he said in that cut-glass English accent which at once intrigued and infuriated Story, that there were two American volunteer nurses working at the hospital and the men would be in good hands.

And so it proved. The hospital was small but immaculate, and the American nurses, two plain, plump sisters from San Francisco, more than made up in kindness and brisk efficiency what they lacked in physical attraction. Tremayne alerted both the British and American Vice-Consuls in the town, and by the time he got back to the dimly-lit station, the *Royal Flush* had been re-coaled and watered and was ready to leave. It was now 3 a.m. The journey from Vladivostock, and the delays involved, had taken almost a full day from his precious schedule and he was anxious to move on, but it was then that he found himself at odds with Tom Story. They paced the echoing, wooden platform, locked in argument.

'We'll leave at first light,' Story said firmly.

'I'm sorry but I think we should press on, Mr. Story,' said Tremayne.

'In the dark?'

'Why not?'

'Hell! We lost six men back there, maybe seven. That was in daylight. If it had been night we'd have crashed plumb into those trees. Next time they could blow the track on us, or a bridge.'

'They won't, old chap, they won't.'

Jesus, thought Story, if he calls me Mister or old chap once more, I'll break a fist over his head. The Englishman's cool politeness was beginning to get under his skin. Aloud, he said: 'How do you know they won't, God dammit!'

'Because Semyonov wants the train. He won't try anything that might put it out of action. In any case, in a couple of hundred miles we'll be out of his territory.'

'Yeah. And some other two-bit General will try shooting us up. A couple of hours, maybe three. Is that going to make so much difference?'

'It could do.' Tremayne spoke quietly, seriously. 'I

mean that. At the end of the day, an hour or so could mean a great deal.'

Story flicked a cigar butt away, and it fell with a sprinkle of sparks on to the track; it glowed in the darkness for a moment or two and then went out. Story did not speak until the red gleam had gone.

'You make it sound mighty important,' he said slowly.

'It is, old chap,' said Tremayne.

'So tell me,' Story said savagely. When Tremayne hesitated, he continued, 'For crissakes, I'm in command of that train, I'm supposed to be in command, and I don't even know how far we're going or where to!'

Tremayne hesitated again. There was no point in holding it back any longer, he told himself. He needed this man's willing support, and he needed it now. His instructions were to inform Story of their eventual destination only after they had picked up Kasakov's men, and he knew that Story had been so informed. But he knew also that this peculiar decision was really only part of the same devious diplomatic game which had delayed him in London. The Americans, like the British, did not want to be seen to be officially involved in the operation – at least, until it was brought to a successful conclusion. So nothing had been committed to paper; all the orders had been issued verbally, for the spoken word could always be denied, and most certainly would be if anything went wrong.

'We're going to Ekaterinburg, Mr. Story – or as near to it as we can damn well get,' he said.

'But the Reds are there!'

'I said – as near as we can get,' said Tremayne. 'And as fast as we can make it. That's your job. To get us there quickly, no more. We'll leave you then, and you can forget all about us. Just turn round and head back for Vladivostock. All right?'

'I guess so,' said Story. He lit another cheroot and in the flare of the match he looked at Tremayne with thoughtful eyes. 'Ekaterinburg, huh?'

'The quicker the better,' said Tremayne. 'How soon can you make it?'

'We'll have a hard time to make it in ten days,' said Story. 'And that's provided we have a free run, no more ambushes.'

'Make it eight,' Tremayne said.

'Figure it yourself,' said Story. 'Ekaterinburg is 4000 miles down the line, give or take a hundred or so. If we travel night and day—'

'We have to do just that, Mr. Story.'

'I said if. We have to stop places for fuel, water, food, right? And allow a bit for accidents, like today. So we can maybe keep on the move 20 hours out of every 24. That Mallett, with luck, can average – I say, average – 20 m.p.h. That's 400 miles a day by my reckoning. Ten days – 4000 miles.'

'Ten days.'

'With luck, a hell of a lot of luck.'

'Right, Mr. Story! Shall we get our skates on then?'

'There's just one more thing,' said Story.

'Yes?'

'It just so happens – I mean, if you want to be formal about it – it just so happens that it's not Mister Story. Not any longer. At this moment, it's Major, and I guess it will be for the duration.' Story grinned, white teeth showing in the gloom.

'I am so sorry, Major,' said Tremayne, 'I really didn't know.' The note of genuine apology in his voice embarrassed Story and he began to regret the impulse that had prompted him to try to put Tremayne down by parading his new rank. It had been a stupid fool thing to do.

'I didn't know myself until a week, ten days ago. Nothing to it. It's not for real. They handed me this temporary, provisional, acting commission in Singapore,' he said. 'I just never got round to picking up the uniform.' He tried to imply that the whole business was unimportant anyway, and that he was sorry to have brought it up.

'I'm not too fond of titles or uniforms myself,' said Tremayne, with more meaning than Story realised. 'Or formality, for that matter.'

Story considered this, chewing on his cheroot. 'You handled yourself real well back there, during that skirmish,' he said. He almost added 'for a limey', but checked himself in time.

'Thank you.'

'On the ship, what did you say your name was? Your given name?'

'Jimmy will do, Major.'

'Tom,' said Story, extending a hand.

The two men shook hands in the solemn fashion of schoolboys after a fight. As their hands dropped, they stood in awkward silence, as though not sure what to do next. It was an absurd moment, in an absurd place, but Tremayne was to remember it always, and not in that way. It was Story who broke through their mutual embarrassment, and he did it in typical fashion. Ramming a powerful fist into Tremayne's shoulder, he made his voice take on a fair imitation of the Englishman's accent.

'Right,' he said, 'shall we get our skates on, old chap?'

2

Taking into account the changing time zones, it took the *Royal Flush* twelve days to reach Omsk, the head-quarters of the White military forces and the seat of the Directorate, the newly-created anti-Red government of Siberia. It was a nominal title, as Tremayne learned to his cost; in practice, the Directorate controlled only small areas of that vast territory, and was split with internal dissensions.

The delay was no fault of Klaus or of his sturdy locomotive, and though they had several light skirmishes with roving bands, there were no more major ambushes. The trouble really began at Yakeshi, just beyond Khabarovsk, where they took on fifty of Kasakov's Volunteers with their horses. They made an impressive force, most of them officers of the old Chevalier Guards, who had been handpicked by Kasakov; stern and dedicated, they were fanatical in their devotion to the monarchy. But they and their horses had to be fed, and this often entailed armed forages into the countryside in search of supplies.

The peasants, tired of the demands of opposing armies and warring factions, were openly contemptuous of the kerenkas, the paper money, which they were offered. It was often necessary to use force, or the threat of force, to make them even discuss a possible trade.

After two such encounters, Tremayne took personal command of the forage-parties, for he had been shocked by the unnecessary barbarity with which the Volunteers treated the peasants. This decision led to a blazing row with Kasakov, but Tremayne, with the support of Story, had his way in the end and was able, in some measure, to curb these excesses.

Other delays were caused by breaks in the line, where the track had been blown, or the rails simply torn up. This meant that they had to clear the debris, pull up the rails and sleepers behind them and re-lay them in front of the train in place of the ravaged sections of track.

'Hell's bloody bells!' said Klaus, after they had performed this tedious operation for the sixth time. 'If we keep doing this, there'll be no line left to take us back to Vlad!'

But it was forward that Tremayne wanted to go. It was already July 8. HMS *Chatham* would be at the mouth of the River Ob on July 17 and would wait only 48 hours. He had nine days, ten at most. They were cutting it fine, too damn fine!

Still, at least they had got to Omsk and it was on this city that he had pinned his hopes. There would be law and order there, some fixed authority with which he could deal, and Ekaterinburg lay only 400 or so miles ahead. So he had imagined the famous 'green' city as a kind of end, and also as a beginning.

As the *Royal Flush* steamed slowly across the bridge over the River Irtish, it seemed as if they were entering a new and incredible world. On the wide and tranquil waterway below, sparkling in the clear bright sunshine, some sort of regatta was in progress; elegant women with parasols, officers in white uniforms, families, children, lined the banks, cheering on two competing eights. Watching the boats slide through the water, the flash of oars as they rose and dipped in rhythm, Tremayne felt a pang of envy, and of homesickness. Memories of his own days on the river echoed in his head, he could feel the thrust of the oars in his hands, smell once again that strange mixture of sweat and liniment which used to fill the changing-room. It was almost unbelievable that he should have crawled thousands of miles across this bitter, fractured land and come across such a scene.

'What in all hell is going on down there?' A frowning Story was standing at his side, looking down.

'A boat race,' said Tremayne. 'Those chaps are not bad, not bad at all.'

'Now I've seen everything!' said Story, shaking his head.

'You've never seen a boat race before?'

'Sure, I have. But now? In this poor, bloody benighted country? Don't they know that the Reds are up ahead, only two or three hundred miles away?'

'Probably a couple of regimental crews. Even soldiers have to relax sometimes,' Tremayne said defensively.

'Maybe. But I'll tell you something, Jimmy. Lenin and Trotsky ain't doing any rowing right now, I'll lay long odds to that.'

'You'd back them, would you?' asked Tremayne, remembering what he had told Lloyd George some weeks before – though it seemed as though a century had passed since then.

'After what we've seen on this trip? They're a cinch. I'd bet the limit.'

'Ah, we have a Bolshevik in our midst!' They turned and saw Kasakov standing behind them. He held his head to one side, and his boyish face was creased in a fixed, charming smile. There had been a growing friction between Story and the young Colonel for the past few days and Tremayne watched them warily.

'You want the truth?' said Story casually.

'It is always better,' said Kasakov.

'I don't know about that, Colonel,' said Story, 'but you asked for it. Truth is, I hate the bastards' guts. But my hunch is that they'll win because they're tough, organised, and as of this moment, they're playing the right music.'

'Not a Bolshevik,' said Kasakov softly, 'but a defeatist. Isn't that so?'

'Nope. I'm just trying to look at things for real. From what I've seen of the Whites, they ain't learned a thing, not a single durned thing. Listen – you got a civil war on your hands, O.K.? A big war, O.K.? Did you ever stop to ask yourself why, Colonel?'

'Ease it, Tom,' said Tremayne.

'I'm just telling him. He don't have to stay and listen.'

'I shall be most interested to hear your views,' said Kasakov.

'Well, I'll tell you. This is what I think, Colonel. I think your side need glasses, good glasses. Because from where I stand, it don't seem to me that you can see a damn thing. Or maybe you don't want to.'

'For example?'

'Like this, for example. For years, since way back, your King – your Tsar—'

'The Tsar?' interrupted Kasakov. The fixed smile dropped away and his voice was arctic.

'Ease it, Tom,' Tremayne said again.

'I'm not fighting, just talking. Like I say, if the Colonel here don't want to listen—'

'You mentioned the Tsar,' said Kasakov in the same icy voice.

'Sure. The Tsar, and all the people round him. You got a great country here – great. But your Tsar carried on like he was God Almighty. And you went along with that. And all the Joe Doakeses of Russia, the ordinary guys, you treated them like they was dirt. Mean, real mean. You did the dealing and you used a cold deck all the time. Don't tell me different because I've been here these three years and I seen it. So comes the time when they say – "Hell, what kind of a life is this? We got no rights, we ain't got nothing, nothing!" They wasn't asking for much, just to have maybe a Congress and a Senate, live like other people, speak their piece when they've a mind to, know what I mean? But what did you do? Time and time again, you told them to go to hell. And that made a perfect set-up for the Reds. And you ain't learned a damn thing from all that, not a damn thing. Instead of a Tsar you got your Hetmans, and your Atamans and your Supreme Rulers and you still treat those ordinary Joes like they was dirt. You got nobody to blame but yourselves, and that's the nut of it, Colonel, the whole nut.'

'And so you blame our Tsar for what has happened?' asked Kasakov.

'The Tsar? Well, sure as hell, he's got to take some of the blame on his shoulders. Taking up with that monk, that Rasputin, for one thing. But now – well, I guess I feel sorry for the poor little bastard.' Tremayne saw Kasakov stiffen at the word, but Story went blithely on. 'He's finding out what it's like to be kicked around, finding out the hard road. He fell a hell of a long way and that can hurt. Yep – I feel sorry for the guy.'

There was a silence. Kasakov's face was white, his lips tightly compressed, his body seemed to be trembling. He was clearly making an effort of self-control, and when he spoke at last the words came out clipped and sharp, as though each carried a cutting edge.

'His Imperial Majesty is not here to defend himself, Major Story. But in his name I tell you now that he has no need of your pity, and only contempt for your lies and your insults.'

'Now, listen here—' began Story, but Tremayne laid a restraining hand on his arm and he stopped.

'I have another, more urgent task to attend to at this time,' continued the Russian, 'but when that has been brought to a successful conclusion, and if we should meet again, I promise this. I will call you out and kill you.' He clicked his heels and marched away, down the coach. Story looked after him with a bewildered expression.

'What the hell did he mean – call me out? A gunfight or something?'

'A duel,' said Tremayne. 'With swords! Or sabres perhaps, I'm not sure.'

'You're kidding!'

'I'm not. He wasn't,' said Tremayne. 'You called his Tsar a bastard.'

'A poor little bastard.'

'Same difference. You have to remember that to the Colonel and his men the Tsar *is* God Almighty. He's something very special. The Divine Right of Kings and all that. They don't recognise his abdication. They swore an oath to him and to him alone, and every one of them would lay his life on the line for that oath. To call him a bastard in front of the Colonel – that's like – like fornicating in church. Worse, in fact, much worse.'

Story lit a cheroot and considered this, watching the blue smoke curl upwards. Then he turned his direct eyes on Tremayne and gave him a slow, shrewd smile. 'Well,' he said, 'I guess I just learned something.'

'Good. Keep on learning while you can – and you'll be a better man.'

'How's that?'

'One of my grandmother's favourite tags. She's got hundreds of them. How about, "Smile, and when you smile, another smiles, and life's worthwhile—"'

'Stop kidding, Jimmy,' interrupted Story.

'It's true. My grandmother has a book of golden—'

'Cut it out! You know what I'm talking about.'

'Do I?'

'For chrissakes! You – the Colonel – Ekaterinburg.

There's got to be only one reason why you want to get there so fast.'

The train slid into Omsk station and jerked to a halt, releasing a noisy gush of steam as though in relief. 'Come on,' said Tremayne, 'let's go. I want to be on the move again in two hours. Two hours maximum.'

'No, you don't!' Story grabbed his arm. 'You didn't answer my question.' He lowered his voice. 'You're going in to snatch His Imperial Majesty, the Tsar of All the Russias etcetera etcetera. Right?'

'Tom,' said Tremayne, 'you made a good speech a few minutes ago. The longest I've ever heard from you. It made a lot of sense.' He opened the door of the coach and dropped down.

'You're crazy!' shouted Story.

'So they often tell me,' answered Tremayne.

Story dropped down beside him. 'Why? The Colonel – O.K. Him I can understand. Like you said – with him it's a religion. But why are you risking your neck?'

Tremayne grinned at him through the swirling, acrid smoke. 'Maybe I'm like you, Tom. I feel sorry for the poor little bastard.'

He turned and strode away. Story paused, shook his head, and then hurried after him.

3

At first, Miss Meg thought that Seraphina was simply acting up again. She had cried wolf so often in the past that when she took to her bed one evening complaining of headache, chills and pains in her arms and legs, Miss Meg largely ignored her. That evening, however, she found that Seraphina was really ill, alternately shivering with cold and sweating with fever. She did what she could to soothe and comfort her, and sent Kolya in search of a doctor. The bedroom door was kept locked, and the children were forbidden access to their aunt.

Kolya returned alone two hours later. He had searched the town, but nearly all the doctors had either been drafted into the Red Army or they had fled. One remained, and the most Kolya had been able to do was to secure a promise that he would try to call in the morning. Kolya reported that the doctor had a long queue of people waiting for attention outside his surgery.

Brushing aside Miss Meg's objections, he took the key and went into the bedroom. Seraphina lay on the sweat-soaked sheets, tossing her head from one side to the other. Her lips were cracked and dry, and she was murmuring incoherently. Kolya touched her arms and forehead with his big, gentle hands, looked deep into the troubled eyes, and without embarrassment, pulled up her nightdress to examine her legs. There was a rose-red sore on the right leg, just above the knee; around it the skin was scratched and stained with streaks of blood where Seraphina had torn at the irritation. The sore looked to be no bigger than a coat-button, but it stood out against her soft, milky skin like some monstrous insect, hideous and menacing.

Kolya lowered the nightdress, replaced the sheet, and beckoned Miss Meg towards the door. He was silent for a moment, as if trying to find the words to explain it to her.

'It is bad, miss,' he said, 'very bad.'

'But what is it?'

'I've seen it many times. The soldiers sometimes bring it from the trenches, sometimes it comes from the dogs. The peasants call it tick-fever.'

'Tick-fever?'

'Yes, miss. Tomorrow, perhaps the day after, she will have many sores, spots – all over. The Madame is very sick. You must keep away, you and the children.'

'I'll keep the children away certainly, but someone must nurse her, Kolya.'

'I will look after her, miss.'

'Nonsense,' said Miss Meg briskly, 'I wouldn't hear of such a thing.'

'It is dangerous.'

'That can't be helped. Now, tell me, what do you advise? I mean, what do the peasants do in such a case?'

'There is very little, miss. Wrap her hands so that she cannot scratch herself. Keep her in the shadow, away from the light, wipe her face and body with clean rags soaked in cold water. In my home village there is a root the people use to make medicine, but I have not seen it in this place.'

'Thank you, Kolya,' she said. 'Will you keep an eye on the children for a while?'

'Yes, miss.' He paused in the doorway, bowing his head beneath the lintel, filling the space with his hugeness. 'We must also pray to God for his goodness, miss.'

'Yes, Kolya,' she said, 'that is something we must not forget.'

When he had gone, she brought water, washed Seraphina from head to foot and changed the wet sheets. In the chest in her room she found a jar of Dr. Morse's Indian Root Ointment, which a friend in England had recommended as a remedy for skin irritations, blemishes, mosquito bites and a dozen other hazards of travel in foreign parts. Without too much hope, she applied a little of this to the sore on the leg. She put a pair of cotton gloves on Seraphina's hands and tied them at the wrist. She made a cold compress and laid that on the sick woman's forehead. Finally she carefully washed her own hands, arms, and face in water to which she had added a little carbolic solution.

She sat up with Seraphina all night, dozing fitfully in a chair for a few minutes at a time only to be aroused by more thrashing and fevered moans from the bed. Occasionally, through the window she saw flashes light up the sky momentarily, like red lightning, and heard the distant crump-crump of gunfire.

The doctor, a thin, scrawny man, red-eyed with exhaustion, arrived early the following morning. He took a brief, almost cursory look at Seraphina, and shook his head. 'Another one,' he said.

'Is it what they call tick-fever?' asked Miss Meg.

'It's what I call typhus,' he said curtly. She sat down suddenly, shocked and frightened by the very sound of that terrible word. He gave her a tired glance. 'What's the matter? Are you surprised? The town is full of it.'

'I didn't realise,' she said. 'I'm sorry. Can you help her?'

'I doubt it. For one thing, I've no drugs or medicines left. I can leave you a little quinine – not really the right thing, but it's all I have. Otherwise, just continue with what you're doing.' He sighed, opened his bag, and handed her a tiny bottle of quinine.

'Thank you, Doctor,' she said, still struggling to bring some order and calm to the confusion of thoughts which had exploded in her mind like a storm. She led the way downstairs, and at the door she opened her purse. 'How much do I owe you?'

'What have you got?'

'Kerenkas,' she said, and showed him the notes. 'Or I have some Soviet money. A little.'

He shrugged. 'Money – paper. What use is that? Tomorrow – who knows? – it could all be useless. Have you nothing else? A chicken? Eggs, perhaps?'

She had two eggs which she had brought back from one of her excursions into the countryside. They had been intended for the children, but she collected them from the kitchen. He gave the eggs a brief examination, put them in his hat and nodded. 'You look worn out yourself. You should try to rest. The living are more important than—' He stopped and shrugged again.

She watched him put the hat in a basket and ride away on his bicycle. The storm inside had died down now, and she felt only a great numbness, her arms and legs seemed like weights dragging at her body.

By the evening, more sores and smaller rash-like spots had erupted all over Seraphina's skin. The fever burned in her like a furnace; to be near her was like standing by the open door of a hot oven.

That night Miss Meg sat in a chair in the bedroom again but the doctor had been right, and sleep overcame her resistance. When she woke it was dawn, and Seraphina seemed to have settled down; she lay with her eyes open, and the hot flush had left her cheeks.

It was only when Miss Meg drew closer that she realised that Seraphina was dead. She felt an odd sense of calm. Poor Seraphina, she thought. She had lived for her imaginary illnesses, made them into a sort of hobby; and now, quite suddenly, as if in revenge, the real thing had stolen up in the night and killed her.

The men came that afternoon and took Seraphina away, without ceremony. They had orders from the local Soviet to collect all typhus victims; there was neither the time nor the facilities for individual treatment. Her body was put into a cart with a dozen others and buried in a mass grave. A priest said a few brief words over the dead. His voice echoed in Miss Meg's head as she left the burial ground with Kolya and the stunned, sad-faced children.

'Holy God, Holy and Strong, Holy and Immortal,

take these your lambs into your bosom. Have mercy on us all.' To which she added silently, earnestly: 'And deliver us from this land of pestilence and war. Please, God. Only let me get the children safely to England, and I promise, I promise in the name of Jesus, that I will never ask another thing from you for the rest of my life.'

It was dusk when they arrived back at the cottage. She gave the children a supper of bread and warm milk, sweetened with honey, and put them to bed. They clung to her as she kissed them good night and her eyes filled with tears. It was wrong, she thought, it was wicked, that children should have to bear so much.

Later, sitting with Kolya in the kitchen, he asked her: 'What will you do now, miss?'

'What is there to do, Kolya?'

'Many people are leaving the town.'

'Leaving? How is that possible?'

'The Red forces are weak. They cannot be everywhere. It is possible to slip through.'

'But where?'

'To the south or the east. The others are there, miss. Not far away.'

She thought about it for a moment only, then shook her head. 'No, Kolya. I couldn't risk the children. They have issued this proclamation. Anyone caught trying to leave without an official permit will be classed as a deserter, and shot.'

'It is a risk to keep them here, miss. That new Chairman of the Soviet, Gromeko, they say he is a holy terror. He has sworn that if the Whites take the town, they will not find one of their supporters alive.'

'But I support no one. I am neutral.'

'If you're not for Lenin, you're against him, that' what Gromeko says.'

'Where do you stand, Kolya?'

'Me, miss? What would I know of such matters?'

'What do you want out of life? That's what I mean.'

'Who am I, miss, that I should want anything? I was born poor, and I shall die poor. That's how it was ordained. Whatever they say in Petrograd or Moscow, whoever rules the roost, that's how it will be.'

'Doesn't that make you angry?'

'Why should I be angry?' He looked genuinely puzzled. 'It is God's will, after all. Do the lower branches of a tree complain because only those above them can see the sun?'

'Kolya,' she said, 'if you feel you would like to try to leave the town—' She stopped, checked by the expression on his face.

'If you want me to go, miss,' he said gruffly.

'No, no, Kolya, you know I don't mean that! It's just – I haven't any right to ask you to stay.'

'Right? What has that to do with it?' He shuffled his feet in embarrassment. 'The samovar's cold,' he said gruffly, 'I'll get it going, make some tea.'

4

That night, Viktor Gromeko, the Chairman of the local Soviet, paid a call on Sergo Mogilov, the Special Political Commissar from Moscow. Mogilov had been in Ekaterinburg for ten days, living in and working from the special train in which he had arrived. He had ordered that another coach be attached to the train, and that a crew was to stand by at all times, in readiness for immediate departure. The train itself was guarded night and day by his own picked detachment of Red Guards.

The two men presented an interesting contrast. Gromeko, the Chairman, gaunt and haggard, with an untidy stubble of beard, and clothes which looked as if they had been slept in, and the Commissar, who always managed to look as though he had been newly-minted. Everything about him seemed to glow, from the Red Star on his cap to the shining clean-shaven face and down to the gleaming black boots. His appearance was a source of irritation to Gromeko, who resented the other man's presence in the town anyway; he took it as a personal slight that Moscow should have taken responsibility for the Tsar out of his hands and handed it to an outsider.

One of Mogilov's first acts on arrival in Ekaterinburg had been to investigate the situation at the House of Special Purpose. As a result he had ordered the arrest of the Guard Commander on charges of drunkenness, theft, and other unrevolutionary behaviour, and replaced the regular guard with his own men. He had put an end, as far as possible, to the petty humiliations and insults to which the Tsar and his family had been subjected and ordered the guards to behave with scrupulous correctness. The regime at the House was also relaxed in other, minor ways. The Romanovs were no longer confined to their rooms; Mogilov ordered that at certain periods of the morning and afternoon they were to be allowed the use of the small yard and garden.

A full report on all these measures had been sent to Moscow, and the German authorities were informed, in turn, that neither they nor the Kaiser need feel any concern for the safety and welfare of the Russian Imperial Family.

Commissar Mogilov put a bottle of vodka and two glasses on the table in the coach, and motioned the other man to sit down. 'What can I do for you, comrade?'

Gromeko gulped down a glass of vodka, and waited as it warmed his throat and stomach. 'I have come from a meeting of the Regional Soviet. We are concerned about the Romanovs.'

'For what reason?'

'There is strong feeling, comrade. Our people are fighting and dying, while they are petted and pampered.'

'We have been all through this before,' said Mogilov in a tired voice.

'Nevertheless, the feeling is growing. Now we hear that you intend to move the Romanovs. Is that true?'

'I have orders from Comrade Lenin himself. You know that. The ex-Tsar must not fall into the hands of the Whites. If the military situation deteriorates further, he and his family must be moved.'

'The situation has deteriorated. Today we had to pull back again. Diterikhs has taken Kystym. His main forces are within eighty miles of the town. Forward patrols have been sighted even nearer.' Gromeko paused, and poured himself another glass of vodka. 'The Romanovs do not have to be moved, Comrade Commissar. Nor do they have to fall into the hands of the Whites.' He took a sheet of paper from his pocket. 'The Regional Soviet has today transmitted a resolution to the Central Committee in Moscow, requesting permission to bring the Romanovs before a Revolutionary Tribunal for sentence.'

Mogilov glanced at the written resolution. His face was impassive, but the scar twitched slightly. 'Have you received a reply?'

'Not yet. But until we do I have been asked to request you not to attempt to move the ex-Tsar.'

'Request?'

'That is what I said, comrade.'

'And if I choose to obey the orders I was given?'

'With respect, comrade. We shall be forced to take steps, certain steps. To put it bluntly, we shall stop you. I am sorry, Comrade Commissar. We do not believe that you understand the strength of the feeling here.'

'I could have you arrested and shot for this, Gromeko!'

'Perhaps. But you would also have to shoot the entire Regional Soviet, and most of the Red Guards.' Gromeko stood up. 'We are simple people here in Ekaterinburg, call us ignorant, if you like. We don't pretend to understand the ins and outs of politics, all this business of treaties and pacts and so forth. But we do know who are our enemies, and how to deal with them.'

There was a shrill edge to Gromeko's voice. As he moved to the door he stumbled and had to grasp at a chair for support. He was clearly at the end of his reserves, living on his nerve-ends. Mogilov went to him quickly, put an arm around his shoulder.

'Do you think Lenin loves the Romanovs? Do you think I love them? Don't you realise? We feel as you do, exactly the same. Nicholas will pay for his bloody crimes, never fear! But not here, not in Siberia. In Moscow, where the whole world will see and hear. A great public trial, before the people. Of course, I understand your feelings – I share them. But we must be objective, isn't that so? We must do what is necessary for the revolution. Trust Lenin. Our Vladimir Ilyich. Doesn't he know best?'

Gromeko steadied himself. 'I have been a member of the Party since 1902. I know my duty.'

'I never doubted it, comrade. But you need rest. These are hard days, we need all our wits about us.'

'Rest!' Gromeko gave a croaking laugh. 'Do you know how long it is since I slept in a bed?'

'You owe it to the Party, to your comrades. You must rest. Stay here – sleep. You will be better for it, believe me.'

'No. I will keep going somehow.' He sighed. 'Remember what I said. The people here don't understand what they are up to in Moscow.'

'You must make them understand.'

'Can you talk to an avalanche? No – they have had enough. They are determined. Depend upon it, comrade Nicholas the Bloody will not leave Ekaterinburg alive.'

Chapter Nine

I

Bureaucracy sprouts in any soil, but in Russia it puts down roots as nowhere else, covering the land like a lush parasitic growth. Russians are, and always have been, numbered, documented, stamped, checked, registered. It is a way of life which they accept as naturally as the passing of the seasons, knowing that whatever else may change, bureaucracy, like fleas on a monkey, will be always with them.

There is a story that, at the height of the Bolshevik Revolution, Lenin sent a Commissar and a company of Red Guards to the State Bank with a warrant to collect money for Government expenses. However, when the officials in charge pointed out that the warrant had no date and no official seal, the Commissar took the point and went away without the money, impressed by their rigid respect for the proper procedure. Even in a revolution, one's papers must be in order.

Tremayne collided head on with the bureaucrats at Omsk. Their ranks swollen by an influx from the areas held by the Bolsheviks, they combined to thwart him at every turn. He had no documents, no written authority, they regretted that they could allow him to proceed no further. The most they would concede was that, perhaps, in all probability, taking into account all the varying factors and without making any firm commitment, he might possibly be permitted to move on when the military situation became clearer.

Tremayne's two hours stretched into six, then ten. It was Tom Story's letter from the American Secretary of State which enabled him to clear the last of the bureaucratic hurdles and at 7 a.m. on July 9 the *Royal Flush* steamed out of Omsk. Suddenly time seemed to have shrivelled, and the hope of yesterday was replaced by a drumming anxiety. The tension communicated itself to his companions and even the normally cheerful, singing Klaus stood at the controls in silence. He seemed to be coaxing the last ounce of power out of the locomotive, willing it to give him the speed. In the coach, Tremayne, Story and Kasakov sat together and made the final preparations.

A few miles west of Omsk the track divided, one track going to Moscow via Ufa and Samara, and the other taking a more northerly route across the Urals to Perm and Petrograd. The main thrust of the White forces was from the south and the military situation on the northern section of the line was uncertain, but Kasakov's plan provided that they should branch off north, and Tremayne decided to stick to it, whatever the risks involved. And it had certain advantages; the northern track would bring them closer to Ekaterinburg and they would avoid the new headquarters of the White forces at Kystym. After his experience at Omsk he had no desire to be bogged down by General Diterikhs and his staff.

By late afternoon, with the *Royal Flush* almost bursting its boilers, they had covered an incredible 300 miles. They were travelling across the Western Siberian Lowland, a flat and seemingly endless plain, but apart from an odd cavalry patrol they saw scarcely any sign of military activity. To Tremayne's relief, Tumen, the

177

biggest town on the route, and an important railway junction, was firmly in the hands of the Czech Legion. The local Commander informed them that the general situation was confused, but the latest reports indicated that the Red units had pulled out of Kamishlov, about 90 miles from Ekaterinburg. He clearly thought Tremayne was mad to proceed further, but he put no obstacles in his path. They loaded supplies and fuel and moved on.

Klaus took the train through Kamishlov in the darkness, without stopping. They caught a glimpse of astonished faces, pale in the lamplights of the station, and heard shouts but that was all. Story ordered the speed to be kept down now, and the *Royal Flush* chugged more steadily onwards for about four hours. At last, they had left the bare plain and were in thickly-wooded countryside, where, in places, the trees almost brushed the face of the train. Story and Tremayne stood together, peering into the night and studying the route, occasionally referring to a detailed railroad map.

'Here,' said Story suddenly, 'about here. Ease her down, Klaus.' The *Royal Flush* slowed to a creaking crawl, and within minutes reached a stretch of track where the single line on which they were travelling was joined for a short distance by a second loop line. 'Hold it, hold it here,' said Story.

The train stopped. The familiar sounds of steam and groaning metal faded slowly, and the night closed in. They were surrounded now by the strange silence of the forest, which is not so much a silence as a stillness, filled with the whisper of trees and the quick, sudden call of the night creatures. Dawn came an hour later, and as the birds greeted it with their silvery chorus, Kasakov and his men disembarked. They were now clad in a motley collection of captured Red Army uniforms, workmen's clothes, peasant shirts and baggy pants. They could pass, without too much difficulty, as a partisan unit. They left the train quickly, expertly, so that hardly a sound came from the patient horses; within minutes the entire group seemed to dissolve into the forest.

Tremayne was the last to leave. He had changed into an oatmeal-coloured blouse which ringed his neck, baggy slacks, dark blue jacket and an old peaked cap. A Mosin-Nagent rifle was slung across his back and he wore a bandolier of ammunition. The transformation surprised even Story, though he refused to admit it.

'Jimmy Tremayne, by thunder!' he said. 'I'd know you anywhere.'

'Well,' said Tremayne awkwardly. 'This is it, then.'

'Yep,' said Story. 'Over the top and the best of luck.'

'I've got a feeling I'm going to need it,' said Tremayne ruefully. 'Luck, I mean.' He held out a hand. 'Thanks, Tom. Have a good trip back.'

'Matter of fact, Jimmy,' said Story, ignoring the outstretched hand, 'I've been doing a bit of headwork on that. Had a talk with Klaus and the other boys. We figured we wouldn't start back just yet a while.'

'You can't stay here!'

'No. We wasn't planning to do that.'

Tremayne looked at the American sternly. 'Your orders are to head back east.'

'We carried out our orders,' Story said. 'We got you here. What we do from now on is none of your goddamned business.' He softened the words with a grin. 'O.K?'

'No. If you're thinking of going on to Ekaterinburg—'

'We're not thinking – we're going,' interrupted Story. 'You game to try and stop us?'

Tremayne looked at the lean, brown face, into the

mocking eyes; all he could do was shake his head in response and murmur, 'You're mad, crazy, out of your mind, you know that, don't you?'

'That makes two of us. You want to know something, Jimmy boy? I reckon we're holding a better hand than you are. What have you got? The Colonel and a bunch of screwballs. That's a subway hand if ever I seen one, so low it ain't worth a bet.'

'Thanks,' said Tremayne drily. 'And what have you got?'

'A train. And we're Americans, official Americans – neutrals.'

'I hope the Reds know that.'

'Hell, President Wilson laid it on the line. No military intervention by the US. We can't take part in such intervention or sanction it in principle. No interference of any kind in Russia's internal affairs. That's what the President said and I got a paper to prove it. You want to read it?'

'Look, Tom, I appreciate what you're trying to do, and I think I know why. But I'll manage, believe me. Far more sensible for you to get out, go back to Omsk.'

'If we were talking sensible,' said Story, 'we'd all head back east. But we ain't.' He paused, then continued more seriously: 'Maybe we can just shorten the odds for you, maybe not. Anyway, we'll stick around in Ek for a couple of days, so if you want to drop in for a hand of poker, look us up.'

Tremayne smiled. 'That reminds me, I owe you 22 dollars from the last game.'

'I trust you,' said Story. 'Let it ride till next time.' This time, he held out a hand, and Tremayne took it. 'See you.'

Tremayne nodded and dropped down on to the track. At the edge of the forest he turned, lifted two thumbs in a smiling farewell and disappeared into the trees.

Klaus joined Story on the footplate. 'Hell's bloody bells,' he said. 'I wish somebody would tell me what is happening.'

'He's just going to collect a parcel,' said Story.

'The British are a very peculiar people,' Klaus said.

'You can say that again,' said Story.

'The British are a very peculiar people,' Klaus said obediently.

Story relit a half-smoked cheroot and blew out smoke. 'Listen,' he said, 'I've been thinking. Before we move on, you'd better get rid of that name-plate.'

'You don't like it?'

'Sure. But in these parts, folks might get the wrong idea if they see a locomotive called the *Royal Flush*.'

'They can't read English!' said Klaus scornfully.

'We might just get to meet some awkward bastard who can,' Story said.

2

The Volunteers moved steadily through the forest, encountering no opposition. They rested at noon, grazing the horses in a small clearing, and Kasakov sent a small patrol ahead to reconnoitre. The scouts returned an hour later with the information that the Red positions were about two miles ahead, beyond the edge of the forest; they had created a network of trenches and defence works on the range of low hills. Beyond those hills lay the town itself, nestling at the foot of the Ural Mountains.

Tremayne and Kasakov went forward with one of the scouts, a local man who knew the area well. Tremayne climbed a tree and focused his field-glasses on the Red forces. They appeared to be composed of a mixture of soldiers and armed civilians, among them some women. The ground between the forest and the slopes was as bare and open as the Siberian plain, it would be impossible for anyone to move across it without being sighted.

Tremayne had to admit that the defensive positions had been arranged with some shrewdness. They effectively blocked any progress westwards, and were protected on the right flank by the broad swiftly-flowing Pysma River, and on the left by the Pecora Marsh, a great depression forced into the land as by some giant fist, and said to be impenetrable. There was no question of a frontal assault, for the whole point of the exercise was to slip as many men through the Red lines as possible without them being detected.

Back in Vladivostock, he had been impressed by the care and detail which Kasakov had put into his plan, but there was one aspect which had caused him some misgivings. He felt that the young Colonel's contempt and hatred for the Bolsheviks carried with it a certain danger; he had a tendency to underestimate the intelligence of the enemy, he just could not believe that the uneducated, untrained mob, the so-called Dark People, could match men like himself in skill, judgment and leadership. It was natural that he should think in this way, it sprang from his whole upbringing and way of life, but it made him vulnerable.

Tremayne climbed down and confronted Kasakov, who smiled broadly, and held up a hand. 'I know what you are going to say! And I agree with you. They have planned the defences well. See, I admit it.'

'We couldn't slip through that lot, even at night.'

'I agree.'

'Well, then?'

'We go where they will not expect it. We cross the Pecora.'

'The marsh?'

Kasakov turned to the scout, a young officer formerly of the Chevalier Guards. 'What do you think, Samarin?'

'It is possible, Colonel. At this time of the year, there is a way. Not easy, quite difficult, in fact.'

'But possible.'

'Certainly possible.'

'Do you know it – could you take us across?' asked Tremayne.

'I believe so,' said Samarin. 'When I was a boy I lived in these parts. I came to the Pecora with my father each summer to shoot. We had one man, a gamekeeper, who could find his way through and I learned the trick from him.'

'How far are we from Ekaterinburg now?' asked Tremayne.

'Fifteen – sixteen miles. The marsh is two miles across, perhaps a little more.'

'Then let's go,' Tremayne said.

As they drew nearer to the marsh, he began to wonder at Samarin's confidence. Thick, fetid slush squelched up to their ankles, the sucking mud protested as they lifted their boots for the next step. The stench was already almost unbearable, the air itself seemed to be heavy and rotten. And this was only the beginning. Ahead of them stretched the Pecora itself, a dark mass of rank vegetation from which clumps of trees, their trunks distorted into weird and freakish patterns, raised reluctant heads. Here and there it was possible to catch the glint of water between the reeds and the coarse marsh grass; water-fowl flew up at the men's approach and circled warily. Mosquitoes rose in swarms from the slimy, stagnant pools, formed themselves into flying columns, and attacked the human invaders relentlessly, giving no quarter.

After an hour of searching, Samarin announced that he had found the path. He pointed to an old birch, on which, scarcely visible, there was a scar made many years ago by someone's knife. 'All the trees along the track are marked in such a fashion. They are like beads on a string. Here and there we shall find tiny islands on which we can rest.'

'I can see nothing – no track,' said Kasakov.

'It is there, Colonel, have no fear,' said the young officer cheerfully. He sought around in a nearby pool and picked up a thick stick. He took ropes from three of the horsemen, knotted them together, and tied one end around his waist. Then, grinning at their solemn faces, he said: 'Gentlemen, I will now demonstrate the crossing of the Red Sea!'

He stepped confidently forward into the marsh, taking a pace at a time, using the stick to test the ground ahead, and paying out the rope behind him. At times the mud and water reached to his knees, but he made it to a clump of trees about 300 yards ahead, and pulling the rope taut, he signalled to the others to follow.

Tremayne led the way, and Kasakov brought up the rear, with the others in between. Tremayne marvelled at the extraordinary composure of the horses; they plodded forward, heads down, sure-footed as mules, following their riders as if this were a common everyday exercise. It was the men who seemed the more nervous as they clung with one hand to the rope and with the other to their horse's bridle; but after a while, when they realised that Samarin knew what he was doing, they too settled down more or less patiently to the tortuous, tormenting journey. As they grew in confidence the pace speeded up a little, but the going was still painfully slow. Tremayne followed Samarin more closely and at several points the

two of them had to hack a way through the lush vegetation with swinging sabres. It was impossible to rest on
the little islands which thrust their heads above the
marsh for more than a minute or so; the mosquitoes and
the stink of rottenness drove them on.

3

At last, at long last, the ground began to harden beneath
their tread, as the ground sloped slowly upwards, and
finally they reached a clump of swamp cypress. The
earth was damp but firm and the exhausted men
squatted on their haunches, drinking in the cleaner air,
scraping the marsh mud from their boots, or wiping their
hands and faces on rags soaked in water. The confidence
began to return to their faces, and they exchanged slow,
secret smiles, as men do when they have shared a joint
endeavour and won through. It had taken them seven
hours, but they had actually crossed the Pecora. If they
lived, it would be a tale to tell their grandchildren.

Suddenly, the jingle of harness cut through the silence.
Kasakov and Tremayne were on their feet at once,
motioning the others to remain quiet. From the cypress
trees the ground rose more sharply, and at the peak of
the slope a small troop of Red Army horsemen appeared.
There were eight in all, and they reined in as they saw
the men and horses below.

'We can take them – easily!' whispered Kasakov.

'Don't be a damn fool!' said Tremayne, and at the
same time he lifted his arm and waved at the patrol.
'Good to see you, comrades,' he called.

The patrol leader hesitated, conferred with one of his

men, and then they cantered towards Tremayne. The leader was young, little more than a boy, but he composed his face into a stern expression as he reined in.

'Who are you? What are you doing here?'

'We're from Tobolsk, brother. 9th Partisan Brigade. We've been through it, I can tell you.'

'But how did you get here?'

'How? I'll tell you how, brother. Across that damned marsh. We had a local man with us, he knew a way.'

'There is no way across the Pecora!'

'Are you local?'

'No. We're from Perm originally.'

'Then don't speak of what you don't know, brother. We crossed the marsh, I tell you.' Tremayne pointed to his boots. 'What do you think this is – horse shit? We had no other choice. Diterikhs is advancing through the forest. Looks to me as though he is planning to creep up on you – mount some sort of surprise attack.'

The young commander laughed. 'Then he must think we're idiots. If he comes at us that way, we'll make it hot for him.' He took off his cap and scratched his head. 'And you came across the Pecora – well, I'll be blessed.'

'We're going to rest up, graze the horses, and then we'll report to the local commander,' said Tremayne.

'We can do with you, comrade,' said the young man. 'The Whites are pressing us hard to the south.'

'Well, we'll drive them back for you, brother,' said Tremayne with a smile.

'We'll drive the lot of them back, the whole lot of them – into the sea! So long, comrade, and good luck!' The commander raised a hand and his patrol trotted off.

'It would have been a pleasure to hang him and his gang from these trees,' said Kasakov. 'If that's the sort of thing we're up against – boys, illiterate children—'

'We're not! Don't underestimate them. If you do,

we're all dead.' Tremayne fumbled in his pocket and brought out a watch. '7 p.m. Time we were moving. It will be dark in two hours.'

The order was given to mount, and they set off, riding in column, with Tremayne doubling-up on Kasakov's horse. They saw small groups of Red soldiers camped in fields or at the side of the dirt tracks which passed for roads, but no one challenged them. Soon they reached a point where the road widened, and at intervals on either side there were large houses.

Samarin pointed to one of these, a spacious white villa with a red flag fluttering from a mast in the front garden. 'That was our house, that's where I lived each summer. The Tsar came there once – that's when my father put up the flag-pole. We flew the Tsar's personal standard then.'

Further on, they came to a fork to the left, and with Samarin in the lead they branched away from the main road. The new track was narrow but well-worn; fields of neglected crops lay on either side. The evening sun flamed fiercely in their faces, caking the marsh-mud which still clung to their boots, and to the legs of the seemingly tireless horses. They were in single file now, riding in weary silence.

Suddenly, Samarin put up a hand, and they reined to a halt. Clearly, across the still air, they could hear the music of an accordion, the sound of men singing. Ahead of them, a few hundred yards up the winding track, there lay a small copse, and beyond that, half-hidden by the trees, it was possible to glimpse the outline of a long, low, white-walled building.

This was the old monastery, set in a walled compound, which was their destination. The monks had abandoned the place some years before and for a brief period it had been used as an official Japanese trading post. Kasakov had assured Tremayne that it was now deserted, and the plan was that the volunteers would billet themselves there for one or possibly two days while he and Tremayne investigated the situation in the town. Isolated, screened from the road, with adequate pasture around for the horses, the monastery was ideal for their purpose. But if Red Army soldiers had occupied it, the complications would be serious indeed.

They sat listening for a while, straining their ears towards the sound. Tremayne recognised the music as that of an old Cossack song; it spoke of the eternal longing of the soldier for peace, to return home to his girl and to walk hand-in-hand with her on the banks of the Don. He found the tune oddly haunting; it plucked at his own heart and feelings, and for a moment his mind was filled with a vision of his family home in Devonshire, the rich red earth, the gentle River Torridge shaded by weeping willows, the laughing face of a girl he had known for one brief summer in his youth, his first, ardent, passionate yet innocent love.

Kasakov brought him back to the present. Dismounting, he signalled to Samarin and two other men to go forward with him and reconnoitre. Unbidden, Tremayne went with them.

As they approached the wood, the music changed to a Ukrainian folk-dance and they could clearly hear men chanting, clapping, dancing. Kasakov motioned to the others to spread out, and they slipped silently through the trees.

The outer wall of the compound had an arched entrance, and two Red Guards, bearded, middle-aged, were standing nearby, talking together. From beyond the wall, smoke and sparks rose from an open, crackling fire, and a tantalising smell of roasting meat wafted towards them, reminding Tremayne of his own hunger.

A distance of about fifty yards, a flat, dusty, open area, separated the edge of the copse from the entrance. It was impossible to cross it without being seen.

Tremayne edged forward on his elbows, and joined Kasakov. 'How many inside, do you think?' he whispered.

'Impossible to say. A good dozen or more by the sound of it.'

'We'll have to take those guards. Quietly, without alerting the others.'

'But how?'

'Be ready.' Tremayne stood up and stepped quietly forward, beyond the trees. The guards, engrossed in their conversation, did not see him until he was halfway towards them. 'Good evening, brothers,' he said quietly. They swung round towards him, startled, and levelled their rifles. He smiled at this, held up a hand. 'No need for that, brothers. I'm a friend.' He moved forward, still smiling, keeping it all casual and easy.

'Where the devil did you spring from?' said one of them, relaxing.

'Heard the singing, saw the fire,' said Tremayne. 'On my way to town.'

'Bit off the track, aren't you, comrade? What's your unit?'

'9th Partisans. Our main group is down by the cross-roads. I came up with a couple of mates to see if we could scrounge some provisions. We've had a hell of a day.' Tremayne turned back to the trees. 'Come on out,' he called. 'It's all right.'

Kasakov stepped forward with the other two men. 'Evening, brothers,' he said, extending a hand as he came towards them. One of the guards accepted the hand-shake, but the other was looking beyond him, to Samarin.

'The devil take it,' he said, 'I know you from some-where, don't I?' He stiffened suddenly, excitedly. 'You're

Samarin, young Paul Samarin! Wait a minute – I heard that you were with the others—' He broke off and turned to his companion. 'It's a trick! This is Samarin, he's on the blacklist, he's—'

The last words gurgled in his throat as Kasakov's arm went round his neck, choking back the breath. As the other man swung his rifle, Tremayne ducked, and put all his weight behind a blow that crunched into the guard's stomach; as he doubled up, dropping his gun, Tremayne chopped down at his neck with the edge of his hand. The man fell face down in the dust and lay still. His fellow-guard was dead, his throat slit from ear to ear by Kasakov's knife, his greying beard already reddening with blood. Kasakov knelt over the other unconscious man, the blade poised to repeat the treatment, but Tremayne pulled him clear, his fingers digging into the flesh of the Russian's shoulder.

'No! No!' he whispered urgently, angrily.

Kasakov showed his even white teeth in a wolfish smile. 'You are too squeamish, Englishman. The only good Red is a dead one!' He bent down, wiped the knife on the blouse of the dead guard, and replaced it in his belt. Samarin and one of the other men stooped against the wall at his signal; Tremayne and Kasakov climbed on their backs and peered cautiously over the wall.

There were about eighteen men in the forecourt before the main building. Some squatted against the wall clapping their hands to the music, while the others danced in the traditional Russian fashion, crouching on their heels, feet moving with incredible speed to the wild rhythm of the accordion. At the fire, an old man turned an improvised spit on which was impaled the carcase of a lamb. To one side, there were two stacks of rifles, and a Maxim machine-gun.

Kasakov and Tremayne dropped down. 'A sitting

duck,' whispered Kasakov. 'Samarin, bring the others up. You others – get rid of this trash.' As Samarin hurried away, the other Volunteers dragged the two Red Guards into the shelter of the trees, while Kasakov scuffed at the dust with his boot, covering the pool of blood as best he could. He grinned at Tremayne, and together they followed the others into the copse. The Volunteers wasted no time; the second Red Guard had already joined his companion in death, and the two bloodied bodies had been tossed into the centre of a group of alders. One man was caught up by a branch, and he hung there, doubled up like some grotesque rag doll, his boots brushing his face, until the branch cracked and dipped under the weight and he slid to the ground.

Kasakov watched Tremayne through narrowed eyes as he turned away. 'Shall I tell you what they did to my mother and my father and my sister?' he said quietly.

'I don't want to know!' answered Tremayne savagely.

'Nevertheless, I will tell you, so that perhaps you will understand.' He spoke in a low, flat voice, without any show of emotion, as if he were repeating a familiar anecdote. 'It was last winter at Tsarytsin. My father was sick, ill, too ill to travel. He begged the others to leave him, to go south, but they refused. Then the mob came – rabble such as those—' He made a gesture of disgust towards the bodies of the guards. 'They made my father watch while they raped my mother and my sister. Not once, not one man, but many times, many men. My sister was fourteen, a pure girl, untouched, sweet as spring blossom. When they had finished, they cut off my mother's breasts, and sliced her open like a pumpkin. They took her body, and they took my father, still living, to the Volga, and they put them into a hole in the ice, into the freezing water. What they did with Glasha, my sister, I don't know. God only knows. She was taken away. All this I learned from one of our servants, a faithful soul, who escaped.' He paused, closed his eyes, and his body shuddered with a long, deep, sigh.

'I am sorry,' Tremayne said, conscious of the feebleness of the words.

'You are sorry. We are all sorry. Every man of my Volunteers could tell you a similar tale. Now, of course, you are going to say that all wars and revolutions bring their own atrocities – that we have been guilty of terrible cruelties also.'

'Isn't it true?'

'Of course. What did you expect – that we should turn the other cheek? I would like to kill them all, one by one. Lenin, Trotsky, all of them. I would fill the rivers of Russia with their bodies.' He sighed again. 'But it won't happen. The American was right. The old Russia, the old, sweet Russia – we shall never see her again.'

Tremayne was surprised, remembering how angry Kasakov had been with Story. 'If you feel like that – why do you continue to fight?'

'What else is left? You think I don't understand, but I do. We – people like me, the old aristocracy – even the Tsar – we're finished, all finished. A dying species. Soon there will be none of us left. It is America that has the future. Perhaps England also – I am not sure. We clung to our old-fashioned, out-of-date world for too long, we built a high wall around our lives and did not see or understand what was happening on the other side. A different sort of world is coming – and we're not equipped to live in it. As for myself, I have no desire to do so.' He smiled suddenly and clapped Tremayne on the shoulder. 'I apologise. It is not my nature to be so sombre. And I am not yet quite extinct! I have a little spirit in me yet. I shall take a few of them with me when I go. And tomorrow – tomorrow or the day after, we shall give their Red noses such a tweak that Lenin will feel it even in Moscow!'

'You're a hard man to understand,' said Tremayne.

'Don't try. The greatest philosophers in the world have tried to penetrate the Russian soul and failed. We have a saying – to understand a man's heart is not so simple as crossing a field.' They stood in silence watching a flock of geese, necks craned, wings beating, heading southwards in the gathering dusk. 'They are the lucky ones,' said Kasakov.

Samarin came to them in the gloom. 'We are ready, Colonel.'

Kasakov nodded. 'Twenty men around that wall, ten to each side. Five to make a back for the others. Ten men to get round to the back and cover the rear. The rest to stay here and take anyone who may try to make a run for it. Five minutes to get into position, then we go – right?'

'The usual procedure, Colonel?'

'Of course. Need you ask?'

Tremayne waited with Kasakov as the minutes ticked away. The Russian replaced his watch, drew his revolver and walked towards the entrance. He stood in the archway for a moment or two, with Tremayne beside him, calmly taking in the scene in the forecourt. Gradually the Red soldiers became aware of his presence; the accordion groaned to a halt, the dancers stopped, the men peered at him curiously, more surprised than afraid. He raised a hand, and the sharp, incisive snap of rifle-bolts broke the silence. Their eyes turned in wonder to the wall, to the rifles which were covering them and the stern faces behind the sights.

One man leaped towards the stacked rifles and Kasakov shot him down. At the same moment, the Volunteers opened up, raking the forecourt with fire, the blast reverberating from wall to wall. Two men put up their hands in surrender, but they, too, were shot. A burly man in shirt-sleeves came to the door of the main building, fastening a belt around his waist. A bullet cracked his face like an egg; he fell on his knees, rolled down the stone steps, and lay still.

They waited for other sounds, other movements, but none came. It had taken thirty seconds, and it was all over. Now only the smoke from the fire danced in the cool evening air, and the bitter smell of cordite smothered the scent of the roasting meat.

Kasakov holstered his revolver and looked at Tremayne, as though expecting him to speak, but the Englishman said nothing. He called Samarin to him. 'Clean up this mess. Post guards. Any trouble – deal with it. My friend and I are going into town. We shall contact you tomorrow – when we know the situation.' He turned his incredible, youthful, charming smile on Tremayne, a hint of mockery in his eyes.

'Would you care to take a stroll? Enjoy the best of the evening?'

4

Despite the map of the town which he had studied until it was imprinted on his mind like an arithmetic table, Ekaterinburg was smaller than Tremayne had expected, and, on the surface at least, more peaceful and normal than he'd imagined. Barricades of sandbags and trees stood at various vantage points, but they were not manned; armed workmen, wearing the armbands of the Red Guards, patrolled in pairs or lounged at street corners, but they offered no challenge. A peasant, half-asleep, sat behind an ox, which plodded down the centre of the main thoroughfare, dragging behind it a cart with huge, solid wooden wheels. The cart was laden with timber and on top of the load sat a young soldier with his arm around a girl. Two droshkys with thin sad-faced horses waited for hire and among the uniformed men and women on the rough sidewalk there was a fair sprinkling of people in neat civilian clothes. Tremayne and Kasakov blended easily into this background; the sight of heavily armed, mudstained men was too familiar to warrant a second glance.

Taking their time, they made their way towards the square and turned right into Voznesensky Avenue, a wide street lined on either side by ornate houses, each set in its own grounds. The sidewalks here were strips of bare earth, bisected by a narrow path. The third house along, long and white, was almost hidden by two irregular-shaped palisades, above which only part of the upper floor and the roof could be seen. Red Army soldiers stood on guard by the gate in the outer palisade. A faint glow of lamplight showed behind the white-washed upper windows.

'The Ipatiev House,' murmured Kasakov. 'The House of Special Purpose.' Tremayne nodded, and would have gone on, but the Russian put a restraining hand on his arm. 'No further. That is enough for now.'

They walked back to the main street in tense silence. Tremayne felt a sense of anti-climax. He had been building up to this moment for months and somehow Ekaterinburg and the House of Special Purpose had taken root in his imagination as grim symbols of tyranny and terror. They had assumed a scale which seemed to be mocked by the reality. The town was unprepossessing, quiet, the people looked comparatively relaxed and unhurried, and Ipatiev House, which its owner had described in such rapturous terms back in Vladivostock, was, from what he had seen of it, simply ugly, over-ornate and tasteless. What he missed was the tension, the sense of occasion which he had imagined would come with his first sight of the Tsar's prison. The palisades might have been thrown up as an afterthought by an amateur carpenter, the guards were casual, bored, indifferent. It was hard to believe that behind those windows, in that dull house, there was a man who had once ruled an area of land which covered one-sixth of the earth's surface, and whose every word and whim had been law to over 150 million people.

The two men made a turn off the square into a small side-street, grandly named Pushkin Boulevard, and lined with little shops, many of them closed and shuttered. The long, hovering twilight had now almost faded, and the few people still abroad seemed to be moving with more urgency. A Red Guard patrol emerged from one of the dark, narrow alleys which sprouted from the street at regular intervals and stood on the corner, casting watchful eyes in both directions.

As Tremayne pulled Kasakov into the darkness of a nearby passage-way, the patrol stopped an elderly man, who produced his identity papers with trembling hands. While one of the guards scanned the documents in the dim light from an upper window, the other called across the road to a young woman who was hurrying past.

'Get a move on there, Elizaveta – curfew in ten minutes!'

'If I move any faster, I shall trip over my legs!' she shouted back cheerfully.

'I'll give them a good rub if you do.'

'Ha! You should have such luck. I've seen better things than you crawl out of the Pecora Marsh!' She smiled, gave him a good-natured wave of the hand as she moved on.

'Off you go, grandad,' said the other guard and the old man went thankfully on his way. The guards paused to light cigarettes, then continued their slow patrol along the street. Tremayne was preparing to try his bluff once more, and Kasakov's hand was on his knife, but the two guards, engrossed in conversation, passed by without a glance in their direction.

'A curfew,' whispered Tremayne, 'and we've got no damn papers!'

'I have this,' grinned Kasakov, touching his knife.

'Don't be a blasted fool. If they find their men knifed in the street, they'll comb the town, search every house! God, you're a madman – if you see anything moving, you want to stick that damned knife into it.'

'Anything Red. I'm very selective,' said Kasakov. 'Come on – it can't be far now.'

They almost missed the street they were looking for; the name, Rubilov Avenue, had been scratched out, and above it there was a crudely painted sign bearing the new title: Leon Trotsky Street. Not much of a compliment to the Soviet Commissar for War, thought Tremayne, as they made their way along the smelly, garbage-strewn sidewalk. A minute later, he was tapping at the back door of a small house. One hand was in his pocket, gripping the comforting butt of his revolver.

Sounds of movement came from within, and through the tiny side window they saw the approaching yellow gleam of a rush candle. A man spoke from behind the door. His voice, low and querulous, carried the distinctive local accent.

'Who is that?'

'Is this the house of Mikhail Tambov?' asked Kasakov.

'What of it? Who wants him?'

197

Kasakov hesitated, frowning, and Tremayne inter-
vened quickly. 'We have a message for him,' he said.
'From his mother in Moscow. She is keeping well, but
Shura the dog is dead.'

A long moment of silence, in which they could almost
hear the man breathing. Then he answered: 'Shura was
an old dog. He had to die sometime.'

Kasakov thumped Tremayne's back joyfully. 'Alexei!'
he called softly.

'Zakhar!' Bolts were drawn, and a thin, stooped man
wearing wire-framed spectacles beckoned them inside.
He made the door secure again, then turned to Kasakov
and grasped his arms with hands on which the blue veins
stood out like ridges. 'Zakhar, my dear boy, let me look
at you, let me look at you!' The provincial accent had
gone now, the voice was dry, academic. The two men
embraced, hugging each other tight, and kissing cheeks
in the Russian fashion.

'Damn you, you old fox,' said Kasakov. 'You know
what happened out there? I forgot the password, all that
rubbish about Shura the dog; it went clean out of my
head. That accent you put on fooled me completely. I
thought we'd come to the wrong house. And your beard,
your pride and joy, what happened to that?'

'One must sacrifice something for a good cause, isn't
that so? I gave up my beard and my beautiful spectacles
with the American horn-rimmed frames. It was a hard
decision, I can tell you.'

'You look like some down-and-out clerk!'

'I do? Excellent! Almost right. Actually you see before
you Citizen Mikhail Tambov, a poor translator and
language teacher, specialising in English, French and
German. Private lessons by arrangement. Oh, you may
smile, Zakhar. It wasn't an easy role to play at first,
believe me, but I flatter myself that I have mastered it

now. Why, I am sometimes called in to translate documents for the local Soviet!' He hugged Kasakov once more. 'Ah, but it's good to see you, my lad. I'd almost given you up. What kept you? And you're the one to talk of appearances! You look as if you've been dragged backwards through a bog!'

'That's a fair description, Alexei,' said Kasakov.

'No,' said the other man sternly. 'Not Alexei. Here I am Mikhail Tambov. At all times.' He turned at last to the patient Tremayne. 'You must forgive us, my friend. It is a long time since we met, you understand. And this rascal is like a son to me.'

'This is the Englishman,' said Kasakov, and added with a grin, 'but he can't help that. He is a good friend, and a good fighter, though a little on the squeamish side.' Alexei paused, his gaunt face tilted sideways on the scrawny neck, his pale eyes suddenly cold. Tremayne felt an odd sense of chill; there was something hooded and vulture-like about the man which repelled him. Kasakov went on anxiously, 'You received our messages?'

'Yes, yes!' said Alexei impatiently. 'We still have our friends. Your messages came through.' He straightened his head and nodded. 'Yes, I like the look of him. He'll do, he'll do very well.' He extended a hand. 'Welcome.'

'Thank you, I am glad to be here,' Tremayne said politely, taking the ice-cold hand. 'And delighted to meet you.'

'Ah, the English!' said Alexei, kissing his fingertips. 'Such manners, so courteous. An example to the world!'

'And where are your manners?' demanded Kasakov. 'Are you going to keep us standing here all night?'

'One moment.' Alexei dropped his bantering tone and became serious. 'It is fortunate that you arrived at this time. You see, the situation has now become quite desperate, the pressure is building up. We have, at the most, 36 hours. Our plan makes it imperative that we make our move the day after tomorrow. I have a visitor in the other room. We were about to discuss the problem.'

'Who is he?' asked Kasakov.

'Don't worry, my lad. He's one of ours, one of our best people. He worked for me when I ran the special division of the Okhrana in Moscow.' He smiled as he saw the look on Tremayne's face. 'Does it surprise you that I was once a policeman? Oh, yes – I also served His Majesty, in my own way. Mind you, I looked different then, I had some flesh on my bones in those days.'

'Don't believe him,' said Kasakov, 'he has always been as thin as a bean-pole. They used to call him Cassius the Red-Catcher. That ugly head is worth a lot – the Bolsheviki have put a big price on it.'

'And so they should,' said Alexei. 'It is no more than my due. Now, let us go through – I'll light the way.'

Taking the candle, he led them down a narrow passage to a small, sparsely-furnished room. A man was standing by the empty stove, and he turned as they came in. He was thick-set, he wore the uniform of a Political Commissar, and there was a scar on his left cheek and forehead which divided the eyebrow in two.

'Here we are then,' said Alexei, 'allow me to present Special Political Commissar Sergo Mogilov.'

Chapter Ten

I

The Red Army detachments patrolling the railway line and defending the approach to the Pysma Bridge could hardly believe what they were seeing. For a train to come from the east was surprise enough, for it had been a long time since that had happened, but for a *bronevik* of this sort to appear was incredible. The Stars and Stripes fluttered jauntily from the front and rear cars, the colours of the American flag had been painted over the camouflage on the main passenger coach, and standing openly on the flat-cars in uniforms that were immaculate were a half-dozen American Marines. When they saw the Red troops, the Americans waved a friendly greeting, and Klaus joined in with a long triple whistle from the engine. The bewildered soldiers waved back while their commanders hastily reached for field telephones to give warning of the approach of the train and to ask for instructions.

Nikolai Dukov, the young officer who befriended Miss Meg in the wood, was now second-in-command of the unit which guarded the Pysma Bridge. His superior had been summoned to a war-council in the town but Dukov had specific orders and he acted upon them. An old locomotive was brought puffing up from a siding and stopped at a point where it could block the single track over the bridge. Field guns mounted on the embankment, manned and loaded, pointed their grey nozzles downwards: riflemen and machine-gunners took up prepared positions. The bridge itself was vital to the town, but even that was to be blown up as a last resort. Dynamite had already been strapped to the supports under the centre span, and Dukov deputed one of his most reliable men to stand by the detonator. If all else failed, the bridge would be sacrificed; but the soldier was ordered to make sure that he took the train with it.

Thus prepared, Dukov waited on the embankment. The light wind, ruffling his sandy hair, faintly carried the unmistakable whistle of an on-coming locomotive, and soon afterwards the train appeared round the bend. Smoke curving lazily from its funnel, flags fluttering, the *Royal Flush* moved forward at a sedate and peaceful crawl, as though to confirm that its intentions were innocent.

Story, standing with Klaus at the controls, ran his glasses over the embankments on either side, noting the guns, the absence of movement, the solitary, hatless young officer standing up there studying them, in turn, through his binoculars. 'O.K. Pull her up, Klaus. Nice and easy.'

Klaus brought the train to a careful halt. The slow squeal of brakes, the rattle of metal, the hissing gush of steam faded, and there was silence.

'The track is blocked,' said Klaus. 'I don't think they like us.'

'Only one way to find out,' said Story. He grinned at Klaus and clapped him on the shoulder. 'Don't look so anxious. Like I said, we're neutral, we're Americans.'

'You are American,' said Klaus carefully.

'You and me, both. We adopted you, remember?'

'I know this,' said Klaus, 'and you know this. It is the Bolsheviki I am thinking of. Perhaps they do not know.'

'Listen,' said Story, 'if you get yourself killed, I'll

personally see that the US Government puts in an official protest.'

'Thank you,' Klaus said gravely. 'How do you say it? Thank you for nothing.'

Story turned to Petka, the fireman. 'You O.K.?'

Petka gave him a broad smile. 'I am very O.K., sir,' he said.

Story nodded, dropped down on to the track and walked forward, treading between the gleaming, sun-bright rails. Dukov watched him for a moment or two, held up a hand to his waiting men, then scrambled down the embankment. He straightened up, brushed his fingers over his tunic, loosened the Mauser which hung in a holster from his belt, and stood, legs apart on the track, waiting for the other man to reach him.

The distance separating them was only a matter of two or three hundred yards, but to Story it felt like climbing a very steep mountain. He could not see the rifles or machine-guns, but he sensed their presence, he felt the watching eyes boring into him. Each crunching footfall sounded hollowly in his ears, and repeated itself like an echo. The face of the waiting Russian grew clearer, young and handsome but stern, unsmiling. Six yards separated them when Dukov spoke.

'That is enough.'

Suddenly, Story saw the humour of the situation. He was reminded of the Western yarns he'd read as a boy in which the cowboy hero approaches a hostile Indian chief with an up-raised hand and the words: 'Hi. I come in peace.' The thought relaxed him, and smiling easily, he said: 'Hello, there.'

'Who are you? What do you want?'

'We're Americans. The train is United States pro-perty. We want to go into town, look up some supplies.'

'Where have you come from?'

'A longways. From the East.'

'From Omsk, perhaps?'

'That was part of it.'

'The Whites are there.'

'Hell, we've met all sorts this trip. Whites, Reds, and all the colours in between. We're neutral, you know that, don't you?'

'I know nothing about you.'

'Step up and take a look.' Story waved a hand in the direction of the train. 'We've got maybe eighteen US Marines aboard, one engineer, one fireman, and me. We're not up to starting a war.' He reached in his pocket and produced two cheroots. 'I didn't bring a pipe of peace but maybe these will do. Smoke?'

Dukov shook his head, but something of the sternness had left his face and there was the hint of a twinkle in his eyes. He was both puzzled and amused by the American's cool, casual manner and certainly impressed by his courage. 'I will look at the train,' he said.

'Sure. No sense in walking back, not in this heat. I'll have her brought up.' Story put fingers in his mouth and startled Dukov with a piercing whistle. As he lit his cigar, the *Royal Flush* purred slowly towards them. The young Russian remained on the track, as if defying the train, and Klaus brought it to a stop a few feet away. Led by Kelly, the sergeant, the Marines climbed down and at his command they formed up before the train in two columns, one each side of the track.

'What is this?' asked Dukov.

'Like I said, a few US Marines. Sort of guard of honour.'

The Red Army soldiers and gunners on the embankment had broken cover by now; they stood in silhouette against the skyline, watching with undisguised curiosity as Dukov walked cautiously towards the train. Story's already considerable admiration for the Marine Corps shot up further at that moment. Kelly barked his orders, and with the beautiful precision of a fine machine, the squad snapped to attention and presented arms. The sergeant turned to Dukov and levered his arm into a magnificent salute.

Dukov hesitated, the perplexity showing on his face. His hand wavered for a moment, the fingers twitching, and then, as if the honour of the entire Red Army was at stake, he pulled himself to attention and returned the salute. It was marginally less good than the sergeant's, but it was enough to satisfy pride. The men above took it as a sign that all was well; a great cheer went up and they came charging forward, slithering and tumbling down the embankment in their haste to get to the train, engulfing the hapless Dukov. There was no stopping them and in the end he joined the celebration. Within seconds the Marines were surrounded by excited, smiling Red soldiers; hands were shaken, shoulders thumped, cigarettes exchanged, guns inspected and admired. Story shook his head and allowed himself a small sigh of relief.

Klaus found him at the approach to the bridge, puffing smoke into the air. 'It is all right, I think,' Klaus said.

'I reckon so,' said Story. 'Klaus, do you see what I see?' He gestured with the cheroot. 'Under the centre span.'

'Dynamite!' said Klaus. 'They could have blown us to heaven!'

'They'd have had a hard time doing that with me,' said Story. 'I think I'm headed in the opposite direction.'

'But is all right now, you think?'

'Sure. We're in,' said Story. 'Now the only problem will be how to get out.'

2

It was not exactly a midnight knock at the door but it was late enough to worry Miss Meg. She put on her worn, woollen robe and went through to the other room. Kolya, who slept there, was already on his feet, and he looked at Miss Meg for instructions.

'See who it is. Don't open the door,' she whispered, and thrust a hand deep into the right-hand pocket of the robe; her fingers closed around the little pistol.

'Who's there?' asked Kolya gruffly.

'Dukov. Nikolai Dukov. I wish to speak to the Englishwoman.'

Kolya turned to Miss Meg. She felt a tiny blush redden her cheeks. She had unpinned her hair for the night and, without thinking, she smoothed it back from her forehead. 'Let him in,' she said, 'but don't leave, Kolya, stay here.' The big man unbolted the door and Dukov, jaunty as ever, stepped across the threshold. He swept off his cap and gave her an exaggerated bow.

'Good evening,' she said primly.

'I like you with your hair down,' he said, 'it suits you. Yes, I like it.' He nodded approvingly.

'What do you want? It is rather late.'

'Really, is that how you welcome visitors in England? I thought you were famous for your courtesy.'

'I am sorry, I have nothing to offer you. Why have you come?' She found his steady, smiling look disconcerting and moved away a little, plucking at the neck of the robe with her free hand.

'You needn't keep your hand on that pistol,' he said in a mocking tone, 'I haven't come to harm you.' He nodded towards Kolya. 'Anyway, I see you have a bodyguard. A real giant! I wouldn't care to upset him.' He

206

reached in his blouse and brought out a small packet. 'See, I've brought you a birthday present.'

'It isn't my birthday,' she said, relaxing a little.

'We'll pretend it is,' he said. 'Here, take it.'

'Thank you.' She went to the table and unwrapped the packet. A rich, nostalgic smell rose from the paper, and there, before her eyes, was something like a half-pound of ground coffee. 'Coffee!' she said, with an expression of pleasure that was only slightly simulated, 'real coffee! Oh, thank you. I haven't seen any real coffee for ages. Where on earth did you get it – or shouldn't I ask?'

'It's American,' he said, delighted with her reaction.

'American!'

'There's an American train in town – it's at the station now. I'm a sort of friend of the Commander.'

'I don't understand – an American train, in Ekaterinburg? How did it get here? Why has it come?' The coffee was forgotten now, her mind was exploding with questions.

'It came from the east. The Commander said they were simply making a survey of the Trans-Siberian. The United States has declared its complete neutrality, you understand. We have no quarrel with the Americans.'

'Where is it going from here?'

'Back to the east, I believe. They came into town for supplies – can you imagine that? – supplies in Ekaterinburg! They'll be lucky to get a wagonload of coal!'

'I can offer you some coffee now, good coffee,' she said smiling.

'No,' he said, 'I really can't stay. I'm on duty again at 5 a.m.' It was his turn to look a little embarrassed now. 'I just thought – well – I'd share my good fortune.'

'It really is kind of you, I do appreciate it.'

'I hope you didn't mind my calling.'

'Of course not.'

'Perhaps – when things settle down – we can meet again. There is a great deal I would like to talk to you about.' He moved to the door, and when he turned back to her, the cheeky smile had returned to his face. 'You should wear your hair down like that all the time.'

'It wouldn't be practical,' she said.

'Perhaps not,' he admitted, 'but it would be better. You are a beautiful woman, you shouldn't try to disguise it. Goodnight.'

He was gone before she could respond. She watched as Kolya closed the door. 'Kolya! Did you understand what he said?'

'Something about the Americans, miss?'

'But do you realise what it means? It's our chance! Tomorrow, first thing – the very first thing – I'll go to the station. I'll talk to them. They can't refuse to take us, they couldn't do that! Kolya, oh, Kolya, it's like a dream come true.' She checked herself, seeing the look on his face. 'Kolya, dear Kolya, I'm sorry. I didn't think, it was selfish of me. You don't want to come, you want to go home to your village.'

'That can wait, miss,' he said awkwardly. 'There is time enough for that. When all the fighting is over. It isn't that.'

'Then what is it?' She searched his face anxiously, and suddenly understood. 'Did you think I would go without you, is that it?'

'If the Americans take you, they won't need me,' Kolya said gruffly. 'That's obvious.'

'They will take us all!' Miss Meg said firmly. 'I will see to that, never you fear! Now,' she added briskly, 'we have a lot to do. We must travel light, take only what is absolutely necessary. But before we start packing – to celebrate – we'll have a real, a proper, cup of coffee.

American coffee!' She would have preferred tea, she thought, tea made in the English style, served with milk and some hot, buttered toast, but she put the idea behind her. One should be grateful for all mercies, great and small.

Later, when they had packed and made most of their preparations, she said goodnight to Kolya and went back to the bedroom. The children lay undisturbed in the narrow beds, their faces rosy with the innocence of sleep. Before she snuffed out the candle, she held it before the mirror, remembering Dukov's words. Of course, he'd been teasing, it was ridiculous to say that she was beautiful. All those dreadful freckles for one thing! But, yes, perhaps she did look better with her hair down; it seemed to alter and soften the shape of her face. She blushed again as she remembered the moment in the forest when Dukov had kissed her.

She slept badly, the thoughts tumbling around in her head, images of England, of her parents, of Dukov, mixed with sudden, sharp, nightmare visions of charging Cossacks and of Aksinia Rostilov lying dead and half-naked on a bed in Petrograd.

3

At the Anton Chekhov Theatre, not far from where Miss Meg tossed and turned in her shallow, troubled sleep, Tremayne and Kasakov were attending an emergency meeting of the Regional Soviet. In those early days it was an inflexible rule of such gatherings that the 'toiling masses' should have the right to see and hear what was being done in their name; thus, armed with passes provided by Political Commissar Mogilov, the two men had been admitted without question and taken their places at the back, on the benches reserved for non-delegates.

It was an extraordinary scene. The theatre, despite its distinguished name, was really not much more than a hall, with rows of slatted wooden benches for seats and a tiny platform for a stage. The only colour was provided by the revolutionary posters which lined the drab walls and the red banners hanging from the ceiling. On the wall near Tremayne a tablet proclaimed that the building had been erected in 1907 by the Ekaterinburg Literary, Drama and Musical Association. They would have been hard put to it to stage a drama to compare with this, thought Tremayne grimly as he looked around.

It was now 11 p.m., the night of June 13, and it seemed that the meeting had been in continuous session since early the previous afternoon. Gromeko, the Chairman, sat behind a bare table on the platform, flanked by members of the Political Bureau and other officials, among them Mogilov himself. Before him lay a turbulent sea of faces, soldiers, workmen, peasants, women, many of them armed and most of them smoking. At one point the Chairman made an appeal: 'In the interests of health, would comrades please refrain from smoking!' It made no difference. The smoke from pipes and cheap cigarettes swirled in the air like fog, the pungent smell of tobacco mingled with the odour of leather and human sweat. Here and there, men dozed openly, squatting on the floor with their backs against a wall, or simply nodding on the shoulders of their neighbours, but for the most part the audience remained alert and eager, following the speeches attentively, shouting their disagreement both with the speakers or other delegates when they felt inclined to do so.

One elderly man harangued the platform because the Soviet had not done enough in the field of education. 'Look at me, brothers,' he cried, 'I have lived for 62 years without being able to read or write. I can't even read those posters! Am I to go to my grave as ignorant as when I was born?'

A young Red Guard demanded that the Soviet should deal ruthlessly with those who looted the artistic and scientific treasures of the nation. 'Preserve the glories of our history, guard the property of the people!' he shouted and they cheered in response.

It was the passionate, simple earnestness of the crowd which intrigued and moved Tremayne. Their faces were lined and yellow with exhaustion, yet still, from some incredible wells of energy, they managed to dredge up the strength to listen, argue, debate. How long would this spirit last, he wondered sadly, how long would it be allowed to last? The Marats and the Robespierres were already beginning to emerge, the tyrants and the tormentors who preached liberty and practised terror, the men with stone faces who built power and prisons on the faith and hopes of simple trusting people.

Kasakov saw it through different eyes. 'Look at this scum,' he whispered. 'The new rulers of Russia! They stink worse than the Pecora!'

'Comrades!' shouted the Chairman. 'Brothers! Please – silence! Please! Comrade-Commander Sablin is here. Comrades, quiet, if you please! Comrade-Commander Sablin has the platform.'

Silence slowly gathered over the hall as a grey-haired man in Red Army uniform came on to the stage. One arm was held in a sling and he walked with a slight limp. A storm of whistling and cheering greeted his arrival; he waited, smiling, for a few moments and then held up his hand. As the noise faded, he began to speak in a flat, dry, unemotional tone, and so quietly that they had to crane forward to catch his words.

'Comrades, brothers. I have just come from the southern front. I will not disguise from you the fact that our position is serious. I am here to tell the truth, not to entertain you with fairy stories. The counter-revolutionary White armies led by Diterikhs are putting our positions under increasing pressure. Ekaterinburg itself is in danger, I make no bones about that.'

He went on to describe the general military situation and to call for more volunteers, arms, supplies. Tremayne found it remarkable that there was no hint of despair or defeatism in the speech, only a steely realism, and the reaction of his audience was much the same. A delegate rose to pledge that the workers from his factory would join the Red troops immediately, an old miner made a similar promise. A young woman was cheered when she scolded the men for their 'reactionary attitudes' towards her sex, and called upon them to encourage women to join in the defence of the town. She reproached them fiercely. 'Some of you still think that women are only fit for a tumble in the hay, to wash and cook. Shame! And you dare call yourselves revolutionaries. Well, let me tell you – we shall fight whether you like it or not! We can load and fire rifles, we can throw grenades! We shall join the struggle alongside our men, die with them if need be!' She sat down to tumultuous applause.

The discussion raged on until the Chairman rose to end it. 'Comrades, it is late. We have talked enough. Deeds will defeat the enemy, not words. I declare the meeting closed.'

'One minute, Comrade Chairman!' A young soldier with a bandaged head was on his feet. 'One minute! What about Nicholas – what about the Romanovs?'

The cry was taken up from all parts of the hall. In a

few seconds, the idealistic fervour which had swept through the crowd like a storm wind disappeared, to be replaced by a hatred no less elemental and powerful. What had been a meeting became a mob, and the half-dozen who tried to protest, shouting that the Revolution should not sully itself with a crime of pure vengeance, were swept aside.

'Death to Nicholas the Bloody! Death, death, death to the Romanovs!'

The cries merged into this single chant, accompanied by the rhythmic banging of feet on the echoing wooden floor. Tremayne glanced at Kasakov; dark eyes blazing like hot coals in a grim white face, hands clasped so tight that the knuckles showed white. He laid a hand on the other man's arm, but the Russian shook it away angrily.

It was three or four minutes before the Chairman could restore order and make himself heard.

'As you know, comrades, we – that is, the Regional Soviet – sent a request to Comrade Lenin, asking that the Romanovs should be put on trial, here in Ekaterinburg. So far we have received no reply to our message.' He waited for the interruptions to die down. 'No doubt Vladimir Ilyitch has much on his mind at this moment, matters of greater importance than rubbish like the Romanovs.'

The young, wounded soldier jumped to his feet again, demanding the floor. He swung round, arms outstretched, turning his hot, excited face to the delegates. 'Comrades! This is not a question for Comrade Lenin or for Moscow! The Romanovs are here – in Ekaterinburg! They are our prisoners. Are we children, infants, that we don't know how to act, what to do? Are we going to wait until the Whites take them? Let us make an example of them all! Let them pay for their bloody crimes now! I propose that they be brought to the Square and hanged!'

'Not only the Romanovs!' shouted another speaker. 'All the others! The Tsarists, the bourgeoisie – they're still here, in this town, skulking behind closed doors, waiting for the Whites. Let us drag them all out into the light of day!'

The chanting and stamping began once more, and again the Chairman had to wait for silence. He glanced at Mogilov who remained impassive. 'Comrades! There is no disagreement among us. But these things must be done in a proper, organised revolutionary manner. I propose that we give Moscow until noon tomorrow to reply.'

Tremayne and Kasakov exchanged a look of dismay. At the discussion earlier, it had been agreed that the rescue attempt would take place on the morning of June 15. Kasakov's friends had insisted that they needed a further 24 hours to finalise arrangements and Tremayne had reluctantly agreed. They turned to hear the Chairman continue: 'If there is no news by noon tomorrow, I further propose that the Romanovs be brought immediately before the People's Tribunal for Revolutionary Justice for trial and sentence. Is that agreed?'

The hands shot up in the air to more cheering. Luckily the crowd was too preoccupied to notice that at least two of those present failed to join in the general acclaim.

Outside, the night air felt fresh and cool on their faces but it brought them little comfort. They walked on in a stunned and thoughtful silence, the delegates from the meeting thrusting by them. Suddenly Kasakov stopped and gripped Tremayne's arm. 'I'm going to the monastery to get the men,' he whispered.

'What for?'

'You heard what they said in there! The day after tomorrow will be too late. We have until noon tomorrow – if that. I wouldn't trust them to wait that long! God in heaven, man, you heard them, baying like hounds for his blood.'

'Now, just ease up a moment,' said Tremayne.

'Ease up! Are you mad? We haven't time, I tell you. I haven't come all this way to be thwarted at the last moment.'

'I mean, let's think it through.'

'I've thought it through. There's only one thing now. Tonight, before it gets light, we'll storm the Ipatiev House and pluck them out. I'll get one squadron to create a diversion, shoot up the local Soviet or something, while we make the main assault. The guards will be half-asleep, they won't expect it.' His voice gathered pace as he spoke, his enthusiasm and confidence feeding on itself.

'It's crazy,' Tremayne said slowly.

'Look, my friend, you don't have to play any part in it. I hereby absolve you. I'm grateful for your help so far – but if you want to step aside, I understand.'

He made as if to go, but Tremayne held him fast, and pulled him into the shelter of an alley. 'Listen,' he hissed angrily, 'listen! I've come a bloody long way too, and I'm not going to sit back and watch you cock everything up! First question. If you get them out, where will you take them?'

'To the monastery. Or some other hide-out. We'll wait there till the Whites arrive, which won't be long by the sound of it.'

'There won't be any hide-outs. They'll comb every building in the area. They'll pull everything down brick by brick if necessary. Suppose you take them to the monastery – do you imagine the Reds won't look there?'

'That place is like a fortress, we'll hold them off.'

'If you're lucky, very lucky, you may have twenty men left. Can they hold out against a thousand, against cannon, mortars?' He was beginning to get through and he pressed home the argument. 'Zakhar, do you want the Tsar and the others alive or dead? Because if you go ahead with this nonsense, you're going to make absolutely certain that they die. The first thing those guards at the Ipatiev House will do when your mob come charging in will be to slaughter the Imperial Family. They're disciplined troops from Moscow, not amateurs. And if – I say if – by some miracle you should get some of the family out, they'll almost certainly perish in that monastery with you and the others. It just won't work, Zakhar, it will not work.'

The Russian stared at him in silence for a moment, his face pale in the moonlight. The enthusiasm of a moment before had evaporated, and he looked more youthful than ever, like a bewildered boy. 'I can't give up,' he muttered, 'I can't. Perhaps it is hopeless, but we must try at least. We have sworn an oath, all the Volunteers. What else can we do but try?'

'We bring everything forward,' said Tremayne.

'What?'

'We bring the whole operation forward. Instead of the day after tomorrow, we act in the morning.'

'Alexei said he needed one more day – the transport, everything—' said Kasakov.

'Then he'll have to hurry it up, won't he? Listen, you go and see him now, tell him of the change. Don't let him argue – make sure he has everything ready by 8 a.m. tomorrow, not a second later. I'll go and see Mogilov in his train at the station and warn him. We'll meet back at the monastery at 7 a.m. Right?'

'Can it be done, can it be done in the time?' asked Kasakov eagerly.

'It will be done, Zakhar, because it must be done.'

The two men faced each other without speaking. Suddenly, impulsively, the Russian smiled, and hugged

Tremayne, crushing him in his arms. 'It will be done!' he said. 'I will see you at 7 o'clock in the morning.'

Tremayne listened to his footsteps die away in the night. He leaned against the wall, closing his eyes as a great tide of mental and physical exhaustion swept over him. He straightened up, struck a match and looked at his watch.

It was almost 1 a.m. It was already tomorrow.

Chapter Eleven

I

Tremayne's conversation with Mogilov was both brief and gloomy. The Political Commissar was in a dark, pessimistic mood. 'I trust you enjoyed the meeting,' he said.

'I found it fascinating,' Tremayne answered truthfully.

'I came too late,' Mogilov said sombrely. 'A month ago, I could have moved the Imperial Family without question. But now – the local Soviet acknowledge my authority in theory, but ignore it in practice. I am watched like a hawk. This evening while I was away, they removed the locomotive from this train, on some pretext or other.' He crossed to the samovar and filled his cup. Turning back, he squared his shoulders and managed a wry smile. 'It is a tight corner. But then, I have been in tight corners before.'

'We shall make our move in the morning,' said Tremayne.

Mogilov nodded. 'Of course, there is no other alternative. It is our only – our last – chance. The transport?'

'Kasakov is seeing about that and the other arrangements now. How many guards will be on duty at the Ipatiev House?'

'Two at the entrance to the first stockade. Four in the courtyard guarding the main entrance. Six in the grounds

218

at the back. Two will be manning the machine-gun at the attic window.'

'Fourteen.'

'There is also a Command Post on the ground floor. The Guard Commander and a couple of orderlies may be on duty there, or they may be in the courtyard while the Imperial Family are exercising.'

'What are the guards like?'

'Tough. Experienced soldiers, Bolshevik to a man. I didn't pick them.'

'So long as we know what we're up against,' said Tremayne.

'There is a further complication,' Mogilov said. 'The boy, the young Tsarevich, is sick. He suffers from haemophilia, as you know – he bruised himself badly yesterday, and today it has grown worse. He may even be too ill to be moved.'

'The Tsar's personal physician is still in the house?'

'No. But he is allowed to make regular visits. I don't know whether he will be there when you – drop in, so to speak.'

'If he is, we'll take him along. If not, the Tsarevich will have to take his chance with the rest.' Tremayne paused. 'Does the Tsar know – I mean, does he know where you stand? That you are a friend?'

'No. He believes that I am one of them. I have said nothing to make him believe otherwise. It would have been too dangerous, we are watched by many eyes. If his attitude towards me had changed, even in the slightest degree, the others would have grown suspicious.' He sighed. 'No, I have been at this game too long to make such elementary errors. All my life, it seems, I've had to live like a man with two souls in one body – to ignore and pour scorn on my friends, and smile on my enemies. It can be hard at times, you understand. I have a wife in

Moscow and two children – she is not a political person, she doesn't understand about such things – but even she believes that I am with the Bolsheviks. I love her too much to tell her the truth. Why should she live her life in fear?'

'Somehow the Tsar must be warned – he must be warned to be ready,' Tremayne said sharply. He was too tired to concern himself with this man's personal problems, there was no room in his mind at this moment for either pity or condemnation. 'It is essential that at ten o'clock tomorrow morning the whole family, plus the doctor if possible, should take their usual exercise in the yard. The Tsarevich must be got out there somehow. If the doctor is there, he must be prepared with whatever medicines are necessary for the Tsarevich. They must all be ready to obey us without question. We shall have minutes, seconds, only. The slightest hesitation on their part could ruin everything.'

'I will get the word to him somehow.' Mogilov shrugged his shoulders. 'Whether he will believe me – that is another matter. He will probably regard it as some sort of trap – and who can blame him?'

'Show him this.' Tremayne held out the ring he had been given in London.

Mogilov ran his finger over the insignia of the falcon. 'Where did you get this?'

'Show it to the Tsar,' said Tremayne, 'he will know who it came from.' He went to the door and looked out into the night. On an adjoining track he saw the *Royal Flush*, the lights still burning in the main coach. 'What will you do?' he asked.

'Do?'

'Will you come with us?'

'No. That won't be possible. I shall sweat it out somehow. I am a survivor.'

Tremayne nodded. He could not understand what motivated such a man, but he had to admit to his courage. 'Good luck,' he said.

'And to you, my friend. Wait.' Mogilov extinguished the lamp. 'Take care,' he whispered, but the night breeze blew his words into the darkness and Tremayne didn't hear.

2

If Story was surprised to see the Englishman he did not show it. He was playing poker with Klaus, the Marine sergeant, and a corporal from Brooklyn named Buzoni. It was Buzoni who opened the door of the coach in answer to Tremayne's knock, and helped him up from the track.

'Look who we got here, Major, sir,' he said.

'Hold it a minute, Buzoni,' said Story. He moved the cheroot from one side of his mouth to the other, studied his cards for a long moment, and then looked at Tremayne. 'Hi. You made it then. Want to join the game?'

Tremayne shook his head and managed a weak smile. He staggered a little as the exhaustion hit him once more and Buzoni grasped his arm. 'Hey, Major, sir, this guy's dead on his feet.'

'I'm all right,' Tremayne said, steadying himself.

'O.K. you fellas – break it up for tonight, huh.'

'I'm holding three of a kind!' complained Kelly.

'I already worked that out,' said Story. 'Beat it.' His eyes were on Tremayne. 'You O.K.?'

'I said, I'm all right,' said Tremayne irritably.

'You don't look it, for crissakes. Sit down, and I'll fix you a drink.'

'If I sit down, I shan't get up again,' said Tremayne.
'That's bad?'
Tremayne nodded. 'Lot to do.'
Story propelled him into a seat. 'I'll see you get up. Here, take a swig of this.' He held out a bottle of vodka.
'I'd better not,' Tremayne said. 'Need to keep a clear head.' He shook himself as though he were trying to do just that, and grinned.
'When you going to collect your parcel?' asked Story.
'Tomorrow. In the morning.'
'You won't have the strength to pick it up if you don't get some rest.'
'It's been quite a day,' admitted Tremayne. 'Tom, what time are you leaving here?'
'You tell me.'
'Could you make it around 10.15 in the morning?'
Story took the cheroot from his mouth and stared at the Englishman. 'You son-of-a-bitch!' he whispered. 'You-are-a-son-of-a-bitch! Back there, up the track, you told me to get back east! You didn't want me around.'
'That's right. But you wouldn't. And you didn't. You're here now. How did you get in, by the way?'
'On the track – how else! That was the easy part. We're Americans, neutral. They're tickled pink to see us. We're honoured guests.'
'Congratulations.'
'Thank you. Now you're asking me to blow all that!'
'Not at all. As I recall, it was you who mentioned something about helping to shorten the odds.'
'O.K. O.K. But I didn't figure that you'd want to use me as a goddamned decoy!'
'You're quick, Tom, very quick. And correct.'
'Do you know what they got out there? Do you want to know what they got? They got dynamite under the bridge, field guns, machine-guns, covering maybe a mile

of the track; that's what they got! They could blow us to Kingdom Come!'

'Fine. It was only a suggestion. If you don't want to do it—'

'I didn't say that!'

'If you don't want to do it,' Tremayne persisted, 'I suggest you leave at first light. Before the rumpus begins.'

'Will you quit putting words into my mouth? I didn't say I wouldn't do it. Did I say I wouldn't do it?'

'Let's put it this way – you didn't react with what I'd describe as real enthusiasm.'

'Jesus!' said Story. 'Are all the British nuts like you? What did you expect – I should turn a cartwheel or something?' He replaced the cheroot and churned it round in his teeth. 'What exactly do you want?'

'Very little,' said Tremayne. 'At 10 a.m. tomorrow the balloon will go up. By 10.30 – perhaps sooner – they'll start chasing somebody.'

'And you want it should be the *Royal Flush*?'

'Exactly. They'll wonder why you came in when you did, why you left when you did. They'll add two and two together, make five, and come after you. As soon as they do that, you stop. You can't understand what it's all about. You let them search the train, top to bottom. The longer they take the better. Naturally, they'll find nothing. You wave them goodbye, and continue on your merry way. Simple.'

'Simple?'

'That's the way I see it.'

Story paced the coach for a full half-minute, then stood over Tremayne, gesturing with the ruins of his cigar. 'I'll do it. I'll do it on one condition. You fill me in – I want the whole works, every detail. I want to know what I'm getting myself and these other guys into.'

Tremayne told him; he outlined the plan for the assault

223

on the house, and of the proposed escape by boat up the River Ob to the Kara Sea, where HMS *Chatham* would be waiting. He gave him the whole picture, omitting nothing. Story listened, nodding here and there, occasionally putting in a shrewd question.

When the Englishman had finished, he said, 'It could work. It's as full of holes as a rusty bucket, but it could work. Just two points. First, if we make it out of here in one piece, we'll wait down the line. You remember that spot in the forest where you got off? We'll wait as near to that as we can get. We'll hang on for, say, 24 hours. Yep. 24 hours. So if anything goes wrong with that boat up-river, you've got us to fall back on. O.K.?'

'I'm obliged,' said Tremayne. 'You said two points. What's the other?'

'Your rendezvous at the monastery is at 7 a.m., right?'

'Right.'

'O.K. I'll wake you two hours before.'

'I beg your pardon?'

'You're out on your feet, Jimmy. You'll be as much good as a spent bullet if you don't rest up. You got maybe two-and-one-half hours. Sleep. I'll wake you.'

Tremayne smiled wanly and nodded. 'In that case,' he said, 'I will have a drink. A night-cap.' Story handed him the bottle, and two minutes later Tremayne was asleep. The American watched him thoughtfully, then went to a locker and took out some equipment which he stowed in his jacket. He found Klaus half-dozing in the cab of the locomotive.

'I'm just going to take a walk,' he said.

'A walk!'

'Yeah. If I'm not back in two hours, wake the Englishman.'

Before Klaus could say any more, he was gone.

3

The AEC trucks and the Putilov armoured cars were lined up in the cobbled factory yard, noses to the wall like so many dark animals feeding at a trough. Ahead, beyond the wall, lay the factory itself; formerly an assembly plant for imported mining machinery, it was now used as a repair and maintenance depot for military vehicles. Yellow light, the clamour of hammers on metal spilled from the workshops into the half-light which preceded the dawn.

From time to time, workers crossed the yard carrying spare parts and tools, talking in low tones. Two Red Guards stood warming their hands by the embers of a fire to one side of the open wooden gates, and another pair maintained a desultory patrol up and down outside. An AEC 2-ton cargo truck, its engine coughing and spluttering, lurched through the gates and was waved on without any check by the sentries.

'Sounds like you're in a bad way, brother!' called one of the guards. 'Don't put it with that lot over there – they're ready for the road. Take it round the back.' The driver's reply was indistinct. He drove past the line of trucks and cars, through an arched entrance in the inner wall, and disappeared.

Samarin signalled to the waiting Volunteers, and in moments the two patrolling sentries were dealt with, and their bodies dragged under cover. The two guards by the fire lived only a half-minute longer than their comrades.

'Right,' whispered Samarin, 'the first two armoured cars and one truck. Move it!' Three men darted forward and took their places at the wheels of the three chosen vehicles. Samarin and two others swung the starting handles. The Putilovs started easily and moved out on to the road. The truck was more difficult, and Samarin cursed softly to himself as he gripped the cold steel and swung it again and again.

A workman came through the entrance from the factory, and Samarin ducked for cover. The man at the wheel lowered his head. The workman paused, pissed up against the back wheel of one of the trucks, then continued on his way across the yard. He was whistling; he would never know how close he had been to instant, bloody death. When the echo of his footsteps had died away, Samarin swung the handle again, and this time the engine roared into life.

Outside, the bodies of the dead guards were thrown into the rear of the truck without ceremony. Ten minutes later, the AEC 3-tonner, commonly called the Russian B, and the two Putilovs pulled to a halt in the forecourt of the monastery.

4

Tremayne woke to the sound of whispered argument. At first he thought it must be part of a dream, because one of the voices was that of a woman speaking clear, rather precise English in a tense, low tone, but then he heard Story answer and knew that he had come back to reality. He peered at his watch. The time was almost 5 a.m.

He stretched and swivelled round. Story and the woman were standing by the door of the coach. Without thinking, still befuddled by sleep, he spoke in English. 'What's going on?'

The woman turned to him in surprise. He got up, stretched his arms, tried to focus his thoughts. If anything, he felt worse for the brief rest, leaden and irritable. You should have kept going, he told himself: a little, inadequate sleep was often worse than none at all.

'Are you English?' asked the woman eagerly. She was dressed like a peasant, in clean but worn clothes, and he guessed her (wrongly) to be about thirty-five. She wasn't exactly a beauty, the face was too angular for that, but the grey eyes were gentle and expressive, and there was character in the firm set of her chin. The voice was unmistakably English middle class.

'Are you English?' she repeated, with less certainty now as he slung on the bandolier of ammunition. He looked past her to Story, who grinned and shrugged. 'You understand English, at any rate,' she continued briskly. 'I am an Englishwoman, my name is Margaret Wellmeadow. I have been trying to explain to this gentleman, this American gentleman, that I wish to leave Ekaterinburg. Indeed, I've been trying to leave for some months, without any success. I heard last night that an American train had arrived. If you have any influence here, I'd be grateful for your help. We must get away. I am perfectly prepared to pay for the journey. He doesn't seem to understand. It is most urgent.'

'I understand, lady,' said Story, stepping forward, 'and I would like to help you. But it just isn't possible.'

'Why not?' she asked.

'I told you, this train belongs to the US military. We're not authorised to take refugees on board, and we're not equipped for it.'

'We are hardly refugees!' Her eyes flashed.

'Whatever you are, Miss Wellmeadow, I can't take you. We've got thousands of miles ahead of us, across country that's full of bandits, partisans, Red armies,

White armies, all fighting each other. It's too dangerous, you'd be safer to stick it out here.'

'You must allow me to be the judge of that!' she said tartly. 'As for the danger, do you imagine that I haven't learned to live with that?' She turned to Tremayne. 'Please, can't you help us?' Her lower lip trembled slightly and she made an obvious effort to control it.

'How did you get here in the first place?' he asked.

'That is a long story, too long to tell now. The point is – I am here. I have these two children—' She checked as his eyes widened and said rather primly, 'They are not mine; that is to say, I am not their mother. Both the parents are dead. They were murdered if you want the truth of it. But the children are in my charge – and I must get them away from this terrible place. They are good children, they would be no trouble, I assure you. You must take us.'

'Have you got permission to travel?' asked Tremayne. 'I mean official permission, from the authorities?'

'No. Does that matter?'

'Essential. They will certainly search the train before it is allowed to leave. If there are any unauthorised people on board there could be trouble, there almost certainly would be.'

'And you could wind up in the local jail, a lot worse off than you are now,' added Story.

She considered this, turning her candid eyes from one man to the other. 'If I get travel documents, will you take us?'

'Let me put it this way. I'd take another look at the problem,' said Story.

'What time are you leaving?'

'Around noon.' As Tremayne opened his mouth to speak, he silenced him with a warning glance.

'Very well,' said Miss Meg. 'I will get the necessary

228

documents. And I will be back here well before noon. Thank you. I really am grateful.' She paused in the doorway, and gave Tremayne a puzzled look. 'You are English, aren't you?'

'On my mother's side,' he replied truthfully.

'I thought so. One can always tell.' She smiled for the first time and the smile gave her eyes and face a sort of radiance. She really is quite beautiful, thought Tremayne. He smiled back, and a tiny current of warmth flowed between them.

It was light outside and they watched her as she walked purposefully away. 'She's sure got guts,' said Story. 'I'd bet the pot on her getting those papers.'

'Why did you tell her you weren't leaving till noon?'

'To get rid of her. I can't take her and the kids, Jimmy, you know that. If they come after me, it may not be as peaceable as you think. They could start shooting, it could turn bad on us. And if that happens, I sure don't want a woman and two goddamned kids under my feet.'

'Poor bitch,' said Tremayne.

'Listen, the Whites will take this place in a week, ten days. She's better off waiting for them. Then she can head south, get away through Odessa.'

'I hope you're right,' said Tremayne. He splashed some water from the washbasin on his face and rubbed a finger round his teeth. His mouth felt harsh and sour, but the blood was beginning to warm up in his veins, and he felt better.

'How do I look?' he asked, picking up his rifle.

'You could set yourself up as a bandit,' said Story, 'no problem.'

'See you around, then,' said Tremayne. 'If you're ever in London, you can contact me at the Travellers' Club.'

'I can't wait,' said Story drily.

'Don't be like that,' said Tremayne. 'It's a good club.'

He took a swig of vodka from Story's bottle, and grimaced as he swished it round in his mouth, then swallowed it. 'A little Dutch courage,' he said with a grin. 'Cheers.'

5

Sister Elizabieta and Sister Lyudmilla left the Convent of the Resurrection at 9 a.m., on their daily pilgrimage to the Ipatiev House. Each of them carried a basket which contained eggs, milk, fresh bread, some darning wool and clean bandages. It was another burning hot day, and they kept to the shady side of the dusty road as much as possible.

They had become used to this regular excursion and even enjoyed it. They would never have admitted as much, for pride is a deadly sin, but it gave them a sense of importance; not everyone had an opportunity thus to serve the Tsar. The Prioress had once suggested to the authorities that other novices should be used, that a rota be drawn up, but the Commissar had rejected this out of hand.

'We know those two by now,' he had said brusquely, 'I don't want any strange faces turning up.'

The Sisters considered this remark to be rather amusing since none of the guards had actually seen their faces. The Prioress had ruled that the novices should remain veiled whenever they went out in public, that only their eyes should be visible. It was not an instruction which they obeyed too strictly, for it was not really part of the Rules of their Order, simply a decision the Prioress had introduced in the first days of the Revolution. She seemed to think that it would help protect her girls from the licentious soldiers and revolutionaries who roamed the countryside – another remark that the novices found amusing.

Once they were clear of the convent, the Sisters threw back their veils and welcomed the air to their skin. They could quickly be replaced if they met any men, and they would certainly cover their faces as soon as they reached the outskirts of the town. They walked on happily, chattering together. Sister Lyudmilla was speaking of a linnet which she remembered from the previous summer. It had come back again this year and flew to her tiny window each morning to receive a few breadcrumbs.

'And he always thanks me!' she added. 'As soon as I've given him breakfast, he bursts into song. Oh, it is so beautiful. I could listen to him for ever.'

'He will leave again when the autumn comes,' said Sister Elizabieta. She was a little tired of hearing about her friend's linnet.

'Of course. He'll fly south. God is truly marvellous in all His works. Such a tiny creature, yet it has the strength to fly over continents, to cross great oceans.'

'God be praised,' said Sister Elizabieta. And with the next breath, she let out a little startled scream. A man, a frightening-looking man with a rifle, had leaped out in front of them, and he was followed by another, while two others closed in from behind. There was no time to lower their veils and Sister Elizabieta almost dropped the basket with the eggs.

'Don't be alarmed, Sisters,' said one of the men, 'you won't be harmed.' He was quite polite, and despite his appearance, the voice was that of an educated man.

'What do you want?' asked Sister Lyudmilla. She tried to stop herself from trembling, and it crossed her mind that God had decided to punish them for raising their veils. She managed to lower the veil with her free hand and felt a little better for it, a little more secure. Perhaps, after all, the Prioress had been right. 'Oh, holy God, holy and immortal, forgive us our waywardness and protect us now,' she prayed silently.

'We don't like to see you walking on such a hot day,' said the man. 'So we're going to give you a ride in one of our automobiles.' He waved a hand towards the fringe of trees where two strange-looking vehicles stood, half-hidden in the undergrowth.

'We prefer to walk, thank you,' said Sister Lyudmilla, recovering now from the first shock. 'Sister – your veil!' She helped Elizabieta cover her face.

'I'm sorry about that,' said the man, 'but I have to insist. We don't want to use force, but we will if you make it necessary.'

'If it's the food you want—' began Sister Elizabieta.

'You can't have it!' said Sister Lyudmilla boldly. 'It has to go to the Ipatiev House. I'm sure you know what that means!'

'It isn't the food,' said the man. 'It is you, both of you.'

Sister Lyudmilla felt herself trembling again. Extraordinary visions and ideas began to tumble through her mind, dreadful things to which she dare hardly put a name.

'You're not going to be raped!' said the man coarsely, as though he were seeing the same visions, thinking the same thoughts. 'Now, come on – we haven't got all day. Are you going to walk to the automobile, or will we have to carry you?'

The Sisters looked at each other. There was really no choice. Clutching the baskets with one hand, lifting their skirts slightly with the other, they picked their way towards the armoured cars. The man made them get into the back seat of one of the monsters, crushed himself in with them, and they were driven away. He gave them an impudent grin. 'Comfortable, girls?'

They did their best to ignore him, looking grimly ahead without answering. Sister Lyudmilla could feel his leg pressing against hers, and tried to edge away, but it was impossible. Disgust joined with her fear; she knew that men were God's creation also but sometimes it was hard to understand why He had fashioned such uncouth, unpleasant, dangerous creatures. Despite his cultured voice, the man smelt like a pig-sty; she had come from a peasant family and the sour, masculine odour of sweat and unclean linen reminded the girl of her own father, whom she had feared and detested.

A much greater shock was ahead of them. They were driven to the old monastery, their baskets taken from them, and they were shown to a small room at the rear of the building. 'Take off your robes,' the man said. 'Your head-dresses, veils, robes and shoes. That's all.'

'We shall do no such thing!' said Sister Lyudmilla in a shocked tone.

'Certainly not!' said Sister Elizabieta firmly.

'I'll give you two minutes!' the man said, clearly losing his patience. 'If you're not out of those habits by then, I'll send in four men to strip you!'

'God will punish you!' Sister Elizabieta said tearfully.

'Why are you doing this?' asked Sister Lyudmilla.

'It is better you should not know,' said the man, not unkindly. 'Believe me, the cause is a good one. When we have the robes, you will be tied up. You will know nothing, or very little, at least. You will be discovered in time, and be none the worse for the adventure.' He smiled. 'It'll be something to talk about in the long winter evenings at the convent.' He went out, closing the door.

'What shall we do?' wailed Sister Elizabieta.

'Do you want to be stripped?' said Sister Lyudmilla.

'Of course not!'

'You have your drawers on?'

'Certainly I have!'

'Then do as the man said.'

'Shouldn't we pray?'

'Later, perhaps. God sees all. He knows our predicament. It is not necessary to inform Him,' said Sister Lyudmilla, as she began to unbutton her habit.

6

It was not until the relief guard arrived at the factory that anyone noticed that the other guards had disappeared. It was then that the manager discovered that a truck and two Putilovs were also missing.

It was a rare occurrence but not one entirely without precedent. There had been occasions in the past when Red Guards and others had deserted with stolen vehicles, either going over to the enemy or, more usually, simply using them to get as near as they could to the homes and villages they had not seen since 1914. With the White armies on the doorstep of Ekaterinburg, it was to be expected that some of the less dedicated members of the Red Army would take to their heels.

That was how the loss was interpreted. However, the Political Commissar at the factory took a serious view of the matter. He had new posters printed, reminding all concerned that the penalty for desertion or the theft of the people's property was death, and had these plastered up on the walls. He dismissed the Guard Commander and took the responsibility into his own hands.

And he sent a despatch rider to Viktor Gromeko, Chairman of the Regional Soviet, with a memorandum which named the guards who were assumed to have defected, described the vehicles which had been stolen, and outlined the steps he had taken to discourage a repetition of the incident.

Gromeko received the despatch at about 9.30 a.m. It landed on his desk with a shoal of other documents and, with other more pressing matters on his mind, he pushed the pile of papers aside. For one thing, this persistent Englishwoman was standing in front of him, demanding permission to leave on the American train. How she had managed to evade his guards and secretaries he would never know, but she had, and short of a bullet, he had no idea of how to be rid of her. The thought of execution did cross his mind, but with foreigners one was on dangerous ground, and it was not wise to act too hastily.

He was a negative man, and it was in his nature to say No to almost every request. Eventually, however, it occurred to him that the simplest way out of the dilemma was to let her go. He would lose nothing by letting her leave Ekaterinburg with the two Rostilov brats; indeed, he and the town would be better off without her.

He struggled against the logic of these thoughts for some time, for an affirmative judgment went against all his principles. In the end, he reached a decision which, in his view, could not have been bettered by King Solomon himself.

'Very well, then,' he said. 'You may go, and the children may go. But the Ukrainian – what is his name? – Kolya. No. That is impossible. He must stay. We need every able-bodied man we can get.'

'I can't go without Kolya!' said Miss Meg, in a shocked voice. 'I couldn't do that.'

'That is for you to decide.' He went to the door and

called a secretary. 'See that this woman is given a travel permit for herself and two children. Note that. One female adult and two children – no others.'

'That is unfair!' said Miss Meg. 'Kolya is our friend! We couldn't leave him!'

I have no more time to argue,' he said wearily. 'Consider yourself lucky. Now, off with you.'

Miss Meg was still remonstrating with him as he closed the door in her face. She collected the travel permit, and went down to the street where Kolya was waiting with the children and two bags containing clothes and food. On the way out she told herself sternly that it was her duty to take the children to safety, that somehow she must find the courage to tell Kolya that he must stay behind. He was tough and strong, more than able to look after himself; it was just something he would have to face.

But when she saw him standing there, his arms protectively around the children, when he turned his face and looked at her with his honest, puzzled eyes, she knew that she could not do it. She crushed the permit in her hand and shook her head, near to tears.

'It's no use,' she said.

'Where there's no sense, there's no reason, miss,' he said in his gruff, gentle way. 'Never mind. We've survived some hard times together, and I reckon we'll live to laugh at them yet, isn't that so?'

Before she could answer they were thrust aside by a Red Guard patrol, which was escorting two women towards the Soviet headquarters. The younger woman, little more than a girl, walked as though in some inner nightmare, her body shaking with sobs, her hair falling around her white face, while the other tried to support and comfort her. Miss Meg recognised them as former neighbours, prosperous, kindly, inoffensive people she'd met once or twice at the old house; she ran forward and grasped the older one's arm.

'What is wrong? What has happened?'

The woman lifted her head. Her eyes were red-rimmed and leaden with despair. 'I don't know. They took us on our way to church. They – they say we are criminals. But we've done nothing – nothing—'

'Get a move on!' growled one of the Guards. He shouldered Miss Meg aside, and prodded the prisoners forward with his rifle-butt. She could do nothing, simply stand watching until they disappeared into the building. The woman's words had reminded her that this was Sunday – the Sabbath day. How could she have forgotten? Perhaps because in Ekaterinburg each day seemed like any other. No church bell had chimed in the town since the Bolshevik take-over, many priests had been arrested and the doors of their churches nailed shut. A picture of the peaceful old Norman church which had once been the centre of her life came to her and she heard again the sweet gentle sound of the bells on those far-off Sunday mornings. Kolya touched her arm, bringing her back to this Sunday and its grim reality.

'We should go back home, miss,' he said. 'God will not forget us.'

'God helps those who help themselves, Kolya!' she said sharply, pride and anger surging back to replace the hopelessness which had gripped her a few minutes before. She was tired of being pushed around from pillar to post, of being the victim or the suppliant. The moment would come when they would seize her and perhaps the children too, arrest them as criminals, throw them into the town prison or worse. Well, she was not, she was certainly not, going to allow them that satisfaction! 'Come along!'

She moved forward briskly with the children. Kolya

picked up the bundles and followed, a bewildered look on his face because they were moving in the opposite direction to the one which would lead them home.

7

It was 9.50 a.m. when Story returned to the train. He had just had a tedious interview with the local Railway Commissar, who had lectured him on the merits of Bolshevism, the evils of Imperialism, the immorality of Allied intervention in Russia, and other kindred topics. But Story's restraint and patience had been rewarded, for he had clearance papers for the *Royal Flush* in his pocket. He paused at the locomotive to tell Klaus to get up steam and went to the main coach. His good humour soon vanished, however, when he found Miss Meg, a boy, a girl, and a huge Russian, sitting together on the floor at the far end. Miss Meg rose and faced him, her jaw set, a determined look in her eye.

'I thought I told you—' he began.

'Here it is!' she interrupted, holding out the crumpled paper. He glanced at her, sighed, and checked the permit. 'That is what you wanted, I presume?' she said acidly.

'Looks O.K.' he said. 'Only one problem. This says for three. One female adult and two children.'

'It is a mistake,' she said, reddening a little, for she abhorred lies or half-truths.

'Mistake or whatever, he's not included, lady,' Story said, jerking a thumb towards Kolya. 'If you want four to travel, you got to have a permit that says four.'

'We are staying together,' she said. 'And we are not leaving this train.'

238

'It wouldn't be hard to put you off,' he said drily.

'I have not come unprepared,' she said, and suddenly covered him with the little pistol.

He looked at her in amazement. 'What are you proposing to do with that thing?'

'I believe they call it holding someone to ransom. I intend to hold you here until the train starts and has reached a safe distance from the town.'

'You'd really use that little pop-gun?'

'I am quite prepared to do so,' she said, with less certainty than she would have wished.

'Let's see, huh?' Story moved towards her. Kolya took a menacing step forward but Miss Meg said quickly, 'No, Kolya, no!' She backed away as far as possible and still Story came on. Her hand trembled as he took the pistol from her, the tears glinted in her eyes. Story tossed the gun in his hand, shook his head, and went to the door of the coach.

'Kelly!' he yelled. As the sergeant came running, Miss Meg huddled the children to her, and stood in front of Kolya.

'Yes, Major, sir?' asked Kelly.

'These people are travelling with us. Take this big guy and dress him up to look like a Marine.'

'Him? I don't reckon we got anything to fit him, Major.'

'Then find something! Petka, the fireman. They're about the same size. Get some gear from him. And move it, Sergeant, move it! We're checking out in twenty minutes!'

'O.K., buster, come with me,' said Kelly. Kolya looked at the sergeant uncertainly.

'Go with the gentleman, Kolya,' said Miss Meg. As they went off, she turned to Story. 'Thank you, Major.'

He tossed the pistol at her. 'Here, catch. Jesus, you

English – you sure are a crazy bunch! Just one thing, lady. Don't get under my goddamned feet!'

'I would prefer that you did not swear in front of the children, Major.' Though the tone was prim, there was a hint of a smile in her eyes.

He bit back a retort, and went forward to the locomotive, which was beginning to spout steam. When he had gone she sat down abruptly, as though all her strength had gone, and wept with relief. The children watched her with wide eyes, bewildered by this unusual display of weakness.

Suddenly, the air was split by the roaring boom of an explosion. It came from the direction of the town centre, and the sound of the blast echoed through the vaulted hall of the station, like a roll of thunder, rattling windows and even rocking the train.

Story was standing on the footplate with Klaus. 'For crissakes,' he said, 'it's started already. Let's get the hell out of here!'

'In fifteen minutes,' said Klaus calmly. He patted the side of the locomotive. 'She is a lady, she does not like to be rushed.'

Chapter Twelve

I

The first explosion occurred on the lower floor of the head-quarters of the Regional Soviet. The blast was so power-ful that it brought some of the masonry crashing down, temporarily blocking the stairs; five people were killed, including the two women Miss Meg had met in the street outside, and seven wounded. Several people in the queue at the doors were also injured by flying daggers of broken glass and the others fled in fear; some Red Guards, thinking that this was the beginning of a White uprising, panicked and fired into the terrified crowd adding to toll of dead and wounded. A child was knocked from its mother's arms by the on-rushing mob, and screaming, trying to pluck it from under their feet, she too was crushed. A young peasant, holding his wife's arm, help-ing her along, felt her sag like a dead weight. He stopped, looking in amazement at the blood bubbling from her breast.

Other explosions followed in swift succession. Bombs were thrown at a Red Army barracks and two factories. An arms and ammunition depot exploded with a roar which shook the entire town, shattering windows for a mile around; sheets of red and yellow flame crackled skywards, columns of black, acrid smoke darkened the clear air. At the same time, a number of heavily-laden wagons and two or three old trucks were driven into strategic positions, blocking off the entrance or exit to certain important streets, and left there by the unknown drivers, who swiftly disappeared.

The Guard Commander at the House of Special Purpose, puzzled by the noise, left his post and went out into Voznesensky Avenue with two of his aides. The sentries on duty shook their heads in answer to his look of enquiry. The street itself was quiet, though the sound of firing and the heavy boom of explosive could be heard all around. A bluff, seasoned soldier, the Commander had been chosen more for his political and military reliability than for any qualities of imagination; he was also a Moscow man, who had a secret contempt for many of the local leaders, whom he regarded as provincial amateurs. His first thought was that the White armies had broken through, but he found that hard to credit. He had important prisoners in his charge, and he would have been the first to be warned of any such danger. The appearance of the two Sisters, arriving on their regular errand of mercy diverted his attention for a moment.

They were approaching the outer palisade in their normal, unhurried, sedate way, as though invested with an inner peace which made them unaware of any disturbance, and reassured in some measure by this, he moved a step or so towards them. 'What's going on, Sisters? What's all that racket?'

There was something strange about them which he could not place, but before he could work it out or they could reply, his mind was further distracted by a movement at the end of the street. An armoured car, a hammer-and-sickle emblem fluttering at the front, was driving towards the house, followed by a big, tarpaulin-covered truck, with another armoured car bringing up the rear.

'What the devil's going on!' muttered the Commander to one of his aides.

'Perhaps – this trouble in the town – it could be serious. They could have sent reinforcements.'

'More likely to be these local idiots. They're after the Romanovs' blood. Not that I blame them for that – but they're not taking them from here without proper authority. I've got my instructions.' As the convoy stopped and Red Guards dropped down from the truck, he snapped out an order. 'Get the prisoners out of the yard and upstairs – and look sharp about it. One of you get on to Comrade Mogilov – use the special line direct to his train. I'll deal with this lot.'

It was at this moment that he felt a chill prickling at the back of his neck. He remembered the two Sisters, realised now what had eluded him before; they were taller and heavier than the usual pair, and there had been something different about the eyes. He turned as the two unsuspecting sentries fell unconscious, clubbed down in a most uncharitable way by the heavy revolvers wielded by the Sisters of Mercy. The baskets had been tossed aside, broken eggs staining the ground with their yellow yolks, milk pouring from the metal cans turning the nearby dust to a creamy mud.

Kasakov and Tremayne levelled their guns at the Commander and his comrades, tore away the irritating veils which obscured their faces and backed up against the outer palisade, out of the line of fire of the machine-gunners in the attic, who could only see their Commander and what they took to be a column of Red Guards moving forward in military order from the truck outside.

'Right, you Red bastard!' Kasakov waved the revolver at the Guard Commander. 'Don't move an inch, not a muscle! Stand naturally. And call those machine-gunners down here. Quick!'

If the other man was slow-witted, he had courage. 'It's a trick!' he shouted. 'Fire! Open fire!' The last words choked in his throat as a bullet cut him down. Led by Samarin, the Volunteers surged forward, overwhelming the other two men.

Tremayne and Kasakov dashed through the narrow entrance. Beyond them lay the house, surrounded by a second palisade, with the exercise area in between. Two of the four soldiers guarding this narrow space wavered, holding their fire in momentary bewilderment at the sight of these strange Sisters with men's faces and revolvers, and before they could recover they were shot down. The third man bolted for the safety of the house and was out of sight before Kasakov could get in a shot. The fourth fired at Tremayne but surprise made his aim erratic even at that short distance; the bullet smacked into the wooden planks behind the Englishman, coming so close that he felt its searing heat. He ducked, instinctively lowering his arm for a fraction of a second, and the barrel of the revolver caught in the folds of the habit. Tremayne let it go and dived forward; his head crunched into the other man's stomach with such force that the air screamed from his body. The guard, thick-set and heavy, dropped his rifle and closed up like a nutcracker, but he did not fall until Tremayne, with cruel precision, lifted the hem of his robe like a woman, stepped over a patch of mud, and smashed a knee into the exposed jaw. The man rolled over and lay still, clutching Tremayne's white veil and head-dress in his hands.

Samarin and another Volunteer had managed to get inside the first palisade and were covering the front door, but the machine-gun, coupled with accurate rifle-fire from the upper windows, had effectively blocked further progress. The armoured cars returned the fire, aiming particularly for the machine-gun, but it was well protected and they had little effect. Six or seven Volunteers already lay dead or seriously wounded, and the rest were pinned down on the wrong side of the wooden fence. Bursts of fire came from the rear of the building at irregular intervals. The man with Samarin made a dash through the door but he was sent crashing back with a shot between the eyes.

Tremayne ran forward to the shelter of the wall of the house, tearing off what remained of Sister Lyudmilla's robes. 'Where's the Tsar?' he shouted, 'and where the hell is Kasakov?' His voice carried only faintly above the steady, incisive chatter of the machine-guns, the clang and whine of bullets on armour-plating and stone.

'They are at the side of the house. There is more cover there. The Colonel has gone to them,' replied Samarin.

'We've got to stop that blasted machine-gun somehow. If we try to move them across that open ground to the truck there'll be a massacre!'

Tremayne moved along the wall, ducking past a window, and looked upwards. At that moment he silently blessed Mr. Ipatiev's taste in architecture; there were enough projections and indentations on the outside, and sufficient ledges, pipes and sheer ornamentation to make his idea possible. He waved to Samarin, beckoning him forward.

'Give me a hand,' he shouted. 'I'm going up on the roof. Tell the others to hold their fire – then keep that front door covered.' He put a foot in the other man's linked hands, and heaved himself up, grasping for a narrow ledge a few feet above. It held, and he clung there by his arms for a few moments, seeking a foothold. By edging along he was able to make use of the crenellations cut into the stonework, and little by little, he picked and pulled his way upwards to the ledge. The real difficulty began here. From his viewpoint on the ground, he had not realised that the ridge of ornamental masonry which ran round the building jutted out so far, forming a sort of overhang which he could not by-pass.

He waited a moment, pressed flat against the wall, wondering whether he should go down and try at some other point. Then he noticed that the ornamentation had been put up in short sections and cemented together to make a continuous line. The joins looked dry and when he explored one to his right, poking at it with the barrel of his revolver, a little stream of sandy powder poured down. He tightened his hold on a small overflow pipe and banged at the overhang with the butt of the gun. A larger shower of grit and dust descended on to the ledge, but the stone held.

He was suddenly aware that the firing had almost stopped, and the near-silence heightened his sense of urgency. They had hoped to achieve their task in seconds almost; now whole minutes were ticking away while he stood there, like a fly on a wall but infinitely more absurd.

With a sense of desperation he reached up and by stretching his right arm to its fullest length found that he was able to grasp the edge of the ornamental ridge. Face to the wall, eyes closed, he pulled at it with all the strength his cramped position would allow, hoping the weakened section would come away and create a gap, but still there was no movement. He rested again; the sweat trickled in tiny streams down his face and dropped in sticky globules on to his boots, he could hear his heart pounding like some inner drum.

Now, taking a deep breath, he gripped the overflow pipe, which creaked ominously, and swung himself sideways, extending his right leg. He put out his right arm and took a firm hold of the edge of the ridge; then, with a silent prayer, he let go with his left hand and swung

246

out into space. For a long, racking moment he hung there one-handed, his body swaying; at last, he managed to get a grip with the other hand and inch by inch pulled himself up until his chest was level with the overhang and he could throw himself forward. His legs still dangling in space, he allowed himself to pause, the stone cool upon his cheek, but a movement in the slab of masonry, a cracking sound which grew louder, spurred him on. He scrambled on to the roof, gripping a length of ornamental wrought iron just above the guttering as an entire section of stone broke loose and crashed to the ground below, sending up a great plume of dust.

Tremayne negotiated the wrought-iron railing and eased his way along towards the attic. It was not so much an attic as a sort of round room, built of solid brick and decorated stone, which rose from the roof like a small watch-tower. The arched window had been removed, and he could clearly see the Goda machine-gun, the Russian-made version of the Maxim. It had a protective steel shield and was surrounded by a barrier of sandbags. Taking a grenade from his belt, he pulled the pin with his teeth, and waited as long as he dared; then gripping the brickwork, he swung an arm in front of the opening and tossed in the grenade. He flung himself down on the angled roof, behind the shelter of the wall, and felt it throb and tremble as the room rocked under the explosion. Clouds of smoke, mixed with debris and sand, poured from the window, the muzzle of the Goda lurched forward drunkenly. A cheer rose from the Volunteers below, and they stormed forward.

Hardly waiting for the choking dust to settle, Tremayne kicked part of the broken barrier aside and climbed in. The machine-gun crew were a bloodied mess of lifeless flesh and bone, the door to the room swung loosely on one hinge. Coughing as the smoke and dust gritted his throat, he moved on. A Red Guard came running up the curving stairway, hesitated, and fell backwards as Tremayne's bullet hit him, rolling over and over like some grotesque tumbler in a circus.

As the man came to rest, and the reverberation of the shot died away, there was a silence so sudden and complete that it seemed almost tangible, something more than just the mere absence of sound. In retrospect, Tremayne realised that it lasted only a few seconds, but he knew also that it was one of those strange, inexplicable intermissions in life for which the clock has no measurement, and time no meaning.

Then, faintly, from somewhere below, he heard the low, sad whimpering of a dog.

2

At 11 a.m. the *Royal Flush* crossed the river bridge safely, but on the further bank they were stopped by Dukov once again. This time there was no barrier, he merely straddled the track with two of his men and flagged them down.

'Do you wish that I should go through them?' asked Klaus.

'Not unless you want those guns up on the embankment to blast us off the rails,' said Story. He leaned over the side as the train ground to a halt and Dukov came up. 'Hi. What seems to be the trouble?'

'I have orders,' said Dukov. 'The train must be searched.'

'But we got full clearance. We just left, for crissakes.'

'Then you have nothing to fear,' answered Dukov

stiffly. 'Don't try any tricks, Major. The guns have the exact range and it needs only a signal from me.'

Story shrugged. 'O.K. Look all you want. Let's go.'

'One moment, Major.' He pulled himself up into the cab of the locomotive and looked around, brushing his fingers over the controls.

'You have a knowledge of these things?' asked Klaus.

'No.' Dukov turned towards the tender, now piled high with coal from the Ekaterinburg depot. The burly fireman was stooping over, stacking some of the larger lumps of coal at the front.

'You!' said Dukov. 'Turn round!'

'He is just the fireman – the stoker,' said Klaus.

Dukov ignored him. 'Turn round. Let me look at you.'

The man straightened up, still holding a huge wedge of coal in his hands, and turned slowly.

'This is not the man you had before, when you came in!' said Dukov sharply.

'Petka? You mean Petka?' said Story. He stood on the iron step, smiling up at Dukov. 'No, I guess not. Petka didn't want to go back east – he quit. Last I heard, he was aiming to go on to Samara to see his folks. So we took this guy as a replacement.'

'I know you,' said Dukov, ignoring Story, his eyes still on the fireman. 'I saw you at the house of the Englishwoman. Let me see your papers!'

'He's just a replacement,' said Story. 'What does he want with papers?'

Dukov ignored the American and drew his Mauser. 'Get down on the track. You are under arrest.' Kolya hesitated, weighing the lump of coal in his hands. He looked at Story, who answered with a brief, negative shake of the head. Kolya tossed the coal aside and clambered down, his face impassive. Dukov followed, covering the big Ukrainian with the gun the whole time.

249

He spoke to one of the soldiers. 'Take this man to the rear coach. Watch him closely.' Turning to Story, he added: 'You will take the train back to Ekaterinburg under guard and make your explanation to the authorities. That man is a deserter, and you have helped him!'

'He's not an army man!'

'Everyone is under military discipline. The penalty for what you have done is very serious. And he will be shot.'

Miss Meg hurried towards them, the breeze ruffling her skirt and the kerchief around her hair, followed by one of the Red Army men. 'Kolya – what is wrong? What are they doing?'

'They're going to run us all in,' said Story.

'Run us in? I don't understand.' She turned to Dukov. 'What is this about?' He simply looked at her in silence, a puzzled expression on his face, as though his thoughts were elsewhere, and she repeated the question.

'He has no authority to travel. He is a deserter,' said Dukov defensively, flushing slightly. 'And where is your permit, may I ask?' he added more sternly.

'Here, Comrade Commander,' said the soldier. 'I have it here.'

Dukov studied the paper briefly, nodding, avoiding Miss Meg's eyes. 'So you are leaving us, eh?'

'I am taking the children to safety,' she said.

'This says only one adult. Female. What about this man, your lackey? Do you know the penalty for what he has done?

'He has done nothing wrong – unless you count loyalty a crime! And he is not a lackey. He is a friend, a friend in the truest sense.' She paused, and continued gently, 'As I thought you were, Mr. Dukov.'

'I have my duty to do,' he replied gruffly. 'And I am not Mister. I am a soldier.'

250

'I'm sorry,' she said, 'I meant no offence.'

He looked down at his feet, and rubbed the heel of one boot with the toe of the other. 'I should like to speak with you a minute.'

'Of course, if you wish.'

They moved away from the others, towards the shade cast by the steep embankment.

'Why do you wish to leave?' he asked in a low, urgent voice.

'Isn't it obvious?' she answered.

'This won't last for ever,' he said. 'The war, the fighting. Peace will come. Then – then a new life, a free wonderful new life. Listen, please.'

'I am listening, Nikolai,' she said.

His face coloured with pleasure at her use of his first name. 'Mar-gar-et,' he said, smiling shyly.

'That's right,' she replied, returning the smile.

He took off his cap, looked down at his feet. 'It is terrible to have to speak here, like this – but there is no choice. I really have no choice, you understand.'

'No. I don't really understand. I'm sorry. Perhaps I'm simply stupid,' she said gently.

'No. It isn't that. What I mean – what I'm trying to say – is that in war, time marches with seven league boots, one can live a whole lifetime in a single day.'

'That is certainly true.'

'In normal times, friendship – all that sort of thing – can develop naturally, grow at their own pace, flourish when the moment is ripe into—' He paused, twisting the cap in his hands. 'I took to you that first afternoon in the forest.'

She saw now what was coming, felt the blood glowing in her cheeks, but was powerless to find the words to stop him. She had sometimes imagined herself in this situation, and always believed that she would meet it with firmness and the plain, down-to-earth common sense which God had given her (as she thought) in place of other womanly attributes, such as beauty. But where was that common sense now, when she most needed it? Her only response to his awkward tenderness was to stand like a shy, silly, tongue-tied schoolgirl!

He took her silence as an encouragement and went stumbling on. 'It was true what I said last night, when I came with the coffee. You are beautiful.' As she shook her head he said earnestly, as though afraid that he had offended her, 'I am not speaking of beauty in the bourgeois, capitalistic sense, you understand. In that world, a woman's looks are all that matter, she is either an ornament or a chattel. In our new Russia, all that will be changed, of course, we shall cherish women – and every human being – for their true beauty.'

'That will be very nice,' she said, smiling a little at his serious tone. These were not quite the words she had imagined she would hear, they were hardly romantic! But then, the whole thing was absurd, outrageous! Here she was, Miss Margaret Wellmeadow, daughter of an English parson, standing in the middle of Siberia – well, not far from the middle, at any rate – with an armoured train nearby, guns bristling from the embankments, the sound of more guns and rifle-fire in the distance, listening to a lecture on women and beauty from a Red Army officer! She should take herself off at once! But another voice sung to her of other things, and she stayed.

'What I am trying to say—' he said hesitantly. 'I mean – when I saw you just now, I felt – how can I explain it? I felt, somehow, I had to tell you, talk to you. You'll probably laugh in my face—'

'I shan't,' she said.

'I have no right to ask – you hardly know me – your home is in England. All that I understand. But sometimes the heart runs away with the head, isn't that so? And in these times, decisions have to be made quickly or one finds that it is too late. If you wish to go, I will not stop you or the train—'

'And Kolya?'

'He can go also. We shall not lose the war for one man.'

'Thank you – oh, thank you!'

'But I – I would respectfully ask – the truth is—'

He did not finish the sentence. There was a shout from the embankment above, and a soldier came scrambling down towards them. Dukov pressed her hand. 'Wait,' he said, 'please wait.' He moved towards the soldier and they spoke together in urgent, whispered voices. When he turned back, she saw that he had changed; the boyish shyness had vanished, and he was once more the young, incisive leader of men.

'I am sorry,' he said, 'please return to the train.'

'What has happened?'

'As I said, in war time moves too quickly.' He moved past her and crossed to the locomotive. Klaus looked down at him from the cab.

'Where is Major Story?'

'He just took a stroll.' Klaus pointed towards the bridge. Story was strolling back towards them, puffing at the inevitable cheroot. Dukov went to meet him.

'I have changed my mind, Major. You may proceed.'

'Best news I've heard today. What happened?'

Dukov spread his hands. 'You will know soon enough, I suppose. The Czech Legion has broken through our lines to the south. We have orders to pull back.'

'You won't hold the town.'

'Perhaps not. But we will give them a good fight. And we shall return.'

'What about our fireman?'

'He can go also.'

Story looked at Dukov, and then glanced towards Miss Meg. 'That's the only reason why you're letting us go?'

'What other reason could there be? We have other, bigger things to worry about than your train, or its passengers. Now, please go.'

Miss Meg was the last to reboard. Dukov helped her up, and as she stood in the doorway, he said: 'Please forgive my foolishness just now.'

'There was nothing foolish in what you said.'

'I allowed my subjective feelings to—' He stopped, and suddenly smiled. 'They say all things are for the best. Please, take this as a keepsake – for luck.' He took the red star from his cap and gave it to her.

'I have nothing to give you—' she began, and then said, 'Wait.' She hurried inside the coach, rummaged, feverishly in one of the bundles, and came to him at last, a forlorn smile on her face. 'It is silly, but I have nothing else.' She gave him a bar of Pears Soap, the last of her supply.

'Soap!' He laughed. 'That is worth a bar of gold! And I need it!'

'I didn't mean it like that, Nikolai.'

'No. But it's true, all the same. The first chance I get I shall take a bath and think of you, Mar-gar-et.'

The *Royal Flush* began to move. He waved once, then turned and clambered up the embankment with the two soldiers. At the top, he waved again.

Just before the train rounded the bend which lay just ahead, they heard the familiar roar of an explosion. Klaus poked his head above the roof of the locomotive and looked back. 'They've blown the bridge,' he said. 'No way we can go now but forward.'

'No,' said Story.

'But it is gone! See for yourself!'

'I mean, no, they didn't blow it. I did.'

Klaus stared at him in astonishment. 'You? Just now?'

'Well,' said Story, 'I figured that without the bridge we couldn't go back and they couldn't come chasing after us. So last night I came down and fixed things up a little. After all, they'd put the dynamite there. Can't blame me for using it.'

'Hell's bloody bells,' said Klaus.

'Never mind that,' said Story, 'just keep this goddamned train moving!'

3

Tremayne moved down the narrow stairs cautiously, stepped over the dead body of the guard, and opened a door. Beyond this, he found a wide landing, with rooms on either side, a black stove, and a broad stairway curving downwards. The rust-red carpet was stained with mud and filth, a series of initials, dates and names had been cut into the woodwork or scrawled on the walls, together with crude drawings and slogans. A garish poster, showing a rugged, bright-eyed worker crashing a mighty fist down upon the top-hatted head of a fat merchant, hung above the stairs, flanked by pictures of Lenin and Trotsky. A stained chamber-pot stood on top of the stove.

The dog's whine, haunting and plaintive, sounded louder now. Tremayne moved from door to door and eventually found the right one. The tiny animal shot past him, leaping down the stairs in its frenzy to reach the lower floor. Tremayne had a glimpse of a bedroom, with one double and one single bed. They were rumpled and unmade, the linen grubby; a prayer-book lay open on a table, a picture of the Virgin Mary hung askew on the wall, a wheel-chair stood in one corner.

He crossed to the whitewashed window, smashed the glass with his revolver and looked down through the jagged empty space. The truck had been backed up towards the first palisade and he could see a girl being helped into the back by two of the Volunteers. From the photographs he had memorised, he thought she was the Grand Duchess Anastasia, but from that distance he could not be certain. Two other girls, their heads bowed, were waiting to follow her.

He left the bedroom hurriedly and ran down the stairs to the spacious hall. A half-dozen bodies lay there, Red Guards and White Volunteers, united now in the common community of death. Once more he was checked by a sound. It was not the dog this time, but the unmistakable scream of a human being at the extreme of agony. And as this faded, he heard an angry, bitter howl from Kasakov.

He found the Russian outside the door of what appeared to be a cellar. He was kneeling on one of the Red Guards, a knife in his hand, stabbing, stabbing, stabbing at the already dead body with the ferocity of a maniac. He fought as Tremayne tried to pull him away, but at last the knife dropped from his hand and he stood up. His face was a blank, his eyes stared with the fixed intensity of a blind man, his body trembled as though it were beyond all control. When Tremayne took his arm, he shook it off, and turned his face to the wall, pressing his forehead against the black tiles. The little dog, squatting outside the cellar door, looked up at Tremayne with limpid brown eyes and wagged his tail.

Samarin came up so quietly that his voice startled Tremayne. 'We're ready, Colonel, we must go, we can't leave it any longer.' Kasakov made no response. 'The Tsarina and the Grand Duchesses are in the truck, Zakhar,' said Samarin with greater urgency. 'Every moment we delay increases the danger.' Still Kasakov did not move or speak.

'The Tsarina – the Grand Duchesses?' said Tremayne sharply. 'What about the others, the Tsar, the boy, the doctor?'

Samarin touched the mutilated body of the dead guard with his foot, in a gesture that was not ungentle. 'We got it out of him. The boy was too ill to be moved, haemorrhaging badly. The Tsar refused to leave him. He ordered the Tsarina and the Grand Duchesses to go out for the morning exercise, but he stayed. The doctor remained also. When we began our attack, they brought the three of them down here.' He opened the door to the cellar, and the dog rushed in.

Sunlight slanting in through the low window divided the room into light and shade. Lying across the diagonal line between the two lay the body of the Tsar, and on either side, one in sunshine, one in shadow, were the bodies of his son, the Tsarevich, and of the doctor. The dog was licking the face of the boy, pawing his shoulder, as though trying to rouse him from sleep.

Samarin closed the door. 'We must go, Zakhar,' he said again.

Kasakov turned slowly. The trembling had stopped and he seemed to be regaining command of himself. 'We must take them,' he whispered, 'we can't leave them here. Burial, Christian burial—'

'We have no time.'

'He's right, Zakhar,' said Tremayne. 'There's nothing we can do now. You must think of the others.'

Kasakov stared at him and blinked as though trying to focus his eyes. He straightened up and even managed a grim hint of his former boyish smile. 'I told you,' he said. 'A dying species. Our little Tsar, people like me – no present, no future, only a past.' He sharpened his tone. 'You take the others, you know what to do. You will go also, Samarin, my friend.'

'What about you?'

'Don't bother about me. I have things to do. My pack is on the truck. Leave it at the gate for me. I will collect it in a moment.' His voice rose to a shout. 'Go, damn you, go! That's an order!' As Samarin stumbled away, Kasakov held out his hand to Tremayne. 'Don't blame yourself, Englishman. You did well. And we almost made it.'

'Almost is not enough,' said Tremayne.

'Still, it will have to do,' said Kasakov. 'What is that saying of yours about half a loaf? Keep them safe, and take them where they can be happy.' He turned, went into the cellar and closed the door.

Chapter Thirteen

I

Because of the changed military situation and the shortage of time, Tremayne decided to cut out the proposed feint to the south and head across country to Krasno on the River Ob, where they were to pick up the riverboat which was to carry them up-river to the rendezvous with HMS *Chatham*. He was gambling that the Soviet authorities would concentrate their attention on the *Royal Flush* and that the blocking off of key junctions by the White underground forces in Ekaterinburg would give his convoy a chance to get clean away.

In the initial stages, the gamble paid off. The trek across country was relatively uneventful. Apart from a threat by a small Red Army patrol whose commander wanted to requisition one of the Putilov armoured cars for his own use, and which was swiftly eliminated, they encountered no trouble. About a mile from Krasno, Tremayne pulled up in the shelter of a wood, and sent Samarin forward with two men to reconnoitre.

Samarin came back ninety minutes later with disastrous news. There was no riverboat. The merchant, who only four days before had confirmed the arrangement at a secret meeting with Alexei, had disappeared with his wife and family; presumably they had either gone into hiding or been arrested by the Bolsheviks. His small fleet of boats, pleasure-craft of various kinds, had vanished.

Tremayne stared at the Russian in disbelief for a moment and then closed his eyes. The excitement which had driven him forward flickered out like a flame as despair and weariness took over. Samarin watched him anxiously.

'What will you do, James Ivanovich?'

'I don't know.' Tremayne shook his head. 'I don't know.'

'We cannot stay here.'

'I know that, for God's sake!'

Samarin looked on in anxious silence as Tremayne turned away, and began to pace among the trees, trying to force his aching mind to grapple with this new problem. He paused twice to study the face of his watch; the figures seemed to be distorted and out of focus, the familiar ticking sounded louder and echoed in his ears like a time-bomb. Whichever way he moved would be a gamble with time, and the wrong move would mean final disaster. He broke a small branch from a beech and began to strip it of leaves; slowly, very slowly, the fuzz in his head began to clear and he was able to assemble his thoughts.

Should they strike north, following the line of the river, and hope that HMS *Chatham* would be waiting as arranged, or turn south to the rendezvous with Story and the *Royal Flush*? He had heard nothing about the British and of the operation since leaving England, and though he trusted the Royal Navy to keep its appointments, he wasn't quite so sure about the British Government. From his experience in London, he knew that they were quite capable of altering course with each change in the political wind; the operation might well have been cancelled. On the other hand, Story had said that he would wait for 24 hours, and he knew him well enough to know that it would take a major disaster to make the American break his pledge.

He struck his leg sharply with the branch and felt it sting through the cloth against the flesh. 'Samarin!' The Russian hurried towards him. 'We're heading south. To the train.'

'The train?' Samarin frowned.

'It will be waiting at the point where we disembarked the other day. Can you lead us there?'

'Of course.'

'Fuel?'

'We have enough, I think.'

'Don't think! Tell me!'

'Perhaps it would be wise to abandon one of the armoured cars. If we drain the fuel from that, and take the reserve supply, we should be able to manage. But it means that some of the men will have to travel in the truck with Her Imperial Majesty and the Grand Duchesses.'

'So?'

'It is hardly correct. The Empress may not permit it.'

'The Empress will have to damn well put up with it!' said Tremayne bluntly. 'I'll talk to her. You get the fuel out of the second Putilov. I want to move off in twenty minutes.'

But dealing with the Empress was not as easy as he had supposed, for the religious fervour which had taken an increasing hold during the months of imprisonment seemed now to have reached the point of mania. She sat in a corner of the truck, clutching her daughters, her eyes glittering as though with fever, and he could get no sense or reason out of her. Despite all his protestations she persisted with the belief that they were being driven off to execution, and her frequent explosions of hysteria

261

were clearly affecting the daughters, who were themselves in a state of some shock. In the end he abandoned the effort to get through and gave the order to move on.

The condition of the women deepened the depression which had settled on the expedition. Most of the Volunteers had preserved in their minds a romantic, traditional picture of the Imperial Family; they had been conditioned to look upon them as superior beings, glittering, aloof, godlike, not to be questioned or judged by the same standards as ordinary mortals. The reality stunned them. The women were not merely shabby, their clothes stained and darned, but they seemed to be reduced in themselves, as if their experiences had drained them of greatness.

Tremayne felt only pity. These women, by an accident of birth, not by any choice, had been brought up as monuments, people apart from, and above, all others. Without any preparation, they had been cast down, worship replaced by insult, reverence by indignity, living under the constant threat of death. It was a miracle, he thought, that they had retained any degree of sanity at all; many strong men would have broken under similar circumstances. He saw them as victims, an infinitely sad group of human beings, and his heart went out to them.

Still, he had no time or mental energy for the luxury of compassion. He was forced relentlessly to press on, counting the miles and the minutes, grudging every stop. At length, the gathering dusk and the sheer exhaustion of his men forced him to call a halt. They pulled off the rugged track into a small clearing on the edge of a wood, and posted guards. Tremayne ordered that no fires should be lit and that the journey should resume again at first light.

As Tremayne settled wearily to rest, he heard the low

throb of a girl weeping. It came from the truck, where the women were sleeping; at first, there was one voice, but then slowly the others joined in. And then, above the rest, there rose a kind of howl, half-animal, half-human, a mournful keening sound, which quickened the heart with an uneerie fear. It was the Tsarina, and as her grief exploded, the voices of the girls increased in volume until the plaintive wailing seemed to fill the wood. It was a moment that Tremayne was never to forget; for years after he was to hear that sound which seemed to express all the terrible suffering of Russia.

The listening men peered at each other in the darkness and crossed themselves, half in fear, half in anguish.

2

Chairman Gromeko's reaction to the flight of the Tsarina and her daughters was at once fierce and typical. He issued an order for six prisoners, among them a Prince, a General, and two former man-servants of the Tsar, to be brought from the common jail to the House of Special Purpose. They were made to load the bodies of the Red Guards and the White Volunteers on to a truck and partially to clean the house, though the cellar was barred to them. When these grisly tasks were completed, they were driven to a wooded area on the outskirts of the town and forced to dig a mass grave for the dead. The six men were then lined up at the edge of the pit, their faces turned inwards, and shot in the head at close range and with cool precision by a Commissar armed with a Nagent Obrazets revolver. They were buried with the others.

In addition, Gromeko formed groups of his most trusted Lettish soldiers into special Terror Squads, with orders to conduct a house-to-house search of the town. Anyone suspected of being a sympathiser with the former regime was to be arrested. The soldiers were given a wide brief; any person unlucky enough to have the wrong sort of accent, to have money or jewels hidden away, even to possess books which might be considered to be anti-revolutionary, was a potential victim. All day long, sad columns of frightened, bewildered prisoners were to be seen shuffling through the streets of Ekaterinburg on their way to the special detention camps.

Once these measures were in hand, Gromeko ordered a complete black-out on any reporting of the morning's events, and went to consult Political Commissar Mogilov. It was their second meeting of the day; the first, at the House of Special Purpose, had been brief and acrimonious, particularly on Gromeko's side, and his mood did not appear to have improved.

'What news?' asked Mogilov immediately.

'The Czechs have penetrated to within six miles of the town. But at the moment we are holding them.'

'I know the military situation,' said Mogilov. 'I was asking about the fugitives?'

'Nothing,' answered Gromeko gloomily.

'A fine pickle,' said Mogilov, shaking his head.

'I was not responsible for guarding the house!' replied Gromeko angrily. 'They were your men, you brought them from Moscow.'

'They did not allow the Tsar or the boy to escape!' said Mogilov calmly. 'And they died to a man in the performance of their duty.' He smiled. 'But why argue?'

He crossed to a cupboard and produced a bottle of plum brandy and two glasses, which he brought to the table. Watching him, Gromeko wondered with envy how the man managed to appear so fresh and immaculate.

'How do you do it?' he asked. 'You always look as though you've just come from the barber.'

'I'm too fastidious,' said Mogilov. 'It is one of my many faults.' He filled the glasses. 'Here, drink. We both need something.'

'I simply want you to understand that I don't intend to be made the scapegoat for this affair,' said Gromeko in a more conciliatory tone.

'Drink,' said Mogilov. 'Let us examine the facts calmly and rationally and perhaps we can reach some solution.' Both men gulped back the drinks and Mogilov refilled the glasses before continuing: 'This is between ourselves, you understand, comrade. In a sense, both our necks are on the block, so it will clearly be in our mutual interest to combine forces. Let us leave the question of the dead Romanovs aside for the moment and concentrate on the ones who escaped. First question. How, in your view, was that escape effected?'

'That's obvious, surely,' answered Gromeko impatiently. 'The entire business was engineered by the Americans in collusion with reactionary elements who had infiltrated the town. Two of the bodies discovered at the house were identified as members of the former Tsar's personal guards.'

'An imperialist plot.'

'Exactly so. It must have taken months to prepare. The bomb attacks, the explosions in the town were deliberately timed to divert us from the main centre of attack. And it was certainly no accident that the American train left Ekaterinburg only a few minutes after the assault.'

'But it was checked surely?'

'Of course. None of the Romanovs was aboard when the train was stopped and searched on the east bank of the river. But someone deliberately blew up the bridge as soon as the Americans had been given permission to proceed. They either arranged it themselves or got someone else to do it. I have no doubt that they had a rendezvous with the Romanov women at some point further down the track, out of range of our guns.'

'It will be hard to prove. The Americans are sure to deny everything.'

'Nevertheless – the facts speak for themselves. And if the Romanov women turn up in Omsk, the whole world will know the truth.'

'Perhaps they won't turn up there. That would look too obvious.' Mogilov sipped the brandy, watching the other man. 'I think we should leave the Americans out of this, my friend.'

'The devil with that! There is a meeting of the Regional Soviet this evening, and I intend to tell the whole story!'

'Then you will be making two errors. First, on a political level. At this moment, the Revolution has enough enemies – the last thing we want to do is to add the United States to that number by making accusations which we can't substantiate. I am sure Moscow will take that view.' Gromeko seemed about to interrupt, but Mogilov over-rode him. 'Let me finish. Next, if you lay the blame on the Americans, consider your personal position. People will ask why you allowed the train to enter the town in the first place. They will also ask why you allowed it to leave when it did.'

'The Railway Commissar gave the clearance!'

'But you are the Regional Chairman, you are supposed to weigh up the political implications in this sort of situation. And apart from the Americans, there are other questions.'

'Such as?'

'Negligence. Sabotage.'

Gromeko stood up angrily, shaking the table. 'If that is your game, comrade—'

'Sit down, sit down!' said Mogilov. 'I am simply suggesting that the facts may be interpreted in an unpleasant way. Unpleasant for you, personally, that is. Why, for example, did you order the locomotive to be taken away from my train?'

'I was informed it needed repair,' Gromeko said uneasily. He resumed his seat, fiddled nervously with his glass.

'Whatever the reason,' Mogilov said, 'the fact is that without a locomotive I could not pursue the American train. That could be interpreted as sabotage, right? I am not accusing you,' he added quickly, 'but others might. Just as they might ask why the local authorities were so negligent that they allowed a force of armed monarchists, posing as partisans, to slip into town, steal military vehicles, and apparently rove around at will?'

As soon as the words were out, Mogilov knew he had made a mistake, and Gromeko was quick to spot it. 'How did you know about the vehicles?' he said quickly.

'I have my sources of information too, you know,' answered Mogilov smoothly. He touched the scar on his eyebrow with a finger, smoothing the hair over it. 'No,' he went on, 'forget the Americans – too many complications. I have a better idea, one that will satisfy everybody, and absolve you from any blame.'

'And you also, of course,' Gromeko said, with a hint of mockery.

'Not entirely. But it will give me a breathing space.'

'I am listening.'

'You simply go before the Soviet tonight and announce that, in accordance with the resolution passed at last night's meeting, Nicholas Romanov and his son, the Tsarevich, have been executed. Which is true, after all.

You discovered a monarchist plot to rescue them, and vigilant as ever, you crushed it ruthlessly.'

'But what about the women?'

'Say that in view of the advance of the enemy forces, they have been taken to another, safer place. Have the locomotive reconnected to my train. While the meeting is in progress, I will leave. I'll pull down the blinds in the coach, make a fuss about the need to get out quickly. People will assume that I have taken the women with me, you understand?'

'And if they suddenly turn up in Omsk? If the Whites parade them before the world press?'

'That will be my problem, not yours. I believe in taking one thing at a time.'

'What about Moscow?'

'I will telegraph Dzerzhinsky informing him that Nicholas and his son were executed by decision of the Regional Soviet. They will accept it, never fear.'

The two men looked at each other in silence for several seconds. Then Gromeko lifted his glass, his face creased into a thin, humourless smile.

'This is an excellent brandy, comrade. Where did you get it?'

'From the cellar of a Grand Duke in Moscow,' said Mogilov.

'And quite right too,' said Gromeko. 'After all, we are the rulers now. I've always said that what was good enough for them is good enough for us.'

He drained his glass, ran a finger round the inside and licked it, smacking his thin lips. 'It hasn't been a bad day, when all is said and done. Nicholas and his son are dead. And wherever the women turn up – well, we will get them. We have friends everywhere, isn't that so? They won't survive long.'

Later that day, Mogilov sent for Alexei, the leader of

the White underground forces in Ekaterinburg, on the pretext that he needed him to translate some important documents from German into Russian. As soon as they were alone, he gave him a full account of his conversation with Gromeko.

'The town is sure to fall in a few days,' he said. 'You must stay behind at all costs. You see, I have been wondering how we might use this terrible situation to our best advantage. First, I want you to get your people to spread the word that the entire Imperial family – everyone – was slaughtered at the Ipatiev House this morning. And when Diterikhs and the Czechs arrive, you must tell them the same thing.'

'The entire family? For what purpose? I don't understand,' said Alexei, frowning.

'You are not usually so slow-witted, my dear fellow,' said Mogilov patiently. 'Listen. When Lenin signed his separate peace with the Germans, he gave the Kaiser a secret pledge that the Tsarina would not be harmed. Once it is said that she has been murdered, it is probable that the Kaiser will tear up the treaty with the Bolsheviks and order his troops to march on Moscow. Do you follow me?'

'And that will provoke the Allies to land more troops and supplies, and attack in their turn.'

'Exactly so. The Bolsheviks will be exposed for the butchers they are, world opinion will harden against them. And they will find themselves fighting on a dozen fronts. Once they have been finally sent packing – in six months, a year at the outside – we can announce that, by some miracle, the Tsarina and the Grand Duchesses escaped alive, and produce them to prove it. They will ride through Moscow in triumph, my friend. Who knows – we may even have a new Romanov Empress on the throne of Russia!'

'God speed the day!' said Alexei, raising his glass. Both men stood to attention, solemnly toasted the future, and hurled the empty glasses against the side of the coach.

That evening Alexei slipped into the crowded theatre to hear Gromeko make his announcement about the Romanovs. It was received in a curious, almost disinterested silence. Despite all exhortations from the platform, the people knew that the enemy was on the doorstep, and they were more concerned with their own fate than what had happened to the Tsar.

As Gromeko sat down, a young man in a long grey army greatcoat rose from his seat and forced his way to the front. It was astonishing to see someone wearing a winter coat at such a season, in such heat, and the surprised delegates gave way as though mesmerised. He vaulted on to the stage.

'What is it, comrade?' asked Gromeko.

'I demand the right to speak!'

'This is not the moment for discussion! Later!'

'Let him have his say!' shouted a member of the crowd, and the call was taken up by others.

There was some applause and laughter as someone shouted: 'Aren't you hot in that coat, brother?'

The young man turned and Alexei saw now that it was Kasakov. He closed his eyes in horror, unable to think or move. When he looked again, Kasakov, that impudent, boyish smile on his face, had stripped off the outer coat, and stood facing the audience in the full splendour of the uniform of an officer of the Chevalier Guards.

'I have brought you a gift. So that you will remember His Imperial Majesty, Tsar Nicholas the Second!'

The crowd sat in stunned silence for a moment. Then, as the howls of anger began to rise, and they pushed forward, a woman screamed: 'He has a grenade!' Some

270

fell back, scrambling for the doors, shouting in panic, others threw themselves to the floor.

The grenade exploded in the young man's hand. He died instantly, as did Gromeko and four others. Many more were wounded: the theatre was still echoing to their cries as Alexei stumbled into the clean, night air.

3

It seemed to Tremayne as if he had scarcely closed his eyes when he opened them to the dawn, and realised that Samarin was shaking him by the shoulder. It took Tremayne a full half-minute to focus on the young officer's grim, white face and to take in what he was saying.

'The Tsarina! She's gone, and the Grand Duchesses with her!'

'Have you searched?'

'Of course. No sign.'

'What about the bloody guards!'

'What could they do? The Tsarina said they wished to go into the woods. The sentry assumed that it was a call of nature.'

'Didn't he follow them?'

'The Tsarina! How was that possible? I mean, one has to have a certain respect.'

'Damn the respect!'

'Naturally, he didn't dream that they would run off. Would you have believed it?'

'The state they were in – yes – I'd believe anything. How long have they been gone?'

'An hour, perhaps.'

'God Almighty, man, why didn't you wake me before?'
'We've been searching.'

Tremayne peered at his watch. 'We've got six hours, give or take,' he said briskly. 'You take the armoured car and three men. Head for the train as fast as you can. Tell Major Story there's been a hold-up, ask him to wait. I'll organise a full-scale search and get there as soon as possible. Clear?'

There were twelve men left and Tremayne organised them into four groups of three, one to guard the truck, and three to search. A single shot was to indicate that the women had been found; it was risky, but there was no other alternative. Tremayne himself led one detachment into the thick of the wood, cutting notches into the trees as a guide back to camp.

Two hours passed before he heard a distant shot, from the left, about a mile away as far as he could judge. It took another half-hour for him to find the spot.

The rising sun cast the shadows of the pines across the clearing like great iron bars. Tatania and Maria were huddled in each other's arms at the foot of a tree, weeping, but there was no sign of the other girls. Two Volunteers were hacking at the ground with bayonets and knives, digging a grave for the Tsarina, the former Empress of All the Russias: a third, an older man, knelt by the body. The tears poured down his unshaven cheeks unheeded as he mumbled a prayer.

'Jesu, most sweet, O glory of the Apostles, O Jesu mine, lauded by the martyrs, Jesu save her; Jesu our Saviour, Jesu most beautiful, have mercy upon her who dost come to Thee, and make her worthy of the joys of heaven, O Jesu, lover of mankind.'

Chapter Fourteen

I

The roads along the coast, and the winding track to Trevellick, were fast becoming as familiar to me as the tortuous route round Lewisham, Peckham, and the Elephant and Castle, which (in the somewhat doubtful belief that it enables me to avoid the worst of the traffic) I often use on my way to and from Westminster and my home in Kent.

This was to be, I hoped, my last visit, at least in terms of the story which had been the burning centre of my life for almost nine months. It had been high summer when I had made that first journey and received a crack on the head for my pains; since then I had seen these Cornish moors in the sepia warmth of autumn and the grim white frost of winter, and though I knew that I could never live in such isolation myself, I had grown to love them.

I had learned also to warn Tremayne of my coming, and the burly, bearded old man called Michael, who had greeted me so inhospitably on that earlier occasion, was always waiting by the gate when I arrived. It was impossible to guess his age with any accuracy; he looked about seventy, but if anyone had told me that eighty-plus was nearer the mark, I would not have been surprised. I'd tried two or three times to get him to talk, but beyond a conventional, muttered greeting or word of farewell, he would say nothing. After locking the gate behind me, he always moved off quickly, stretching his legs in a stride which would have done credit to a much younger man. In the end, I put it down to a natural surliness, and tried no more.

Tremayne, I think, had grown to trust me, though it had taken some time. He'd opened up slowly at first, tempting me, as it were, with morsels of information, giving me a lead here and there, but holding back much that was vital until he had tested me out. There were many questions to which he refused to reply though I guessed that he knew most of the answers. He had warned me that I would have to dig out the full truth, and he clearly intended that I should do just that. To do him justice, I think he wanted me to check for myself, so that I could be certain that the extraordinary story which unfolded gradually as we talked was not the romantic exaggeration of an old man's memory, in which a molehill of fact is often the foundation for a mountain of fable.

And so, in between our conversations at Trevellick, I tackled the difficult business of research, moving in ever-widening circles from the Public Records Office in London to Europe, America, Canada and finally the USSR.

The Russian part of it was, perhaps, the most disappointing. I'd taken the Trans-Siberian from Moscow to Kharbarovsk – foreigners are rarely allowed to go on to Vladivostock – and stopped off at Sverdlovsk, which is what Ekaterinburg is now called. It wasn't only the name that had changed. I didn't really expect the town to live up to the mental image I'd formed, but I doubt if Tremayne himself would have recognised it, for what I saw was a modern city, a great industrial centre, three or four times the size of the original Ekaterinburg. To give them their due, the local authorities had done a great deal to preserve some of the best features of the old town and there was a fair quantity of parks and open spaces. On the whole, the new buildings seemed to have been put up more with an eye to utility than style, but I'd seen worse. I've always believed that two architects should be shot at dawn every Wednesday morning simply as a warning to others and Sverdlovsk did nothing to change this view.

Still, the new theatre which had been erected in place of the old building where the Regional Soviet had held its meetings sixty years before looked graceful and welcoming, and I was told that the Pecora Marsh, drained and levelled in 1948, was now an airfield. It must have been an enormous undertaking. Through an interpreter, I asked some of the older people about the marsh; they were surprised that I knew about it, and with good reason, proud of the achievement. One ancient described its horrors in graphic detail. When I asked him if it had ever been crossed he said: 'Some said there was a way. But I have been in these parts all my life and I never knew anyone who crossed the Pecora and lived to go to church the next Sunday!'

The locals were less keen to talk about the House of Special Purpose. Preserved more or less intact, the palisades gone, the house is open to visitors and an Intourist guide arranged for me to see over it. It was a depressing experience. Perhaps it was my imagination, but the place seemed to have the dank, mummified atmosphere of an old sepulchre. I noticed, with interest, that a party of local schoolchildren who were being shown round ahead of me appeared to be affected in much the same way. Their shrill voices dropped and they grew more subdued as we moved from room to room. It had nothing to do with any feeling for the dead

275

Tsar, I was sure of that; to these youngsters Nicholas was little more than a footnote in a history book, as remote and impersonal as King George V or the Duke of Windsor are to children in Britain. No, it was the house itself. Somehow it had never been cleansed of its ghosts; they invested each room and corridor with a sense of desolation and the sour scent of death.

I stood at the entrance to the cellar but did not go in. Something held me back, perhaps a certain reluctance to indulge my morbid curiosity. Oddly enough, the sun was coming from the same angle as on that summer day in 1918, its light dividing the room exactly as Tremayne had described. It wasn't difficult to imagine the bodies lying there. It was only then, I think, that I felt the full enormity of the tragedy: not simply the death of the little Tsar, his son and the faithful doctor, for in a sense, their fate had been inevitable, its roots reaching back through the history of this strange, turbulent land. They were three dead human beings among hundreds of thousands, millions perhaps, who had perished in the Revolution and the civil war. Many of them had died for no reason, without knowing why; others had sacrificed themselves willingly, their hearts and minds filled with a dream of a new Russia which would be a lighthouse for all humanity, an exemplar of liberty to the world. I had seen much on my journey and from the people, with rare exceptions, had experienced nothing but kindness. What they had achieved was there to be seen and measured.

But a lighthouse? Liberty? Ah, the brave music of a distant drum!

Standing in the doorway of the cellar, I turned to my guide, a crisp grey-haired woman with the word reliability stamped on her serious, humourless face. I was in no mood to be tactful, the question tumbled from my mind to my tongue without refinement. 'Is this the room where the Tsar and the others were murdered?'

She looked at me more in pity than anger, as a schoolmistress might look at a stupid child. 'The former Tsar was held back here in the house, with his family, for his own safety. At an appropriate time, he was tried by a properly-constituted court for crimes against the people and executed.'

'And the others? His wife, the Tsarevich, the four girls?'

'They were tried and executed at a later date.'

'For what crime?'

'Really,' she said, 'such things are of no interest today.'

'They are to me.'

'The Tsarina was of German origin. It was discovered that she was involved with the Germans and the Whites in a plot to overthrow the Revolution and re-establish the monarchy, with herself as Empress. All this is a matter of historical record,' she added irritably.

'It all depends who writes the history,' I said.

'We will go now and see the monument to the heroes who fell in the revolutionary war,' she said briskly.

2

The memory of this incident was still very fresh in my mind as I arrived at Trevellick on that last afternoon. It was early April, the weather was mild and Tremayne and his wife welcomed me on the sheltered terrace, where we shared a pot of tea. I was on one of my regular if spasmodic diets, and I declined the offer of scones and cherry-cake.

He listened to my account of the journey across Russia, asked one or two questions about Sverdlovsk (which he still referred to as Ekaterinburg) but otherwise showed a surprising lack of interest. For much of the time he sat with his eyes closed, though I knew him well enough by now to know that he was not asleep, merely drifting on the tide of his thoughts. I cut a long story short, lit a pipe, and waited.

'Ekaterinburg,' he murmured, half to himself. Then, with something of his old briskness, he said, 'What else do you want to know?'

'Many things,' I said, and heard him give a tired sigh. 'I'm sorry,' I added quickly.

'No, no,' he said. 'Press on.'

'The Tsarina. Tell me a little more about what happened on that last day.'

He glanced at his wife and took her hand. 'The Tsarina? Poor, poor woman. She was – was unbalanced, to say the least. Who can blame her? She had been forced to leave the Tsar and her son, she was certain they'd been killed. She could not believe that the rescue was not just another Bolshevik trick – we were disguised as partisans and she took us to be just that. During the night, she arranged the escape. Tatania and Maria were opposed to it, but they were over-ruled. The Tsarina knew that we weren't far off Krasno – she had some notion of seeking refuge in a nunnery near the village.'

'How did she die?'

'Quite suddenly. One minute she was hurrying, urging the girls forward – then – it was too much for her. Her heart – a seizure of some sort.'

'She was buried in the forest?'

'As good a place as any,' said Tremayne, and his wife nodded. I could see the tears glinting in her eyes. 'The Volunteers fired a salute over her grave. I tried to argue them out of it – because of the risk of attracting the local Reds – but it was useless.'

'And the other two?'

'Olga and Anastasia? We continued the hunt, of course, but in the end we had to give up. No trace. We went back to the truck and pushed on. A couple of hours later we met Tom Story and Samarin, coming to meet us. And the day after we were in Omsk.'

I was reluctant to press them any further because their distress was so evident. Tremayne sat forward in the cane chair, enclosing the china teapot with his frail hands, as though to warm them. We sat in silence, our minds on a cellar in Ekaterinburg, a grave in a forest near the River Ob. Then the long moment passed and, straightening up, he took an envelope from the pocket of his woollen jacket and handed it to me. 'I came across this among my papers. Thought you'd like to see it.'

The envelope contained a faded photograph, a full-length portrait of a handsome young man in the glittering uniform of the Russian Imperial Chevalier Guards. I could just make out some writing on the back. It was in Russian and it said: *Passing Out Day, June 13th, 1908. Zakhar Nicolayevich Kasakov (Lieutenant).*

'I picked it up from his sister in Paris, some years after the war,' said Tremayne.

'She wanted you to have it, dear,' said his wife.

'Yes.' He nodded, took back the photograph, and framed it in his hands. 'Zakhar Nicolayevich Kasakov,' he said, almost to himself. 'He couldn't go like other men. He had to be larger than life, even when he decided to leave it. They were right about him, of course, he was a kind of madman. I never knew anyone who could be so human one moment, so utterly a savage the next. Half-hero, half-wolf. He should have been a feudal knight. Perhaps that's what he was, a sort of relic, a throwback. But at least there was this to be said of him. Not many of us are able to possess a truly pure, unselfish emotion; we hedge and qualify our feelings. Kasakov was not like that. His love for his little Tsar, his hatred for the Tsar's enemies – they were pure emotions, there was no margin to them, no limit.'

I watched him as he sat back and pulled loosely the jacket around his shoulders. 'If you're cold—' I said.

'No. This is the best of the afternoon.' he smiled. 'Come on, let's have the rest of your questions, my boy.'

'Did you ever have contact with Mogilov or Alexei after 1918?' I asked.

'I saw Alexei in Berlin in 1926,' said Tremayne. 'Things were getting too hot for him – he'd decided to get out. He told me all that happened. As for Mogilov, he survived until 1929, when he was exposed and shot.'

'Did you hear any more of Dukov?'

'Oh, the world heard of him! Even you, I'm sure! General Dukov, one of the heroes of the defence of Stalingrad during the war against Hitler. His troops were among the first to enter Berlin, didn't you know that?'

'I'd heard the name, but I hadn't connected the two.' A picture of a young soldier with sandy-coloured hair straddling a railway line flashed into my mind, like a clip from an old film. But I had other points to settle, and I pressed on.

'After the Whites captured Ekaterinburg, they set up an official enquiry,' I said. 'The report confirmed that all the Romanovs, the men and the women, were murdered at the House of Special Purpose.'

'I read it,' said Tremayne. 'As Tom Story would have said – that report was as full of holes as a rusty bucket.'

'But some of the Red Guards that were captured

testified that the entire family were taken to the cellar and shot.'

'Prisoners will testify to anything to save their skins – or they can be made to do so. No, the Whites believed the report because it suited them to do so. Mogilov and Alexei did their work well. They even explained the absence of the bodies by putting it about that they were all thrown into the Pecora Marsh! And the world believed them!'

'Still, the British Government at the time – Lloyd George and so on – they knew the truth. They knew that the women, at least, had been rescued. They'd been responsible for mounting the rescue mission, after all. Yet they also seemed to accept the story that all the Imperial family died at Ekaterinburg.'

'Lloyd George,' said Tremayne. 'Now there was a politician! Did you ever hear him speak? No, I don't suppose you did. You missed something, I can tell you. Best orator I ever heard. They don't seem to make them like that any more.'

I tried to bring him back to the point. 'The rescue mission,' I said. 'How did the great orator talk his way out of that one?'

He chuckled again. 'I don't believe he thought we had one chance in a million of success. But he'd got the old man on his back, badgering him to do something. George V, I mean. He had a dreadful conscience about his failure to help Nicholas the year before, you see. When Lloyd George saw me at Buckingham Palace that night, I think he simply grasped the opportunity to appease the King.'

His wife, smiling gently, rose from her chair. 'I think you should take your rest now, dear.'

'I'm not tired!' he said gruffly.

'That's what you always say,' she answered. She put a

hand on his arm, and helped him up. A look of affection, which I found oddly moving, passed between the two old people.

'See how she bullies me!'

'You can continue your talk later,' she said.

3

I watched them move carefully inside, and then went to stretch my legs and my mind by a stroll over the moors. Walking is not one of my favourite pastimes, but I was driven to it on this occasion by a growing impatience.

If I'd learned one thing about Tremayne, it was that he could not be pushed. All the way through, he had insisted on telling me the story in his own way, section by section, always stopping short when he reached some sort of dividing line between the events he described. Whether this was sheer cussedness on his part, or simply because he had that sort of mind, I'd never been able to decide.

The real problem was that without him I was pretty well helpless, as I'd discovered to my cost in the course of the research. I was not only following a trail that was almost sixty years old, which was hard enough in all conscience, but this particular one, for all kinds of political and personal reasons, had been deliberately obscured, overlaid by false scents, criss-crossed by other trails which led nowhere. I'm not saying that I had wasted my time. The background material and detail I'd collected proved to be invaluable and, in all essentials, it confirmed what Tremayne had told me so far; but he had been only one of the leading players in the drama. The others were either dead, or could not be found.

Klaus Striebeck, by a strange and tragic irony, was taken prisoner on the Moscow front in 1943 and sent to a camp in the Urals only a few miles from the city which had once been Ekaterinburg. In Vienna I saw his grandson, who told me that Klaus had been put into a penal battalion and ordered to Russia as a punishment for his anti-Nazi attitudes. He showed me a paper from a department of the Austrian War Office which recorded that, according to Soviet records, Private Klaus Striebeck, aged 49, had died on October 2nd, 1944.

Of Tom Story or Miss Meg I could find little trace, and at times, it seemed to me that Tremayne was being particularly elusive about them. He did give me an address in Dallas, Texas, for Story, but it proved to be a very old address indeed, and led nowhere. To do him justice, Tremayne warned me that this would happen but I'd been to Los Angeles to talk to the film-producer son of a former Russian Grand Duke about the Romanovs, and I decided that I would go on to Texas and take a chance.

There were several Storys in the telephone book, one of whom turned out to be an elderly cousin, who was on the verge of senility. All I extracted from this amiable but eccentric man, apart from a lengthy and rambling version of his own life, was one fact I knew already; that Tom Story was, or had been, an expert on railway systems and had spent most of his life abroad following this profession. And I also saw a photograph of Story, taken in 1916; a tall, lean, young man whose eyes seemed to be mocking the camera.

I came up against similar problems with Miss Meg. There was a record of her birth in the Parish Register of the little village in Wiltshire where she had been brought up, and a record of her father's tenure as minister at the local church. Few people remembered him which was sad, but not surprising. One spry old lady recalled Miss Meg, whom she referred to as the vicar's daughter.

'Nice girl,' she told me, 'but shy, you know. Her father was very strict, even for those days. Went off to Russia, she did, as some sort of governess. Russia, of all places! Talk of the village it was!'

'But she came back after the war?'

'Not to my knowledge,' she replied firmly. 'No, she went off to Russia and we never saw her again. The vicar wouldn't talk about her – shut his mouth tight as a trap if you asked. In my opinion, she must have died out there. I mean, stands to reason – living in that climate, among all those foreigners!'

It would have taken the resources of a very large detective agency to pursue either Tom Story or Margaret Wellmeadow any further, and I doubt if even they would have got very far. So I was left with Tremayne and I knew that he would tell me nothing more about them until he was ready.

I'd been lost in these thoughts, hardly noticing my surroundings, but as I turned to make my way back to the house, I saw the old man, Michael, and realised that he must have been following me. He turned and began to walk away, as though to suggest that his presence was just an accident, and suddenly, looking at his broad back, an idea flashed into my mind.

'Kolya!' I shouted.

I might as well have stunned him with a hammer. He pulled up quickly – too quickly – and stood as still as stone for a moment. Then he shuffled round and stared at me, with a puzzled, bewildered expression on his face, like a man who had heard a voice from the past. I had no doubt now who he was, but as I took a step towards him he moved away, hurrying as though in panic.

284

4

When I got back to the house, Lady Tremayne was waiting for me, and I knew from the look on her face that she had spoken with Kolya. But all she said was: 'Did you enjoy your walk?'

'Very much,' I said.

'Michael told me he saw you.'

'Michael?' I asked.

'The moor can be difficult, especially at this time of the year. I think he was afraid that you might lose your way. He is very conscientious, perhaps a little too much sometimes.'

'You have known him a long time?'

'Yes. Quite a long time.'

'Since you first went to Russia? When you were Miss Margaret Wellmeadow – or shall I say – Miss Meg?'

Tremayne came into the room at that moment and she turned to him with a smile. 'I think our guest might like a drink, dear. Let us all have one.' He poured two generous measures of Scotch and a vodka and brought them over to us.

'Cheers,' he said solemnly.

His wife turned to me. 'Sit down. I think we owe you an apology. You see, we have nursed our secrets for so long, it is hard to part with them.' I was still standing, and she touched my arm. 'Please. Sit down and we will talk. I think you know most of the story, but perhaps there are still some questions?'

We sat down together. She remained silent for what seemed a long time, as though gathering her thoughts. Then she gave a small, sad sigh. 'There is a custom in Russia,' she said, 'or perhaps it is a superstition. There, the people always sit down for a few moments before beginning a journey. It is supposed to bring good luck And we are going on a kind of journey, isn't that so?'

As she spoke, I had the feeling that I had got something wrong, very wrong indeed.

'You are still asking questions?' asked Tremayne wryly.

'There are just one or two loose ends,' I replied.

'Fire away.' The words were casual, almost hearty, but I could sense the tension underlying them, as if he knew that we were nearing the end of the long road. His wife sat forward, gripping her glass, her eyes fixed on my face.

'What happened to Tatania and Maria – the two you brought out? There was never any report about them – nothing about their arrival in Omsk.'

'It was by their own wish,' said Tremayne. Once again that look of deep affection passed between him and his wife. 'They'd had enough. Suffering changes people, you know – and if you think that is a platitude, I have to tell you that all platitudes have a foundation in truth. They wished, for all sorts of reasons, to remain anonymous, assume other identities if you want to put it that way. And we respected that wish. Of course, we couldn't stop the rumours, some of the Volunteers talked, but nothing could be proved. I informed the British Government that my mission had failed, and they accepted it.'

'Had they sent the gunboat to the Ob?'

'I never bothered to ask. I doubt it. All governments are perfidious,' he said tartly, then continued in a softer tone: 'Tatania entered a religious order, and went to West Africa as a nurse. She died there, twenty years ago.'

'And Maria?'

'Haven't you guessed?' He smiled and laid a hand on his wife's shoulder. 'Why do you think we moved here –

that we guard our privacy so well? We fell in love on the train, on the long journey to Vladivostock, and we have been in love ever since.'

I shook my head, not in disbelief, but at my own idiocy. 'I thought, I really thought you were Miss Meg,' I said.

She laughed. 'Oh, no. Dear Meg. She became my greatest friend.'

'She took the children to America, to relatives of the Rostilovs, and settled there.' added Tremayne. 'We saw a good deal of both Tom and Margaret during the twenties and early thirties.'

'They were married?'

'No. Tom was never the marrying kind. But they – they were good friends, as the saying goes.' A twinkle brightened his eyes. 'And we brought Kolya here, to help look after Maria. Re-christened him Michael – more English, you see.'

He got up, and gently kissed his wife's cheek. 'Well, there we are, my dear,' he said, 'it's all out in the open now.'

5

Death has been too regular a visitor to this story, but I have to record that Viscount Tremayne of Trevellick died four months after our last talk, leaving no heir, and that his wife, Maria, followed him two days later. They were buried together, as was fitting, and I stood at the graveside with men and women from Zennor, St. Just and other villages to pay my last respects.

Tremayne left me all his books and personal papers, a

fascinating record of a fascinating life. Everything else went to Kolya, for his lifetime, and he, at least, still survives happily in a cottage on the coast near Trevellick.

Maria – I find it hard to think of her as Lady Tremayne or a Grand Duchess – also left me a small but precious souvenir. It is a signet ring, bearing the falcon, the personal crest of the Tsar.

Whether it is the ring which once belonged to King George V of England, I neither know nor care. It is mine now, by lawful inheritance, and I intend to keep it.